Indiana Wild

Spirit Pass: Book 1

By S. E. Smith

Acknowledgments

I would like to thank my husband Steve for believing in me and being proud enough of me to give me the courage to follow my dream. I would also like to give a special thank you to my sister and best friend, Linda, who not only encouraged me to write but who also read the manuscript. And to my friends who have kept me writing: Sally, Julie, Jackie, Chris, Narelle, and Lisa.

—S. E. Smith

Paranormal/Time Travel Romance
INDIANA WILD
Copyright © 2013 by Susan E. Smith
First E-Book Publication April 2013
Cover Design by Melody Simmons

Synopsis

Indiana Wild is as wild as the Montana ranch she was raised on. The youngest of four children, she was a delightful surprise for her older parents. She spends her time training horses and cow dogs and loving the freedom of the wide open spaces. When her grandfather dies, she finds her much older brothers have different plans for the ranch she calls home and for Indiana.

Indiana's oldest brother is determined to tame Indiana and bring her to live with him in Los Angeles, where he can keep an eye on her and the money she is inheriting. He believes with a little taming, he can control the wild spirit of his little sister and find her a good husband who can manage her.

Furious with the court order giving her older brother's guardianship over her, Indiana turns to the only place she feels at home…. the wide-open spaces of Montana. She is determined to avoid her controlling brothers and their greed, even if it means hiding from them until they give up. An unexpected trip through Spirit Pass takes Indiana further than she ever expected…. by almost a hundred and fifty years.

Jonathan Tucker is as tough as they come. He and his twin brother have cut a successful horse and cattle ranch in the harsh Montana territory. When cattle rustlers try to steal his cattle and shoot one of his men, he is grateful to the young boy named Indy who comes to the rescue, even if the boy does have an attitude. The last thing he expects is to find the 'boy' is in fact an independent, freethinking, stubborn female who is not afraid to voice her opinions. She is as wild as the untamed land around them and he is determined she is the wife for him.

When Indiana is taken from him, Jonathan finds he will do whatever it takes to bring his Indiana Wild home for good, even if it means following her to the future.

Contents

Chapter 1

"How could you? How could you do this to me?" Indy whispered in disbelief, staring at her brothers as if she had never seen them before.

"Indiana, it's for your own good," Hayden said sternly. The oldest of the four Wild family kids, he was also a successful attorney in California. "Grandfather was old and senile. A new Will needed to be done. It was well within our rights for me to help him draft the new one."

"Grandfather was not senile! You bullied him into signing the papers making you his legal guardian. We were doing just fine until you came out and stuck your nose in our business," Indy said angrily.

"Now Indy, you know Hayden is right. We were only thinking of your best interests," Gus said, leaning forward as if to pat Indy on the knee.

"Touch me Gus and I'll slice your greedy fingers right off your thieving hands," Indy said through clenched teeth.

"Indy, there is no need to speak to Gus like that," Matthew said, moving a little further away from where she was sitting.

"Shut up, Matt. You are nothing but an opportunist gambler who sees another way to support your lifestyle. You'll blow your inheritance in less than a year and be begging at Hayden's door for more," Indy said coldly.

Indiana "Indy" Wild looked at her three older brothers in anger and disbelief. She couldn't believe they had been so underhanded as to steal the only place she had ever called home from her. Hayden sat looking at her from behind her grandfather's old desk. The oldest at forty-seven, he was an imposing figure taking over their father's side of the family. He was six foot one with broad shoulders and a slight pouch around the middle from all the days of sitting in courtrooms making millions. His dark brown eyes stared at her coolly as he waited for her to calm down.

Calm down like hell, Indy thought dispassionately. *He just wants me to sign on the dotted line so he can add more millions to his bank account.*

Hayden had come to the Wild Ranch in Montana six months ago when their grandfather had a slight stroke. Until then, it had been ten years since he had returned and then only to bury their grandmother and parents who were killed in a car accident. Indy had no idea that during the two weeks he was there he had their grandfather sign a new Will and other documents giving him power of attorney.

Indy glared at her brothers feeling her stomach tighten with nerves. She had been a surprise to her delighted parents when her mother became pregnant unexpectedly in her forties. There was a twenty year difference between her and her youngest brother, Matthew. She was twenty-two to his forty-two.

Her parents raised all of them on the ranch, living in the same house as her grandparents. When her parents died, her grandfather took over raising her since her older brothers had their own lives to live. It had worked out well. Indy had always been close to her grandfather and after the accident, they had grown even closer. While Indy's brothers left as soon as they were old enough to live elsewhere, Indy never planned on leaving. She loved every aspect of ranch life from the cattle, to the horses, to the old cowpunchers that came and went each year.

"Indy, accept it. The ranch has already been sold. You will receive a sizable amount of money which should help you. The money will be set up in a trust account and you will receive monthly checks until you reach the age of twenty-five. At that time, you will receive the full amount. The company that purchased the ranch will take over at the end of the month. Everything goes to them except personal belongings, of course. I have made sure you have enough money to cover your first six months of living expenses so you can find a job. I suggest you plan on attending graduate school. You will have a better potential for finding a job with a higher level degree. If you need funds to cover it, I can release them as I have control of your trust fund."

She just stared at Hayden in disbelief as he continued describing how he was taking over the ranch, her money from the sale, and her life. Gus fidgeted in his seat as he watched the emotions crossing Indy's face. Out of the three brothers, Gus at forty-five was the most compassionate of the three. He was married to a nice woman and had four kids. He was currently working at Montana State University as a math teacher.

"Indy, you can come live with Marge and me in Billings. Bob and Todd are moving out to go to college and their rooms will be open. You might like it there," Gus said quietly.

Indy's eyes filled with tears, but she refused to let them fall. She would be damned if she would give any of them the satisfaction of seeing her cry. Standing and walking over to the window, she stared out over the mountains she loved so much.

"That won't be necessary," Indy said quietly.

She kept her shoulders straight. She knew there was nothing she could do. Hayden wasn't just good as an attorney; he was cut-throat good. He would have made sure he had all his bases covered before he presented the sale of the ranch to her. Her other two brothers didn't give a damn about the ranch. Gus, though the nicest of the three, needed the money to pay for his kids' college tuitions. Matthew just wanted the money to live the good life in Vegas and would be broke before the year was out. Hayden, well, he was just greedy.

"Midnight, Kahlua, Chester and Tweed are mine. I paid for them out of my own money. They go with me," Indy said with her back still turned. Midnight and Kahlua were two horses she had bought and trained for rounding. Chester and Tweed were her two cow dogs. "I'll have my stuff out and be gone within the next two weeks."

"I took the liberty of looking at several places you might be interested in living at...." Hayden began.

Indy turned sharply, staring coldly into Hayden's eyes. "Hayden, you can take your liberties and stick them up your ass. I go where I want, when I want. I don't need your or anyone else's help. Once I'm out of here I don't give a damn if I ever see any of you again. Now, if you will excuse me, I have some packing to do," Indy said in a stiff voice.

Indy walked out the door of her grandfather's office. She felt numb inside as she headed toward the stairs and her bedroom. It wouldn't take her long to pack as she didn't own much. She had never needed much living on the ranch. Anything she had ever wanted the ranch had supplied.

* * *

"I think that went well. What about you guys?" Matthew said as he watched Indy walk out the door.

"Matt, sometimes you can be such an ass," Gus said as he stood up. "We shouldn't have done it this way to Indy. This ranch is all she has ever known. We should have discussed what we planned with her."

"You are too soft on her, Gus," Hayden said pulling all the paperwork together and placing it in a large envelope. "This ranch is worth a fortune and we were lucky to be able to sell it for what we did. Indy will adjust. This is no place for a young girl anyway. Once she calms down, I'll let her know I took the liberty of purchasing her a condo in Los Angeles. She'll thank us one day," Hayden said as he stood up and brushed an imaginary piece of lint from the pants of his expensive Armani suit.

"Los Angeles?" Gus stared in disbelief at Hayden. "You can't put Indy in the middle of a big city! She hates cities."

"As I said before, she'll adjust," Hayden said grimly before heading out the door. "I have to fly back to L.A. tonight as I have a case on Monday morning. I'll let Sam know to make sure Indy has everything packed and moved out by the end of the month. I'll let you know when the final payment for the ranch has been made and make sure it is deposited into your accounts."

Chapter 2

"Indy, are you sure about this?" Sam Whitewater asked for the third time as he handed her another pack. "Winter is still upon us and it can be brutal out there. What if we get a late winter storm?"

Indy ignored Sam for a moment as she cinched the ties onto the packs she had loaded on Kahlua. She had enough gear to last her a couple months if she was careful. The air was still frigid from the snow that fell last night. It had been a light dusting though and shouldn't hold her up. The horses and dogs could easily handle it. Staring out at the mountains to the west she knew her brothers would think she was just being difficult, unreasonable, and immature but she knew differently. When she had read the letter from Hayden last night it had taken everything in her not to call him up just to cuss him out. It wouldn't make any difference anyway. How did you cuss the devil out? He just enjoyed your pain.

"Sam, I'll come by your place sometime in early spring to visit and resupply. I know how to survive in the mountains so don't worry. I had the best teacher after all," Indy said with a slight curve to her lips.

"You're damn right you did. Now you make me wish I hadn't taught you so well," Sam replied sadly. "Your brothers do not understand your heart. Hayden would never have demanded you move to the city if he did."

Indy had shown Sam and his wife, Claire, the letter she received. Hayden had gone before a judge and had a court order giving him guardianship of

Indy until she was twenty-five on the basis she was unable to make clear, rational decisions ensuring her mental and physical health and finances. She had been ordered to live with him at his L.A. home until further notice. A certified copy, delivered by the local sheriff along with an airline ticket, had been enclosed. In addition, the document stated any livestock or animals were to be placed in the care of the new owners of the Wild Ranch until further notice by her guardian.

Indy stared out at the mountains for another moment before she called out to Chester and Tweed. Pulling her gloves on tighter and securing her hat, she mounted Midnight. She reached down, taking the lead rope for Kahlua that Sam held out.

She looked down at Sam with a sad smile. "I would rather live in the mountains for the next couple of months to a year before I live in a city. Hayden might cause a fuss, but they won't find me. I'll be moving around a lot, so don't bother trying to look for me. This way, if Hayden asks, you don't know anything," Indy said quietly, looking at the man who understood her better than her own family.

Sam observed the young woman sitting upon the solid black horse with a mixture of sorrow and respect. She had chosen a hard path most men couldn't survive. He knew she could. She had been raised to be a part of the land and would die anywhere else.

Lifting a beaded necklace from around his neck, he handed it to Indy. "*Okoblaya icimani.* Peaceful journey, little one," Sam said sadly, gazing up at his slender goddaughter.

Indy grasped the necklace tightly in her fist before sliding it into her pocket. "*Wowahwa. Atewaye ki.* Peace, my father, " Indy replied with a tight smile.

With a click of her heels, Indy moved off slowly heading for the mountains looming far to the west. She knew she could die, but figured she had a choice this way. She could die on the land she loved, doing what she was born to do or let her spirit die a slower, more painful death at the hands of her brother in a city. She had a much better chance of surviving in the mountains.

***

It had taken her two days to reach the mountains. She had to keep moving, using as many different methods as possible so she couldn't be tracked. She had headed out through the lower cattle pastures first making sure her tracks were mixed in with those of the cattle. It hadn't snowed again so she couldn't use it to help her.

Once she was closer to the mountains, she moved along the river where the ground was harder and didn't leave as many tracks. She crossed over the river and headed up the mountain following little used trails Sam had taught her about when she was younger. There were a number of caves and shallow rock overhangs she could use for shelter in the higher regions.

She would head north now. There was a huge ranch on the other side of the mountain range. Maybe she could hire on as a cowpuncher in the spring. If she kept a low profile she should be alright. By then, Hayden should have given up looking for her.

The snow had gotten deeper as she moved further up and light snow flurries mixed with the heavy snow that was falling. Tweed and Chester ran ahead, bouncing up and down. If it became too difficult for them, she would have to make a sled to pull them on. For now, though, they acted like the two year old Australian Cattle dogs they were.

Days turned into weeks and before Indy knew it almost a month had passed. It was getting to be late March. She was close to a hundred miles from her grandfather's ranch from her calculations. She had to stop a few times for several days as late winter storms blew through the upper elevations.

Luckily, she had purchased specialized camping gear several years ago made just for the cold Montana winters. The arctic tent and sheet metal stove had kept her, Tweed and Chester nice and warm. She had extra tarps she had strung up to make a portable lean-to for the horses.

She had supplemented her food supplies with small animals she had trapped or the dogs had run down. The first two weeks had been the worst. She had heard the sound of planes making a crisscrossing pattern and knew Hayden had discovered her missing. She had to travel mostly at night during that time until she moved out of their search field. Once, she heard dogs far off in the distance. She had put Tweed and Chester up onto Midnight and Kahlua and used a small stream to help hide their scent. After the third week she figured she was far enough away to be safe and had been able to gain more ground during the daylight hours.

It wasn't until she reached Spirit Pass that she felt totally safe. Sam had told Indy about it when she was little. He had brought her up here only once and told her of the legend of Spirit Pass.

It is said those who travel through the sacred ground would complete a journey that would change their lives. When Indy asked what type of journey, Sam had told her he once had traveled through the Pass only to find himself in another world. There he had met Claire and fallen in love. The world he found himself in had been a dangerous place, for red man and white man did not like each other.

Claire had been traveling with her family when her parents and little brother had taken ill. Her parents had died, leaving Claire and her little brother alone. Sam had come upon them lost and frightened on the other side of the mountains. He helped Claire nurse her brother back to health.

During that time, Claire and Sam had fallen in love and Sam had convinced Claire to come back with him over the mountains where he owned the ranch next to her grandfather. Indy had always liked Claire. She had always acted like a second mother to Indy, teaching her stuff like how to cook using ingredients not found in a box. Those lessons had come in very handy over the last couple of weeks.

"Come on guys. Once we get through the pass we should be safe. We'll head down to the lower elevations where it shouldn't be so cold. Maybe we can find work on a ranch," Indy said, suddenly excited. Tweed and Chester wagged their tails as if to agree and took off ahead of her.

Laughing, Indy nudged Midnight on with Kahlua following behind. The cut through the pass was long and narrow. Indy looked up as small rocks and bits of snow fell off the sides. She vaguely wondered what world she would end up in. She hoped it was one with wide open spaces, no big cities, and no big brothers.

The air around her swirled and a cold shiver ran down her spine as she passed the halfway mark. Turning on Midnight's back, Indy looked behind her. She was surprised to see a mist of snow so thick she couldn't see the entrance to the Pass any longer. Shrugging her shoulders, she turned back around and focused on the path ahead of her.

Yeah, she thought to herself, *it would be nice to find a world where I can be who I am and not have to worry about my brothers anymore.*

Indy made good time after she made it through the Pass down to the lower elevation. She stopped on a ridge about half way down to take a break and give the horses and dogs time to rest. She sank down, sitting on the ledge looking out over the valley below. It was beautiful. There were patches of snow dotting the landscape and probably a hundred head or more of cattle grazing.

She would make camp down near the timberline and scope things out before she approached the ranch. She wanted to make sure it was safe. She hoped her brothers hadn't sent notices out to all the ranches.

She decided she would take it slow and see if she could find a cowpuncher or two alone. She would approach them and make polite conversation, checking to see if they said anything. If they didn't, she would see if there were any positions open. If they did say something or acted strange she would head back up into the mountains to hide.

Chapter 3

Indy set up her tent and just a top covering for the horses' lean-to. It was warmer down here and she could keep their blankets on them to help keep them warm at night. She spent the next three days enjoying the peace and quiet of the woods.

She took the opportunity to wash some of her clothes out in the nearby river and even warmed up enough water to take a nice shower using the portable solar shower she had. It felt good to wash her hair out and feel clean again.

"Come on boys; let's go see if we can find us any cowpunchers to talk to," Indy said as she saddled Midnight. She looped the lead rope over Kahlua's neck, knowing the mare would follow Midnight anywhere.

Riding down to the lower region, she was almost to the stream crossing over to the cattle when she heard gunfire. Pulling in the reins, she listened carefully as the gunfire continued. Moving across the stream to a low rise on the hill above them, she slipped off Midnight's back and motioned for the dogs to lie down.

Pulling out a pair of binoculars from a saddlebag, she laid down on the cold ground and looked to see what was going on. It was downright stupid to be shooting guns around that many cattle. It wouldn't take much to start a stampede.

Indy watched as three men on horseback charged at another two who had been sitting around a fire under one of the few trees dotting the landscape. One of the men on horseback fired a gun, hitting the old man in the chest.

Oh shit, Indy thought stunned as she watched the man fall backwards onto the ground.

The young man who had been sitting moved to grab the injured man and dragged him behind the tree firing his own gun at the masked man on horseback. Indy turned her binoculars towards the other two men. They were trying to round the cattle up.

Rustlers? In broad daylight? That took some balls, she couldn't help thinking silently to herself.

Swinging her binoculars back to the two men who had been sitting under the tree, she could tell they were in a world of hurt. The scene playing out below her had to be real, she thought in dismay as she watched bark flying from the tree and the trail of blood on the ground.

Getting up, Indy motioned for the dogs to go after the cattle. "Round 'em up, boys," she said grimly.

Indy swung up onto Midnight's back and pulled her Ruger semi-automatic rifle from her saddle. Laying it across her lap, she kicked Midnight into a full run knowing Kahlua would be right behind her. Charging at the masked man shooting at the two men behind the tree, she stood up in the stirrups to get a steadier ride clutching the saddle with her knees to keep her balance.

Raising the rifle, she let out a series of shots close enough in front of him to let him know she meant business. The masked man on the horse swung around, startled to find someone shooting at him from behind. The young man behind the tree took advantage of the rustler's sudden distraction. He stepped out from behind the tree and fired a shot, hitting the man in the arm and causing him to drop his gun.

The masked gunman yelled out in pain, clutching his wounded limb against his chest. Unarmed now, the man pulled back on the reins and headed after the other two men who had tried to take the cattle. He rode through the herd, which was heading back towards the camp, the two dogs barking and nipping at their heels.

Indy pulled her jacket up higher around her neck and pulled her hat further down. She needed to check on the two cowpunchers to make sure they were okay, but didn't want to take the chance of them recognizing her. She would play it safe for now by keeping her face covered as much as she could. Hopefully, if her brothers put out posters looking for her they didn't include anything about her traveling companions.

Midnight slowed to a walk with Kahlua right on his hind quarters as Indy approached the tree. The last thing she wanted was to get shot. Stowing her rifle back into the gun harness attached to her saddle, she held up her hands to show she was unarmed.

"That's far enough!" A young voice called out from behind the tree.

"I'm unarmed. I just wanted to make sure you two cowpunchers were okay," Indy called out trying to deepen her voice. "Looked like one of you might have been hurt."

A gruff voice murmured something to the young man. "Get down off your horse and keep your hands up," the younger man called out.

Indy slowly lowered her hands long enough to get down without falling before raising them again and taking a step toward the young man.

"Do you need some help?" Indy asked.

A young boy of about fourteen slowly emerged from behind the tree. He looked scared and the gun in his hands shook as he pointed it towards Indy's chest. He took a deep breath as he studied Indy for a moment.

"Jake took a bullet to the shoulder. You know anything about bullets?" The boy asked.

Indy tried not to smile. "I know if you keep pointing that gun at me, I might be learning more about them than I want to."

The boy flushed as he lowered the gun in his hand. "Sorry about that. Didn't know if you were with them others or not."

"Not, is the correct answer," Indy said. "Let me take a look at your friend. The boys will bring your cattle back." Indy walked slowly towards the boy and around the tree where she saw an older man in maybe his early fifties leaning up against the tree. Blood soaked one shoulder and he held a gun in his other hand.

"Hey, looks like you've had a rotten morning," Indy said huskily. Bending down, she carefully looked at the man's shoulder.

"Hell, that's an understatement if I ever heard one," Jake replied in a deep, pain-filled voice.

"Looks like the bullet went all the way through. I've got some first aid stuff to patch you up with until we can get you to a doctor," Indy said rising and moving over to the pack on Midnight.

"Did you know any of those men who came at you?" Indy asked as she gently unbuttoned Jake's shirt.

Pushing the shirt down, Indy cleaned the area around the wound carefully before pulling out a bottle of Novocain and a small syringe with a hypodermic needle attached. Filling the needle with a small amount, she gently numbed the area on the front and the back so she could sew up the wound. Taking an extra fine needle, she wiped it with an alcohol swab before threading it with stitching thread. Sam had taught her how to take care of cuts and other wounds while out on the range. Most of the time if you were going to get hurt there wouldn't be a doctor around so it was common sense to learn advanced first aid. Indy had taken it a step further and had gone to college for nursing. She had finished her bachelor's degree in a record two years because she hated being away from home for so long.

She quickly sewed up both wounds and wiped it down with another alcohol swab. Cleaning up the used material she walked over to the fire and dumped everything but the hypodermic needle into it. She would put it in a container to depose of later.

"Shit, I didn't feel a thing, but a few pinches after you stuck me with that needle. What the hell did you do?" Jake asked in astonishment.

Indy laughed. "I thought you might prefer a less painful way of getting stitched up. I could have opted for the old fashion stick between the teeth and hope you passed out if you would have preferred."

"Hell no," Jake grumbled. "My name's Jake Turner. The boy here is Calhoun Tanner. We're much obliged for your help."

"No problem. I'm Indy." Indy looked over to see if there was a flash of recognition on either man's face. Not seeing anything she turned to look out over the cattle. Tweed and Chester were barking madly, pushing the cattle into a tight circle. She let out a loud whistle, causing both dogs to stop and look towards her. With a flick of her hand, both dogs trotted away from the cattle and moved towards her.

"Cal, you did a good job. I owe you my life, pulling me out of the line of fire like that," Jake growled out.

Cal turned red at the old man's compliment. "Thanks, Jake. I hit one of 'em, the one that shot you. I hit him," he said excitedly.

"Know you did, boy. Good shooting. Boss men will be proud of you," Jake said turning to Indy. "Those are some dogs of yours. You train them?"

"Yes, sir. The one with the black patch around his eye is Tweed. The one with the brown face is called

Chester. I've had both of them since they were born. They are the best cattle dogs in the country." Indy knew that for a fact after the last rounding competition, she had participated in a year ago when they had still been pups.

"The boss men are always looking for new hands. You need a job or you just passing through?" Jake asked curiously looking a little closer at the kid in front of him. It was hard to see the kid's face as he kept it turned slightly away and had his hat pulled down and collar pulled up. He didn't look much older than Cal did. Still soft in the face like Cal was.

"Looking for a job. You think your bosses will hire me and the boys on?" Indy asked nodding towards Tweed and Chester.

"Hell yeah, after what you saved them today. Those thieving butchers would have killed the two of us and took damn near a hundred head of cattle if it hadn't been for you." Jake spit into the dirt next to the tree.

"I've got to break camp. I can be back before nightfall if you think you can get me a job. This way it will also even out the odds if those men decide to come back," Indy said rising and moving towards Midnight.

"You wanted by the law, boy?" Jake asked suddenly watching Indy carefully.

Indy jerked to a stop, not turning around at first. "Maybe." Indy turned to look Jake in the eye. She never lied if she could help it and she wasn't about to start because of her brothers. "I don't lie, steal, or hurt other people. I just want to be left alone. There are some men looking for me. I would prefer it if they didn't find me. Why they are looking is between me and them. If you have a problem with that I'll head out now and keep going."

Jake studied Indy for a moment, seeing the truth and pride in the kid's stance. He believed Indy didn't lie, steal or hurt other people, not after the help he had been to them. He was of the mind if it wasn't any of his business he stayed out of it. He just didn't want to make a mistake that would cost his bosses.

"I don't have any problems. Go get your stuff," Jake replied with a nod.

Indy let out the breath she had been holding. She meant what she had said. If Jake had had a problem with what she had told him, then she would have gotten on Midnight and left, never to return. Now she was riding back to break camp. She knew instinctively she could trust Jake and Cal. They were good men.

It didn't take Indy long to break camp as she had been doing it so much over the past month or so. In no time at all, she was heading back down the trail out of the timberline and towards the camp by the tree. It was just getting dark when she rode up. Cal was riding around the herd making sure they were okay. He nodded as Indy rode by followed by her band of misfits. Pulling up near the fire, Indy slid from the saddle. She moved with quick, efficient steps, pulling her remaining supplies off of Kahlua's back and removing the lead rope. Next, she pulled her saddle and bridle off of Midnight. Giving them both a hand signal she watched as they moved off to join the cattle and graze.

"You train them too?" Jake asked as he stirred a thick stew in a pot over the fire with one hand. He had the other in a sling.

"Yes. I have something that will help you with the pain if you like," Indy said reaching for her saddlebag. She had noticed the tight lines around Jake's mouth as he moved. She removed a couple of tablets, holding them out to him. "They won't make you sleepy or anything, just cut the pain. You'll feel a difference in about fifteen to thirty minutes," she explained.

Jake took the two green gel tablets. He looked at them with a puzzled expression on his face. He didn't question Indy about them though he looked like he would have liked to. He swallowed both of them down with a swig of water from his canteen.

"How'd you learn so much about doctoring?" Jake asked.

"School and a friend," Indy replied shortly not wanting to say too much. "Tell me about the ranch and who you work for. You said boss men. How many own the ranch?"

Jake swallowed back the grin. He could tell an evasive move when he saw one. The lad didn't want to talk about his self. "Twin Rivers is the name of the ranch. It's owned by twin brothers, Jacob and Jonathon Tucker. They mostly raise horses, but keep a nice stock of cattle for their own food supply. They have one of the largest ranches in the area."

"How many men do they employ?" Indy asked pouring a cup of coffee. She wrapped her gloved hands around it for warmth. It had cooled off considerably after the sun went down.

"About fifty at any given time," Jake responded quietly. "Sometimes more, sometimes less. It's hard to find good help out here. Most men are either passing through, looking to make a little money, or not cut out for the life," he added scooping up a bowl of thick stew and handing it to Indy.

Both of them turned when they heard Cal ride up. He quickly dismounted and pulled his saddle off. "Smells good, Jake. How you feelin'?" Cal asked as he grabbed a bowl and filled it with stew.

Jake looked up in surprise at Indy. "Good. Damn lad, those pills you gave me took the pain away like you said. If'n I didn't know better I would never have guessed I'd been shot this morning."

Indy just grinned before taking another bite of the stew. She hadn't missed the use of the word 'lad' again. Maybe his thinking her a boy would help her establish herself and give her time to make sure she was safe. "You said the Tuckers raised mostly horses. What type of horses?"

"Mostly Mustangs for the army and local ranches. They have a few race horses too they breed and send back east," Jake replied before letting out a loud belch.

Indy smothered a grin. She remembered having belching contests with Sam's boys. She never seemed to win as she could never eat as much as they did.

They used to call her the runt because they all towered over her. Sam was tall for a Lakota. He stood at six foot one. All his boys were at least six two or three. Claire used to say it was from all the milk they used to drink.

Indy's own five foot four was not nearly as impressive. She was small boned on top of that and it made her seem even smaller than she was. She had inherited her mother's features. She had large dark green eyes framed by dark lashes. Her face was heart-shaped leading to the impression she was more feminine than she really was.

She had braided and covered her light brown hair, streaked with sun-bleached blonde with a black bandana before covering that with her large Stetson. Her figure was hidden in layers of clothing. She wore a pair of light-weight thermal long Johns covered by her jeans and a pair of leather chaps. Her dark brown coat covered her almost to her knees and had a thick wool lining. She finished out her outfit with a thick scarf she kept tucked into the collar of her coat. She figured she probably looked about the same age as Cal.

Cal looked at Indy then at Jake. "Do you think those men will be back tonight, Jake?"

"Might, though I doubt it." Jake scratched his chin, the whiskers making a sound similar to someone rubbing sandpaper on a piece of wood. "Might want to take turns keeping watch."

Indy nodded. "Jake, why don't you take the first watch? Cal, I'll take the second if you don't mind. The boys will help out as well. I'll set them to making the rounds and keeping an ear out." Indy looked over at Tweed and Chester, with a flip of her hand they took off like ghosts in the night.

Cal looked at Indy in awe. "How'd you do that?"

"I trained them to protect me as well as the cattle. I studied guard dog training videos and read books, then spent hours and hours working with them on hand signals. Not all dogs are as good as those two. The boys and I have been together since they were born so there is a large amount of trust built into our relationship," Indy replied.

It's a shame that same thing can't be said about my own brothers, she thought sadly.

Jake poured the remains of his cup into the fire before he stood up. "You two get some shut-eye. I'll wake you at midnight, Indy."

Indy nodded. She cleaned up the dirty dishes, stacking them neatly back into the box next to the tree. Pulling her sleeping bag out, she laid it near the fire. She would leave her boots on tonight. She didn't need any surprise visitors in them when she went to put them on. Unzipping the thick bag, she pulled her coat off and rolled it up to use as a pillow before she slid in and zipped it back up. She hadn't realized Cal was watching her with wide eyes until she had laid back down.

"What type of bed roll is that?" He asked, looking at her thick sleeping bag before glancing down at his thin wool blanket.

"It's a thermal sleeping bag designed especially for cold weather country. I can zip myself in this puppy and stay warm in sub-zero temperatures if I have to. The worst part is getting out of it. It keeps you so warm you don't want to get up in the morning," Indy said. "It also has a little extra padding so you don't feel the ground as much." She couldn't help adding with a grin before rolling over. She might be a softy, but she had learned a long time ago never to give up her sleeping bag.

Jake woke Indy up at midnight eyeing her sleeping bag with envy as he threw another log on the fire. Indy unzipped the bag and softly whistled for Midnight. The black horse was impossible to see at night. A moment later the sound of hooves could be heard.

Indy quickly saddled Midnight and led him out of the firelight before mounting him. She rode down toward the stream first to take care of her personal business. One thing she desperately missed about home was indoor plumbing. She would kill for a hot soak in a tub and a real toilet.

She spent the next four hours making the rounds. She motioned for Tweed and Chester to return to camp to stay near the men. If she was right, the two dogs would snuggle up next to each one of them. They loved to snuggle with her at night. At four she woke Cal to take over and crawled back into her sleeping bag. Chester quickly resumed his snuggling duty next to her since he'd lost Cal.

Indy rose early the next morning. She was just coming back from the stream again when she heard the sound of horses approaching. She pulled her toiletry bag closer to her and felt for the nine millimeter semi-automatic pistol she kept under her coat.

She quickly motioned for the dogs to go on alert. If they were expecting trouble, she would need the element of surprise. When she topped the rise, she could see a group of about six men. One of the men climbed down off his horse and shook hands with Jake and clapped Cal on the back. It looked like the men knew each other.

Indy rose and slid the nine millimeter handgun back into its holster. Pulling her hat further down to cover her face and pulling up her scarf so the lower half of her face was covered fairly well, she moved cautiously toward the group of men now standing around the fire.

Jonathan Tucker watched as the small figure moved cautiously towards them. He had listened as Jake and Cal told them about how this kid named Indy had come riding in firing his rifle while the kid's dogs had gone after the other two men and rounded up the cattle they had tried to steal. The kid then patched Jake up better than the doc from town. He couldn't see the kid's face because of the way he was wearing his hat and coat. Jake said the boy was looking for employment and the Twin Rivers would be getting a deal between the kid and his dogs.

Indy glanced warily at the men, giving them a brief nod before moving over to her saddlebags and tucking her toiletry bag away. She knew she was being rude, but after having been in hiding for so long she didn't feel comfortable around so many people. The man standing near Jake took her breath away. His dark hair and chiseled features made her think of dark nights and steamy beds.

Shaking her head lightly at her bemusing thoughts, Indy wondered if she was beginning to lose her mind from being out on the range for so long. Turning, she gave a silent motion with her hand to Tweed and Chester. A few moments later, Midnight and Kahlua were walking slowly towards her followed by the two dogs.

"Boss, this here is Indy, the lad, I told you about. Those two bringing up the horses are Tweed and Chester. Best damn cattle dogs I've ever seen," Jake said.

Jonathan had watched as the lad walked right by them with barely any acknowledgement. It surprised him as most boys his age usually wouldn't shut up, especially if they wanted a job working for the Twin Rivers. He watched closely as the boy barely moved his hand, giving the two dogs a signal.

The two dogs sitting next to him immediately took off. His eyes widened when a few moments later the lad looked over towards the two horses moving toward him. Another slight hand movement had the horses standing still and the dogs returning to their spot behind him.

"Nice trick," Jonathan said waiting for the lad's reaction to him noticing the signals.

"Not a trick, training," came the calm, husky reply.

Jonathan felt a shiver run down his spine at the husky voice. His eyes narrowed as he studied what little he could see of the kid's face. It was baby smooth with lush pink lips and a small nose.

He let his gaze wander further down, but couldn't see much under the thick coat and chaps. He felt his body stir to life in sudden interest. He frowned in shock and disbelief. What was he thinking? It had been a long time since he had been with a woman so he could understand having a reaction like this to a woman but for a boy? He scowled as his eyes moved back up to the boy's face. Dark green eyes narrowed on his as he jerked his eyes back up.

"Nice training," Jonathan corrected. "Jake says you're interested in working for the Twin Rivers."

Slim shoulders barely moved in a shrug. "Yes," came the short reply.

"You old enough to be working? The last thing I need is your ma to come looking for you," Jonathan replied, beginning to get irritated with the boy's attitude.

"I'm old enough to shave. And for your information, my ma is dead. So's my pa," came the short response.

"Sorry to hear that," Jonathan said.

Again, the slim shoulders shrugged, drawing Jonathan's attention to the figure hidden under the thick coat. Jonathan turned before he said something he knew he would regret. He needed to pay a visit to the brothel in town if he was having reactions like this to some smooth-faced kid. It had definitely been too long.

"Jake, I want you to head back to the ranch house and have doc take a look at your shoulder. Indy, you're hired. You'll stay here with Cal, Levi, and Duke. I want you to bring the cattle to the pasture closer to the homestead." With a nod of dismissal he turned toward his horse.

Indy let out a sigh of relief as she watched her new boss and two other men ride away. She felt good about her act. She could tell he misinterpreted her comment about shaving.

He didn't have to know she was talking about her legs and not her face. If she could keep out of everyone's way and keep a low profile she didn't have to correct their views on her, at least not at first.

She didn't owe anyone anything as far as she was concerned, except a full day's worth of work. Moving quickly, she saddled Midnight and motioned for the dogs to follow her. She wanted to put as much space between her and the other cowpunchers as possible.

Chapter 4

Indy spent the next three weeks out on the range. At times it was tough. Since she was a girl she couldn't just whip it out and go like the guys did. She also liked to bathe more than they did.

In order to do that she had taken to leaving early or coming back late. She used Tweed and Chester as an alarm system to let her know if anyone was around. There had been a couple of times when she had almost gotten caught.

She knew she would have to do something when it came time to return to the ranch. There was no way she was going to stay in the bunkhouse. For one thing, all the men seemed to take great pleasure in releasing gas from both ends of their body.

While accustomed to working with ranch hands and being around Sam's boys, these guys seemed to take it to a new level of competing with each other to see who could be the most obnoxious. Even Cal had joined in after the first night. Indy had quickly taken to building a camp away from the others saying it was better for the dogs to be alert for danger.

The weather had started to warm up a little more as it moved into the middle of April. Indy still hadn't seen the ranch house yet. Jake had come out once to let her know he had healed up right pretty and the doc wanted to meet the lad who had done such a fine job of sewing him up. Indy had talked with Jake for a while before he headed back to the ranch.

It was about midday two days later when Indy heard her name. Turning in her saddle, she watched as Jake rode up again. She turned Midnight around to let him know she had heard him.

"Indy, boss man says to come in," Jake said, pushing his hat up onto his forehead.

"What for?" Indy asked. She hoped it wasn't to fire her. She liked the job even if she had trouble with the overabundance of gas the men put out.

Jake spit before answering. "Seems Jacob is bringing in a herd of mustangs and they need some help with them. Things are quiet out here. Trace and Butler can handle the cattle."

"I need to pack my stuff up," Indy said, nodding towards her camp.

Jake looked at her in surprise. "What are you doing camping out here by yourself?"

"I'm not by myself. I have the boys. I prefer their snoring to the gas geysers going off with Trace and Butler," Indy said as she turned Midnight towards her camp. With a whistle, Kahlua and the dogs followed.

Jake and Indy were heading back to the ranch within the hour. It took them half a day to get there and it was getting dark as they rode into the yard.

"You must have left right at first light. I didn't realize we were still so far out," Indy murmured softly, looking at the ranch house in awe. It was huge! Even bigger than her grandfather's house. It had a large wraparound porch with plenty of windows.

"Wow, some house!" Indy said, staring in open amazement at it.

"Yeah, pain in the ass if you ask me. Jacob and Jonathan's folks built it. They wanted a place big enough to entertain. Their ma was from a rich family back east used to big houses, hard to heat during the winter months if you ask me," Jake said spitting again. He groaned as he got down off his horse. "I'm getting too old for those long rides," he muttered under his breath.

"Where will I be staying?" Indy asked getting down.

"No room in the bunkhouse. Boss said you can stay in the old cabin near the river. Needs some work, but he figured if you wanted to stay there you could do it. If not, he said the barn would have to do until a space was freed up. Since you was the last hired you don't get much choice."

"Why don't any of the other men want the old cabin?" Indy asked curiously. If she had a choice of staying in a smelly, overcrowded bunkhouse or have a place of her own she would choose a place of her own any day.

"None of them want to waste time fixing it up. They would rather be going to town on their time off to spend it with the ladies," Jake said with a grin.

"Oh. Well, my luck then," Indy said. "Which way to the cabin and when should I report for duty?"

"Cabin is down that trail about a quarter mile. The rivers not very big but has been known to flood a time or two. The cabin is up high enough so it usually just gets water to the steps. The boss wanted to give you a couple days' time off since you ain't had none so you could work on it. He had two of the men deliver some materials down there yesterday figuring you might prefer it to the barn. Jacob is supposed to be in with the horses in about three days. That's when we'll need you."

Indy nodded. So, she had three days to get the cabin fixed up which shouldn't be a problem as long as it wasn't too bad. She wondered if it had a tub or a shower. She really didn't care as long as it had a real toilet.

She thanked Jake for his help and told him she would be back up to the barn at sunrise three days from now. Mounting Midnight again, she turned the horses toward the narrow road Jake had pointed to and rode off.

* * *

By the middle of the first day, Indy was thinking Jake needed to clarify what 'some work' meant. She had spent the better part of the first night just cleaning out all the local inhabitants who had moved in, which included a family of raccoons and mice, in addition to all the ugly bugs. Chester had even found the remains of a rattlesnake that hadn't survived the frigid temperatures of winter.

Indy was just glad it was dead. She ended up tossing what was left of the mattress outside and built a bonfire with it to help light up the night so she could see. After setting up her sleeping bag in the finally clean cabin, she fell into an exhausted sleep. The next morning she took a survey of what needed to be done. First, there was no tub, no shower, no toilet because there was no bathroom or indoor plumbing! She had screamed out her frustration for a good ten minutes.

The cabin consisted of one room. The kitchen consisted of a long shelf with what looked like a wash tub and a hand pump along with more shelves above it and an old wood burning stove. The dining room consisted of two rickety chairs around a small rough wood table set in the middle of the room. The bedroom consisted of an old wash stand, a charming chamber pot, and a rope bed that looked more like a medieval torture chamber rack along the far wall.

Indy finished cleaning the sparse area inside until it shone before she moved to look at the outside. The roof needed repair in several places. As she moved around to the back, she noticed an outhouse that was leaning slightly. Moving over to it, she carefully opened the door and peeked inside. A wooden seat with a hole cut out of the center greeted her.

She closed the door and pushed gently on the small structure. It didn't move at all. It must have settled into the ground after one of the floods. Well, at least she had a toilet of sorts instead of a pot to piss in.

Beside the house was a small enclosed area with some of the fencing missing and an old double stall lean-to. Midnight looked up as Indy walked around the structure testing it for weaknesses. He whinnied softly when she shook her head in dismay. It needed a new roof as well, but seemed to be sound otherwise.

"I know, boy. Not like home, is it? Guess we'll just have to make a new home for you. Custom built by Indiana Wild," she said patting his head as he leaned over her shoulder.

"Well, daylight is wasting. Guess I'd better get busy," Indy said, moving toward the little cabin.

The weather had become unexpectedly warm for an April day and Indy knew it was only going to get warmer as she worked. Changing out of her jeans into a pair of low-cut tan shorts and pulling on a sports bra and a button up shirt, she finished her work clothes out by sliding her feet into a pair of tennis shoes. They had a better grip than her boots and would have to do.

Pulling her long hair into a ponytail on top of her head, she pulled out her iPod touch and a set of ear buds. She had bought one of those new cases that used solar to charge it. It had been a life saver over the last couple of months as she liked to listen to music or read one of the many ebooks she had downloaded before her escape. It helped to fight the loneliness too. Setting her iPod to shuffle the music, she cranked up the volume as she tied a small fabric utility belt with pockets around her waist and knotted the shirt under her breasts. She was ready to do some serious damage.

* * *

Jacob Tucker was never as glad as he was now when he caught sight of the main house. He had ridden ahead to make sure everything was ready. He left his foreman, Ed Rawlings, to finish bringing in the herd of Mustangs. He had been on the trail for the past six weeks and was ready for a hot bath and a decent meal.

Right now, he would take the hot bath. He smelled like horse, smoke, and sweat. Pulling up in front of the barn, he dismounted with a fluid ease born from years in the saddle.

"Hey boss, didn't expect you back for another two days," Jake said coming out of the barn. "I'll take Roam if you like."

"Thanks Jake, appreciate it. Hell, it's good to be back," Jacob said as he moved towards the huge ranch house.

"Jacob, welcome back. We weren't expecting you for another couple of days," Jonathan said, meeting his younger twin before he even had a chance to put his foot on the first step.

It was almost impossible to tell the two apart when they were cleaned up. Six foot two, with broad, muscular shoulders built from years of hard work had given them hard bodies the women liked. Jonathan and Jacob couldn't go to town without the women flaunting their daughters and sometimes themselves before them trying to catch one of the bachelor brothers' eyes.

They both had dark blue eyes and dark brown hair that hung almost to their shoulders. The only difference was Jacob had a slight scar above his left eye from a fight a few years back. They often liked to use their close looks to sample different women. If one liked a woman, he might see if the other did and vice-versa. At that moment, though, they looked nothing alike. Jacob was covered in filth from the long ride and had a couple days growth of beard on his face not to mention his hair was down below his shoulders.

"Looks like you could use a bath. Come on in and I'll get Wally to prepare you one." Wally was a Chinaman they had found in the back alley a few years ago. He had been drunker than a skunk and smelled like one too. He had come out to work on the railroad and didn't like it. He had been beaten pretty badly by the time Jacob and Jonathan stumbled upon him while taking a piss outside the back of the saloon in town. They had brought him home and Wally had been with them ever since.

"Wally, can you draw a bath for Jacob here?" Jonathan called out.

"Yes, sir. Yes, sir. Welcome home Mr. Jacob. Wally, have you bath in no time," Wally said as he moved with lightening quick reflexes to pull out a huge copper bathtub and dragged it into the middle of the kitchen. In a matter of minutes, Jacob was lowering himself into the steaming tub with a groan.

"Damn, that feels good," Jacob said as he leaned back.

Jonathan sat at the table studying his brother's tired face. "How did it go?"

"Great. All the ponies made the journey, I have a signed contract with the army to supply them with a hundred and fifty trained horses by the end of the summer, and I got laid while I was in Jackson," Jacob said with a grin.

"Shit. Was she good?" Jonathan asked, rubbing his crotch. Damn, it had been the better part of six months since he had gotten laid. He didn't like visiting the local brothel but he just might have to before too long.

"Good enough," Jacob replied before dunking his head under the water. He washed it and then leaned back as Wally cut it for him and gave him a shave.

"Do you think it is possible to train a hundred and fifty horses by the end of the summer? That doesn't give us much time. They wouldn't agree to sign unless I could promise it," Jacob asked looking over at Jonathan.

"We have at least five of us who can do the training, six if you count the new kid," Jonathan replied pouring a glass of whisky for himself and Jacob.

"What new kid?" Jacob asked reaching for the glass of amber liquid. Damn, but it was good to be home.

"Some kid traveling through. He looks like he's about fourteen maybe fifteen. He has a real attitude problem. Anyway, some rustlers shot at Jake and Cal while they were watching the cattle out near the timberline. Jake took a bullet to the shoulder, but Cal was able to hit one of the guys. This kid comes riding up shooting at the rustler taking shots at Cal and Jake while two of the other rustlers tried to take off with the cattle. The only thing is, the kid has these two cattle dogs he has trained go after the men and the cattle. Before long according to Jake and Cal, the kid has Jake patched up better than the doc could do, with no pain, and his dogs have all the cattle back," Jonathan said before taking a drink.

"You don't think it was a setup do you?" Jacob asked looking at his brother.

"No. I watched as the kid gave out the signals to the dogs. The kid has his horses trained too. I watched as he controlled them with just hand movements. When I commented on it the kid gave me an attitude. Anyway, he's been out for the past four weeks with the herd. Every cowpuncher I sent out there came back with the same story. The kid and his dogs keep the herd in place and the kid knows what he is doing. I kept him out there for a while to see how he'd handle it. He made his own camp away from the others claiming it was better for the dogs but never complained. Jake said he didn't even appear to be in that big a hurry to come in yesterday." Jonathan looked out the window before grinning."I told Jake to tell him the bunkhouse was full and he had to stay either down at the old cabin or in the barn. Last night there was one hell of a fire down there. I could see it from my bedroom window and this morning I swear I heard some cursing before the hammering started. That should give the kid a little bit of an attitude adjustment." Jonathan finished his drink laughing.

Jonathan didn't want to admit he was trying to keep the kid as far away from him as he could. He didn't understand why just thinking of the kid did things to his body, he had never felt before, not even for the experienced women in town. It worried him and he didn't know how to handle it.

"Damn, but you have a mean streak in you," Jacob said, getting out of the tub and wrapping a towel around him. Wally placed a hot plate of food down on the table in front of him. The men spent the next half hour talking about the army deal Jacob had signed while he ate.

* * *

Jake felt sorry for Indy. The kid had been good through all the trials the boss had set up for him. He knew what the boss was doing when he had changed out all the men except the boy. Seldom did the boss make any of the men stay out on the range for more than a week at a time. He also knew for a fact there was plenty of room in the bunkhouse for the kid. He had felt guilty as hell for lying to Indy, but he had his orders.

Jake listened to the non-stop hammering all morning until his guilt got the best of him. He figured Indy probably hadn't had anything to eat last night or this morning so he fixed a couple of biscuits with bacon to take down. He would even see if the kid needed any help with the repairs while he was there.

Walking down the road, he rounded the bend and froze, staring up at the roof in disbelief, the plate of biscuits and bacon falling from his numb fingers. Moving backwards, he didn't take his eyes off the figure standing on the roof until he almost fell in a rut in the road. Turning quickly, he practically ran all the way back to the ranch house.

* * *

Indy wiped the sweat running down her face on the shirt she was wearing. It was definitely hotter up here than down on the ground. She finally decided if she was going to be out in the sun, she might as well work on her tan.

Pulling her shirt loose, she laid it down on the roof next to her before pulling the bandana off her head to wipe the sweat. She was almost done. Another five rows and the roof on the cabin should be good.

At first, she had been afraid she would fall through the damn thing in a few places. Now, after working on it for the past three hours, she could appreciate the workmanship that had gone into the building of the cabin. While it had been neglected for quite some time it was still very solid.

Her mind turned over different options as she worked and she decided if she added on a bathroom it wouldn't be such a bad place to live. She could add the indoor plumbing. She had helped her granddad add two bathrooms to their old homestead.

She sang along with the songs as she worked enjoying the tempo and even doing a little jig, or a booty shake, as she worked. Midnight, Kahlua, and the dogs were in heaven, laying in the sun and enjoying a day off too.

Indy was moving to another spot when she had the feeling she was being watched. Standing up on the roof, she used one hand to shade her eyes while she looked around letting her eyes travel around the perimeter of the cabin. The dogs were still lazing in the front yard under a tree. Turning, she looked back toward the river.

Indy's eyes widened as she saw a Lakota Indian brave standing on the other side of the river watching her. She could tell he was Lakota from his traditional clothing. If she hadn't been looking, she probably would have missed him. She frowned a moment, wondering what he was looking at.

Hadn't he ever seen a girl working on a roof before? Probably not, Indy thought after a moment grinning.

Smiling, Indy waved a hand to say hello and returned to her roof. She didn't have time to waste if she was expected to be back at work day after tomorrow. She still needed to finish the lean-to for the horses and fix the fence. Plus, she wanted to see what she could do about making a mattress for the bed.

* * *

Maikoda stood staring in disbelief at the white woman on the roof of the old cabin. He had been traveling through this part of the valley on his way north. He knew the white men who lived here and they did not mind when he traveled through the land they called their own.

He had been wounded once many years before by a bear and one of the white men named Jacob had saved him, nursing him back to health. Since then, he had moved through their lands with a sense of brotherhood not often found among the white skins. He made camp not far from the river and was hunting when he heard the singing above the loud sounds of the hammer.

He had never heard songs like those floating on the wind. When he followed it to the river, he thought at first it was a water spirit singing until he looked up and saw the nearly naked white woman working on the roof as if she did it all the time. She seemed unconcerned about her state of undress which surprised him. All the white women he had ever seen wore so much clothing he did not know how they moved.

It also surprised him that she seemed to sense his presence. When she stood up, his breath caught at her beauty. Her hair was pulled back carelessly, but the colors seemed to glow in the sun. She wore a small piece of cloth to cover her breasts and the breeches she wore were almost non-existent. When she turned to stare at him, he noticed how she had frowned at first looking around. He thought to hide so as to not scare her off, but had not been able to move.

When she looked at him, he was surprised at her lack of fear. The white woman had not been afraid at all. She smiled at him, raising her hand in welcome before turning back to work on the roof uncaring that a Lakota brave was watching her.

Maikoda pulled back into the woods when he heard the dogs bark. He had not seen them so they must have been in front. He would remain close should the woman need help. He wanted to know more about her.

Chapter 5

Jake was wheezing by the time he got to the big house. He was in shock. How could a kid as young as Indy get a naked woman to fix his roof? Hell, how could a kid as young as Indy get a naked woman as beautiful as that?

Jake might be an old man, but he was still a man. He had to let the boss men know what was happening because if the other men were to go down to the cabin and see that there was a naked woman on the roof, they just might tear it down to get to her. Women were few and far between, especially ones as beautiful as the one working on Indy's roof.

Opening the back door to the kitchen, Jake tried to draw in a deep enough breath so he could talk coherently. His heart was hammering and all he could do was wheeze as he drew air into his heaving chest. He opened and closed his mouth like a fish out of water, but he was still having trouble getting anything out.

Jonathan stood up as Jake burst through the back door. "Boss…. Boss man…." Jake gasped, trying to breathe.

"Shit. What happened to you?" Jonathan asked in concern as he pushed Jake into the chair he had just left.

"It's the kid," Jake began, wiping at the sweat running down his face with a trembling hand.

"What about the kid? Did he take off? Did he get hurt working on the cabin?" Jonathan demanded in aggravation.

"No, no, the kid…." Jake tried to speak looking a little frantically between the two brothers.

He nodded his head in thanks to Wally when he handed him a cup of water. He took a deep drink of it to help with his parched throat before he set the cup down on the table with unsteady hands. He looked back and forth between his two bosses trying to think how to describe what he had seen.

"Well, speak up. What did the kid do?" Jacob asked impatiently.

"He's got a naked woman up on his roof fixing it," Jake finally choked out in awe.

"He's got a what?!" Jonathan and Jacob exclaimed at the same time in disbelief.

"I'm telling you. The kid has a naked woman, a beautiful naked woman, up on the roof of his cabin fixing it. I've never in my life seen a woman more beautiful with hair the color of ripe wheat and legs that go on forever." Jake suddenly looked like a kid who had just discovered he was getting everything he had ever wanted for Christmas.

"Damn, I have to see this!" Jacob exclaimed, looking up at his brother. "I need to get dressed. I'll meet you out front in two minutes. Get the horses," he said with a grin. "I've also got to meet this kid. Hell, a naked woman fixing his roof. Shit!" He added as he jumped up out of his chair.

Jacob grabbed the towel that almost fell off and took the stairs to his room two at a time. He pulled on his pants and grabbed a shirt. He almost fell on his face as he tried to get his socks on before taking the stairs back down as fast as he could.

By the time he got out the front door, Jonathan had a wagon that one of the men had just brought in turned around and ready to go. The man driving barely had time to jump down before Jonathan climbed over him and grabbed the reins. Jacob hopped as he slid his foot into his boot. He was still buttoning his shirt as Jonathan called out to the mules to move it. Jake hung on in the back for dear life as the mules move out at a fast trot.

* * *

Indy had just finished hammering in the last of the shingles on the roof in relief. She cranked the volume up on the iPod for one of her favorite songs as she finished up the last row. Standing up and giving a high five to the sky, she didn't hear the dogs bark out a welcome to her visitors as she was celebrating completing the damn thing. Singing as loud as she could to the song that was playing, she swayed back and forth using the hammer as a microphone as she belted out the last chorus to the song.

Jonathan pulled the mules up and stared in wonder at the roof of the old cabin. He knew he would never look at the old place the same again. Jacob's face reflected the same thoughts as he looked at the woman moving so sensually and singing a song he had never heard before.

When she shook her ass all three men groaned. The sun was shining down on her, highlighting the blond streaks running through it as her pony tail swung back and forth. As they moved closer, they could tell she was wearing some type of light blue top, but there wasn't very much of it as it left her practically bare all the way down to her slim waist.

She was wearing a pair of tan colored pants that were cut extremely high up her thighs and fit her low on the hips. They looked like they had been painted on her ass the way they hugged it. A small, cloth pouch was tied around her hips. Her tanned legs were bare all the way to her ankles where small white shoes covered her feet.

"I thought she was naked, but she's not," Jake whispered, never taking his eyes off the figure swaying up on the roof in awe.

Jacob and Jonathan turned to stare at Jake in disbelief. The little bit of clothing the woman wore was just enough to make them wonder what else was underneath it. Both of the men had raging hard-ons. It was a sight neither had ever dreamed of seeing.

"Damn! Where do you think the kid found a woman like that? I sure as hell know it wasn't from Meeteetse," Jacob said, thinking of the small town closest to the ranch.

"I don't know, but I plan to find out," Jonathan said grimly, jumping down out of the wagon onto the hard packed ground. He turned to give Jake an order to make sure no one else came down this way. The old man's eyes were glued to the woman's swaying figure on the roof. Jonathan knew if anyone else saw the woman there would be hell to pay. "Jake. Jake...," Jonathan growled out, trying to get the old cowpoke's attention. "Jake, damn it! I want you to make sure none of the men come down here. If they hear her singing we could have a rebellion on our hands."

"Sure thing, boss man," Jake whispered in response, not moving.

"Now, Jake," Jacob growled out coming to stand next to his brother.

Jake swung his eyes to Jacob before swallowing, his Adam's Apple moved up and down with the motion. "Right, no men allowed down here." Jake slowly slid out of the wagon and moved off down the road, glancing backwards repeatedly until he was too far to see anything.

Jonathan watched as the woman on the roof seemed to come to the end of the song she was singing. She took a bow to an invisible audience before turning around with a graceful twist. He watched as her eyes widened in surprise when she noticed she was no longer alone.

"Shit," Indy breathed out under her breath. "Busted."

She was going to be pretty damn pissed if they fired her after she worked her ass off last night and today fixing up the cabin. She wanted at least a week to enjoy the fruits of her labor before she was told to leave. She sure the hell earned it.

Indy carefully turned off her iPod and removed the ear buds. She stowed them in the pouch around her waist before gingerly walking over to the edge of the roof. She looked down at the two men who were now standing in front of the cabin staring up at her.

Both of them had dark expressions on their faces that she couldn't interpret.

Neither expression looks good for my continued employment, she thought with a sinking feeling in her stomach.

"Hey boss. Welcome home, Mr. Tucker, it's a pleasure to finally meet you. I thought you weren't supposed to be back until the day after tomorrow," Indy said nervously as she stood looking down at them.

She drew in a deep breath to steady her nerves. She'd be damned if she would apologize for being who she was to another man. She had proved she was a hard worker and a good cowpuncher. She dared them to say she couldn't hold her own against any of the men in the bunkhouse. Especially if they considered the fact that she was doing a pretty damn good job of repairing the cabin too! They were getting a bargain with her, experienced cowpuncher and a handyman all in one.

Jonathan jerked in surprise, the shock on his face turning to disbelief. The kid with the attitude who had been driving him crazy since he had seen him.... her, was a woman with an attitude *and* nice full breasts. He felt his cock jerk, as if it was telling him it had known from the beginning that Indy was a woman.

"Indy?" Jonathan choked out in shock.

"This is the kid you were telling me about?" Jacob asked in disbelief as he stared at the ripe figure in front of him.

"Hold on. I'll be right down," Indy said before disappearing over the top of the roof. She grabbed her discarded shirt, slipping it on before she moved over to where she had the ladder propped up against the side of the cabin.

"How in the hell did you mistake her for a boy?" Jacob muttered the minute Indy disappeared from their sight. "Either your eyesight is going or you've been alone too long."

"Shut up, Jacob," Jonathan growled at his brother as he tried to get his flaring temper under control.

A rush of emotions coursed through him as he watched Indy walk around the side of the cabin pulling her long hair out from the shirt she had draped loosely over her shoulders. Every step she took showed off a hint of the bare skin that had been on display a few short minutes ago. She appeared to be unaware of the amount of flesh she was showing.

Jonathan couldn't remember any woman, including the few widows in the area he had visited recently, showing as much skin or being as comfortable as Indy appeared to be with her state of undress. The idea that she was used to showing off so much skin didn't sit well with him, especially as he could feel his brother's eyes lighting up with appreciation as she approached them.

"I finished the roof. I had to re-shingle almost half of it," she was saying as she walked toward them. "I cleaned out the inside as well. There is still a lot that needs to be done, but I have most of it under control, I think," she added, glancing at them with a defiant expression. "Would you two care for a cup of tea or coffee?" Indy asked stiffly as she moved by both men heading for the front door of the small cabin.

She untied the work pouch from around her waist with trembling fingers. She wasn't going to give them a chance to fire her, or at least she wasn't going to make it easy for them to do so. With a bitter twist to her lips, she figured it might be better if she put the hammer up first because if they did she might use it on one of them. Besides, she thought with a twinge of guilt, her granddad had always taught her to be polite to company unless they came bearing bad gifts, then she was allowed to shoot them.

Both men watched in disbelief as Indy pushed open the front door to the cabin and disappeared inside. They followed a minute later, standing inside the doorway and watching as she poured water into a pot before setting it on a strange looking stove.

"I haven't had a chance to look at the wood stove yet. I don't want to take a chance of burning the place down now that I have it cleaned," she said with a wave of her hand at the old blackened potbelly stove. She paused a moment to look at the two men who were still staring at her as if they had never seen a girl before. "Coffee, tea, or me?" She asked with a humorous twist to her lips as she wondered if they even heard anything she was saying.

"You," they both breathed at the same time in low gruff voices.

Indy chuckled and shook her head before turning back to the small propane stove she had. Well, that blew that theory out of the water. They were listening, at least to some of what she was saying.

"That was just a joke, I'm not on the menu. Do you want coffee or tea? If you want coffee, it will have to be the instant stuff," Indy said pulling three old tin cups off a long shelf over the long wooden plank that acted as a countertop.

She normally didn't drink the instant stuff as it was a little strong for her but she felt it might help her right about now. She glanced over her shoulder when neither one answered her right away. She waited patiently until Jonathan finally swallowed and answered her.

"Coffee would be nice," Jonathan replied hoarsely still staring at Indy's face.

In all his life he had never seen a woman as beautiful, or as different, as her. She had a coating of freckles across her delicate little nose. He decided he wanted to kiss every single one of them before he checked out the rest of her to see if she had any more.

Indy nodded once, turning back to focus on the little Sterno stove she was using to heat the water instead of the two men who continued to stare silently at her. When it was hot, she emptied the little packets of instant coffee into each cup and poured the hot water over it. She stirred it before turning back to hand a cup to each man.

As she did, she studied each of them under her eyelashes for a moment trying to gauge what they were thinking. Both had a range of emotions crossing their faces. Jacob's was speculative and curious while

Jonathan's face was dark and intense. A shiver passed through Indy as she flushed and looked away.

No, this does not bode well for my continued employment, she thought in despair.

"If you want any cream or sugar I have some packets," Indy said waving the two men toward the rickety chairs next to the table.

She jumped up and sat on the wooden plank that acted as a countertop in the kitchen. The only other place to sit was on the bed and that was not the place she wanted to be sitting if the heated looks she was getting from Jonathan were anything to go by. She swore if his stare got any hotter she would catch fire. As it was, she could feel her skin flushing from the intensity and it took everything in her not to fan herself.

"Where in the hell are your clothes?" Jonathan finally choked out as his gaze was captured by something sparkling near Indy's belly button which was peeking out from her unbuttoned shirt.

Indy looked down and frowned in confusion. "It was too hot to wear my jeans. Besides, it isn't often we get a warm day like today and I wanted to work on my tan," she added with a shrug.

"Tan?" Jacob whispered, following Indy's legs as they swung back and forth.

Indy shook her head in frustration. "Listen, I don't think you came down here to discuss my attire. Do you need me to start back to work sooner?" She asked Jonathan before directing her next question to Jacob. "Mr. Turner, how many horses did you purchase? I heard you needed help with training them. How much time do we have before they need to be ready for resale?" She asked in a tone that she hoped was business-like.

Indy thought it would be better to direct the conversation back to the business at hand. What she chose to wear or not wear was insignificant compared to whether she still had a job or not as far as she was concerned. Besides, she still had a lot of work to do on the cabin. She was going to have to work even harder at getting it ready if they needed her to start back tomorrow instead of the day after.

"Work?" Jacob asked distractedly as Indy leaned back to pick up a little pack of cream and sugar to put in her coffee. The sun coming in behind her reflected off the sparkle at her waist again.

"What in the hell is that?" Jonathan finally asked, standing up so fast he almost knocked the chair over.

Indy frowned down in confusion at the little white packets in her hand. "Cream and sugar. I don't really care for black coffee," she responded, looking up at Jonathan as he stood unexpectedly.

Shaking his head, Jonathan walked slowly towards the counter where Indy was sitting. "No, on your...." Jonathan swallowed past the sudden lump in his throat. "On your stomach," he said, nodding to the glittering crystals.

Indy leaned back again so the sun could shine on her smooth, toned stomach. Stretching out, she looked at her belly button ring. Puzzled, she said, "It's my belly button ring. It is one of the few concessions to my feminine side. I thought it would be nice to get my belly button pierced but wasn't brave enough to do it at first. Sam's son, Taylor, dared me to get it. You should have seen his eyes the time I wore my bathing suit. I thought I was going to have to give him mouth to mouth," she responded with a chuckle. "It served him right," she added looking up with a mischievous grin at remembering Taylor's reaction to her in her two-piece at a barbecue Sam and Claire threw at the end of summer this past year.

"Ah, shit," Jacob said, looking at the glittering jewel hanging down. He had never seen anything so sexy in his life. He had never seen anything like it in his life. He pulled at the front of his pants trying to find a more comfortable position as his cock swelled at the glimmering jewel.

Jonathan didn't even try to hide the bulge in the front of his pants. He was so turned on at that moment he was ready to take Indy right there on the counter. Moving to stand in front of her, he reached out a finger and touched the tiny jewel. His heart hammered as his finger brushed the soft, warm skin of her stomach. He drew in a swift breath as a wave of possessiveness surged through him with an unexpected ferocity that left him shaking.

Indy looked up, startled as she felt the light touch of Jonathan's finger as it slid along her skin. "Guess you guys have never seen a belly button ring before, huh?" She whispered out.

Pushing back against Jonathan, she jumped down off the counter. She moved toward the old black wood stove in an excuse to throw the papers from the packets into it. She didn't understand what was happening to her, only that his touch left her feeling hot and - bothered.

It felt like he had sent an electric jolt through her. His closeness was doing stuff to her insides she didn't like and definitely wasn't sure of how to handle. Distance was her best bet until she had time to analyze what was happening.

"So, do you need me to start tomorrow or do I still report the day after?" She asked breathlessly as she turned back around to stare at both men.

"You won't be reporting for anything!" Jonathan responded as he turned to stare at her, suddenly furious.

Anger, sexual frustration, and an overwhelming feeling of possessiveness coursed through him in wave after wave of unfamiliar feelings. She had tricked them. She had tricked him! She knew he thought she was a 'he' and never said anything. Not only that, but she had been out on the range for the past four weeks with just about every cowpuncher on the ranch - all alone, damn it.

"You lead me to believe you were a boy," Jonathan accused between clenched teeth.

"I never said I was a boy," Indy clarified defensively. "I never lied to you or anyone else," she added stubbornly.

"You said you were old enough to shave," Jonathan pointed out, looking at Indy's smooth face.

"And I am. I shave my legs regularly as well as other places," Indy replied calmly, lifting up her right leg to show him how smooth it was.

Her comment had both men's eyes swiveling to her long, smooth leg with its toned muscles and light tan. Jacob choked back a deep groan. Jonathan didn't bother to contain the hiss that escaped his lips as the pressure in his pants increased tenfold. The image of those long, smooth legs, wrapped tightly around his waist, floated through his mind in vivid detail.

"Jacob, step outside," Jonathan growled out in a low, dangerous voice.

"What?" Jacob looked up, startled at Jonathan.

"Leave, now. Wait for me outside," Jonathan said harshly. He turned a strained look toward his brother as he silently pleaded with him to understand. "Please."

Jacob looked for a moment between Indy and Jonathan before a slow, small smile curved his lips. "Sure, I'll be outside checking out the horses." Tilting his hat to Indy, Jacob walked out of the cabin leaving his brother and Indy alone.

"Who sent you?" Jonathan asked quietly as he took a menacing step closer to where Indy stood next to the old black stove.

Indy watched Jonathan, not understanding what was going on but feeling like she had suddenly jumped in the deep end of the pool only to discover she couldn't swim. "No one sent me. I was passing through when I heard gunfire. Jake and Cal told you what happened," she said, nervously pushing a loose strand of hair behind her ear as he took another step closer to her.

Jonathan's mind was in a whirl. She had to be lying to him. There was no way someone hadn't sent her. Every mother and father within a hundred mile range wanted their daughter married to one of the Tucker brothers. But how could she have tricked all of his men for so long out on the range?

He remembered Jake telling him she had set her camp up away from the others. Someone must have brought her supplies or helped her survive. There was no way a woman could have traveled, must less survived, without help.

"Who are your parents? Where is your family?" Jonathan asked in a deceptively calm voice. "Where are you from?" He continued, firing off one question after another.

Indy looked at her boss with growing anger. She wasn't going to tell him anything. If Hayden had put out a missing person's poster with a hefty reward for information on her, she sure as hell wasn't going to help her older brother by making it easy to find her. Besides, she didn't owe anyone anything. It looked like she was going to have to be moving on whether she wanted to or not.

"I told you my parents were dead so there is no need to know who they were," she stated coldly, clenching her hands by her side. "Where I am from is my own business. You hired me over four weeks ago to do a job and I proved I could do it. That is my reference," she insisted passionately.

Jonathan took the last step bringing him within touching distance of the small, defiant figure standing proudly in front of him. "You'll tell me who your parents are and where you are from so I can notify them to come get you immediately," he demanded in the same calm, deadly voice he had been using since Jacob left them alone.

"I'll tell you when hell freezes over," Indy responded hotly. She would never go back. She would never let Hayden get his greedy hands on her. "Do I start tomorrow or the next day? If not, tell me now and I'll be out of here first thing in the morning," she said bitterly, tossing her head and tilting her chin in determination.

Jonathan stood looking down at Indy's defiant face. He could tell from the way she was pursing her lips together, she wasn't going to tell him anything. Just the thought of those lush lips caused him to wonder what she would taste like. Hell, if her mother and father were so desperate as to send their daughter to his ranch without a chaperone, the least he could get from the aggravation was a kiss.

Jonathan pulled Indy against his hard body, not giving her a chance to protest. He crushed her lips with his own in a passionate kiss that told her without a whisper of doubt just how much he wanted her. He would see just how she felt about that.

Chapter 6

Indy was shocked when Jonathan grabbed her, pulling her into his strong arms. She was even more astounded when he crushed his lips to hers in a kiss that left her head spinning. Moaning, she slowly raised her arms up to wrap them around his neck.

It had been a long time since she had been kissed. Even then, it had been Sam's boys just trying to teach her how it was done. She had never really had time to have a real boyfriend. Between her schooling, taking care of her grandfather and the work demanded by living on a working ranch, boys had been at the very bottom of her list of things to do.

Indy opened her mouth when she felt the nip of his teeth along her bottom lip. When he slid his tongue into her mouth, she gently closed her teeth down around it, sucking it in before pressing back with her own. God, he tasted so good.

Jonathan groaned at the response Indy was giving him. He had never wanted a woman as badly as he wanted the one he held possessively against him right now. His arms tightened around her soft curves, pulling her even closer against his hard body.

He pressed his throbbing shaft against her wishing he could rip both their clothes off right then and there. When he had first crushed her lips to his, he half expected her to pull back and slap him. The last thing he expected was the passionate response he was getting. She met him head on, giving back as much as she was taking. When she sucked on his tongue, he almost came right there in her arms like a young boy kissing his first girl.

Pressing Indy up against the counter, Jonathan finally pulled back just enough to look down into her flushed, dazed face. Both of them were breathing hard. He drew in a shuddering breath as he tried to clear his head enough to think.

"Tell me who sent you. I'll let them know their ruse worked. Do they want money or just the honor of saying their daughter belongs to one of the Tucker men? Tell me who I need to contact," Jonathan demanded tersely. He wanted Indy, and if it meant marrying her to get her, he would.

It took a moment for Indy to understand what he was demanding. Anger burned at the thought that he was willing to use any underhanded method he could to get information from her. The passion-filled cloud surrounding her brain suddenly cleared as anger took over where uncontrollable desire had been only seconds before.

Well, two could play this game, she thought savagely as self-preservation returned with a vengeance to her lust-filled body.

Leaning up and pressing her breasts against his chest, Indy ran her tongue over his bottom lip seductively before replying in a cold voice. "You can take your demand and shove it up your ass before I tell you anything," she bit out softly before pushing him out of the way and walking over to the door. She looked at him over her shoulder as she lifted the latch on the thin wooden door. "Now if you don't mind, I have work to finish before it gets dark," she added coldly as she yanked the door open.

She stepped outside onto the small covered porch and grabbed her work pouch and hammer off the small shelf near the door. She tossed her head in challenge to Jacob as she walked past him toward the lean-to that desperately needed attention. She ignored his startled look, refusing to show him how embarrassed she was at responding to his brother's underhanded methods of trying to get information out of her. As far as she was concerned, Jonathan, Jacob, Hayden, and every other controlling, conniving, deceitful male could go to hell. She was better off on her own.

Jonathan stormed out of the cabin after her, his long legs eating up the distance between them as he came up behind her in determination. He grabbed her arm as she stepped toward the sagging horse stall. Swinging her around, he clenched his teeth trying to hold back his temper.

"Tell me who sent you, damn it. I said I would let them know I would marry you," he snarled in frustration.

"Marry?" Indy repeated in confusion until his words sunk in. "Marry you!" Indy screeched the second time in disbelief as his words finally penetrated the red haze of rage swirling through her brain. "Who the hell said I wanted to get married? I just hired on as a cowpuncher, not a whore. I wouldn't marry you if you were the last man on earth!" She snapped heatedly looking at him as if he was insane.

"Your days as a cowpuncher on this ranch are through," Jonathan growled deeply, cutting the air with a wave of his hand to emphasize his point.

"Are you firing me, then?" Indy asked, glaring up at Jonathan.

"You're damn right I'm firing you. I'm also going to haul your ass back to Meeteetse and find out who sent you in the first place," Jonathan replied hotly glaring down into Indy's green eyes that had darkened with emotion as his words cut through her.

"Fine! You don't have to fire me. I quit! I never wanted to work for this two-bit dump anyway. But, for your information I am staying at least one more night in that damn cabin since I spent so much time cleaning and fixing it up. Now get the hell out of my sight before I sic the boys on you," Indy yelled, furious he had the nerve to fire her.

She was so mad she was ready to scream. Of all the arrogant jerks! To think she wanted to marry him after one little kiss. If she had married every guy she had ever kissed she would have been married at least three or four times by now!

..*

Jacob came up behind Jonathan and laid a calming hand on his brother's shoulder. He was warily watching Indy. Fear, defeat, and resignation crossed her face before her lips tightened in determination. He watched her hand tremble slightly before her fingers tightened around the hammer she was holding. From the look on her face, he had no doubt she would either follow through with sic'ing the dogs on them or using the hammer to knock some sense into his stubborn-headed brother.

"Come on, Jonathan. We need to talk," Jacob said softly, pulling his brother back a step.

Jonathan stared at Indy a moment before turning sharply on his heel and striding over to the buckboard with a curse. He was still reeling from the kiss they had exchanged in the cabin. Hell, he felt like someone had cold-cocked him in the head. He didn't know if he wanted to kiss her senseless or throttle her for being so damn hard-headed. Climbing up next to Jacob, he picked up the reins before looking down at Indy who was standing by the leaning horse stall, defiantly glaring back at him.

"Be ready to head to Meeteetse first thing in the morning," Jonathan said before pulling the mules around and heading back down the road toward the main house.

* * *

Indy was so mad she felt like her head was going to explode. She turned and headed for the river, throwing the hammer down when she reached the edge of the shallow, rocky shore. Standing on the edge of the bank, she threw her head back and screamed out her frustration.

"Argh! I hate big, bossy, arrogant, knuckle-headed males!" Indy shouted out in frustration as she clenched her fists into tight balls and stomped her feet in an effort to get mad, so she wouldn't start crying but it was no use, overwhelming defeat swamped her already overtaxed emotions.

* * *

Maikoda watched from the woods across the river as the white woman yelled at the white man named Jonathan. He couldn't help but smile as she faced the big man unafraid. She was different from any woman he had ever known, white or Indian. She was fierce like the mother bear protecting her cub.

When she walked toward the river, he watched curiously as her two dogs followed her sitting and watching as she moved back and forth screaming, cursing and yelling dire threats to all males. He observed as she suddenly stopped and closed her eyes, standing motionless as if waiting for something.

She stood there breathing in and out slowly. He could tell she was saying something as her lips moved, but no sound escaped from her. She did this for several minutes before she opened her eyes.

Even from the distance separating them, he could see the tears glistening in her bright green eyes as she stared blindly at the river. It was only when she moved to sit on a low rock near the water that he made the decision to approach her. He could not stand listening to the quiet, agonizing sobs shaking her slender body.

Moving silently out of the woods and through the shallow water, he paused only when he heard the dogs give a low growl of warning. They stood protectively near their mistress. The hair on their backs standing straight and their deep growls warning him not to come closer without their mistress' permission. He waited calmly to see how the white woman would react to him being so close to her.

Indy heard the soft growls of warning from Tweed and Chester. She looked up to see what they were growling at and recognized the Lakota brave who had been watching her earlier. Motioning for the dogs to lie down, she turned and looked at the man standing in the middle of the cold river bed in resignation.

"Your feet are going to turn to ice if you don't get out of there, you know," Indy said, releasing a shuddering breath and wiping her wet cheeks on the sleeves of her shirt.

Maikoda stared at the white woman a moment before slowly crossing the rest of the river. "You are not afraid of me," he stated quietly.

Indy smiled glumly and shook her head. *"Takuwe iyecetu mis un kokipe un mitiblo ki?"* Why should I be afraid of my brother? Indy asked in Lakota with a weary, dry humor.

Maikoda jerked to a stop, staring in disbelief at the white woman sitting so calmly in front of him as if she did it every day and speaking to him in the tongue of his people.

"How is it you know the language of my people?" Maikoda asked, confused. Nothing about this white woman made sense to him, not the way she dressed, not the way she acted, and definitely not the way she spoke.

Indy laughed softly at the surprise and confusion flashing across the face of the man standing in front of her. "My godfather is a Lakota medicine man. It was pure survival if I wanted to know what his kids were up to when I was growing up."

"Your godfather is an Indian?" Maikoda asked curiously. "What is his name? Perhaps I know him."

Indy shook her head. She was through with men wanting to find out more about her. With her luck, Hayden might have taken into account she might hide out on the reservation near the ranch. She was sure he would have posted a missing person poster on her there as well. She was better off just moving on. It would be safer in the long run if she didn't stay in any one place for long.

She looked at the man standing in front of her and shook her head again. "No way, I'm not telling anyone anything," Indy informed him firmly, standing up. "If you want to stay that's fine, but I have work to do before I leave. I hate leaving any job half-assed," she told him as she walked over to where she had thrown down her work pouch in her anger.

Maikoda watched as the white woman picked up the hammer and the bag of nails she had dropped earlier. She walked around him, heading toward the lean-to where the horses stood nibbling on the grass growing around it. Hanging her pouch on one of the vertical posts, she walked over to the side of the cabin and pulled the ladder down so she could use it. Without a word, Maikoda walked over and took it from her. He carried it over to the lean-to and set it against the side.

"Thanks," Indy muttered.

"Will you tell me what you are called?" Maikoda asked, watching as Indy tied the cloth belt around her slender hips.

He couldn't help but look at the glittering jewel in her belly button. He felt strangely protective of the white woman climbing up the ladder. He would need to reflect on it later tonight when he was alone. It was as if the Spirits guided him to her. He felt that it was important that he watch over her. He did not understand why, but something told him she was to be protected.

"Indy. What's your name?" Indy asked, pulling pieces of loose wood off the roof of the lean-to.

"Maikoda," he replied, reaching up and taking the pieces of aged wood from her and piling them up next to the side of the stall.

"Well Maikoda, can you hand me some of those wood shingles over there? It would make the job go a lot faster if I had some help," Indy said with a small, hopeful grin. "I'll make you dinner in return, how's that?" Indy asked, looking down at the handsome, brave who was frowning up at her with a bewildered expression on his face.

"Why do you do the work of a man?" Maikoda asked curiously even as he handed a piece of shingle up to Indy.

Indy shrugged her shoulders. "I've been working on a ranch my whole life," she replied nonchalantly.

"You learn how to fix things. Why should I have to depend on a man to fix it for me when I am perfectly capable of fixing it myself?"

Maikoda handed Indy another shingle. "You are different from other white women I have seen," he admitted ruefully.

Indy chuckled at his reluctant admission. "I guess so. I like who I am and I don't feel like I need to explain myself or answer to anyone." Indy looked down on the Maikoda with a sad smile. "My grandpa and my godfather both used to tell me I was born to the land and this way of life. Who am I to argue with such wise men?"

* * *

Maikoda and Indy worked for the next two hours side by side, talking quietly about a wide range of things from fishing and hunting, to the weather, to his family. Indy enjoyed his company and they were able to finish not only the roof of the lean-to but the fencing around the paddock as well.

Stepping back to look at the finished product, Indy couldn't help but grin with pride at all they had accomplished in such a short time. Life sucked at times, but usually not for long. She might be out of a job again and back to living in the mountains, but at least she had met some really nice people along the way.

Smiling at Maikoda as he carried the ladder over to the cabin and slid it underneath, she thought it would have been nice to introduce him to Sam's daughter Aleaha. She was currently doing her residency at a hospital in Billings but would soon be home to help Doc Emerson at the local clinic in town.

"Come on in and I'll make you some dinner. It won't be anything fancy, I'm afraid. My supplies are getting a little low," Indy said, moving towards the cabin. She pulled off her gloves and tool belt and set them both on the shelf near the door.

Within minutes, she had a thick beef stew simmering over the little Sterno stove and was slicing some bread she had left over from the range. It wasn't the softest but it would be good dunked in the stew. Setting the table, she turned to Maikoda and motioned to the old metal pail sitting on the end of the counter.

"If you'd like to wash up the water is fresh. Dinner will be ready in a few minutes. You have a choice of beverages: water, tea, or coffee. I don't have anything else, I'm afraid," Indy said with a smile.

Maikoda liked the easy way Indy moved about. She acted like she had known him for years. Unlike the few white females he had encountered, she was not hesitant at all around him.

She was even more unlike the Indian maidens. She did not try to catch his attention in any way. He was considered a catch among the females of his tribe as he was an excellent hunter and could easily provide for a family. He was not sure what to make of the slender white female who treated him as if he was her 'brother' as she called him earlier.

"Why are you so comfortable with me? You are not afraid to be near me, not even as it grows darker outside. Yet, you have not tried to make me want you like the young women of my tribe. I do not understand you," Maikoda blurted out as he sat in the chair across from Indy.

"Why shouldn't I be comfortable with you?" She asked in surprise. "If you tried anything the boys would tear you apart," she said, nodding to where Chester and Tweed lay sleeping by the bed. "Besides, I just don't think you are that kind of guy. I enjoyed your company today, not to mention all of your help. And while I think you are very handsome, I just don't get that 'feeling' with you. Not like..." Indy's voice trailed off as she thought of Jonathan and his kiss. She had definitely gotten a 'feeling' from that. She was honest enough with herself to admit she had been dreaming about kissing him from the first time she saw him out on the range.

"As you do with the one called Jonathan?" Maikoda finished with a mischievous smile.

Blushing, Indy waved her hand to the bowl in front of him. "Oh, shut up," she muttered as she blew on her food to cool it so she could eat.

"You are different from women here. I would like to find a woman such as you," Maikoda said quietly. "I like your strength. I like how you talk with me about different things. I like how you look," he added with another smile.

Indy laughed. "You would like my friend Aleaha. She is absolutely gorgeous, a great listener, and the sweetest person in the world," she teased.

Maikoda looked up in interest. "Who is this Aleaha? She lives near here?"

Indy paused a moment, trying to think. She figured it wouldn't matter if she told him about Sam and his kids, especially Aleaha. After all, she would be gone tomorrow morning as soon as she collected her pay for the past four weeks.

"Aleaha is Sam and Claire Whitewater's daughter. Sam is a full Lakota Indian and a medicine man of his tribe. They have six kids, four boys and two girls. The girls are twins. Anyway, Aleaha has been studying to be a doctor. She's doing her residency in Billings right now and should be done by this fall so she can move back home to set up her own practice. She's really smart. I have a picture of her if you would like to see her," Indy said, getting up to go to her saddle bag where her iPod was. She had all kinds of pictures on it.

Indy turned and looked at Maikoda, holding the iPod against her chest and biting her lip as she carefully studied him. "Listen, I would appreciate it if you didn't tell anyone you saw me, except of course Aleaha and Sam. I have some men looking for me, I would just as soon not see again for a while. I won't ask you to lie. It would just be helpful not to say anything if you can," Indy asked nervously looking into Maikoda's eyes to see how he was taking her odd request.

"I will protect you with my life, little sister. You have no need to worry," Maikoda promised sensing it was very important to her.

Indy smiled her thanks before pulling her chair around so it was next to Maikoda. "Okay, this is Sam and his wife Claire. This next one is Aleaha and her new pickup truck. She was so excited when she got it." Indy went through the pictures explaining each one of them unaware of Maikoda's reaction.

Maikoda looked at the small shiny box in Indy's hand in wonder. What type of magic was this? He wondered silently. He had never seen images of people so clear before. It was almost like the people had been captured within the thin, silver and black box. When Indy laughed at one picture showing her, Aleaha and a group of boys standing next to a pool of clear water in nothing but small pieces of material, Maikoda couldn't contain his growl of disapproval.

Indy looked up, startled. "What's wrong?" She asked startled.

"Who are these other males who would see you and Aleaha with so little clothing on?" Maikoda growled in anger.

Laughing, Indy replied with a shake of her head. "It's okay. Those are Aleaha's older brothers. We had gone to one of Taylor's rodeos down in Texas. This was taken at the hotel. It was a fun trip," she explained, looking at her adopted family with affection.

"All those males are her brothers?" Maikoda asked in relief.

"Yes. Don't worry. Aleaha and her sister Allie can more than take care of themselves," Indy said, turning the iPod off and putting it back in her bag.

She let out a big yawn. She hadn't had much sleep last night and she had worked hard today. Between the hard work and the emotional roller coaster she had been on, she was exhausted.

"I don't mean to be a party-pooper, but I'm beat. I need to get some sleep. Tomorrow's going to be another busy day," Indy said, yawning again.

Maikoda stood immediately. "I thank you for sharing your company and your food," he said, walking toward the door of the cabin.

Indy followed him to the door and opened it. It was dark outside. "Can you make it back okay in the dark?" She asked, worried that she had kept him so late.

"Yes, little sister. You do not need to worry. I will be fine," Maikoda paused, looking down at Indy with an intense expression before he made up his mind. "May I ask you one more question?"

"Sure," Indy said with a raised eyebrow.

"Where could I find this Aleaha?" Maikoda asked almost hesitantly, as if he was afraid Indy wouldn't tell him.

Indy laughed softly. "On the other side of the mountains. You have to go through a place called Spirit Pass to get there. Sam showed it to me. He said it was a magical pass to another world. From there you can ask just about anyone and they can point you to the Whitewater ranch. Sam can contact her for you if you really want to meet her. She comes up pretty frequently considering how busy she is," Indy replied as her shoulders drooped in exhaustion. "Be careful on your way home," she added sleepily as Maikoda paused as he stepped through the door.

Maikoda lifted his hand and ran it softly down Indy's cheek. "*Okoblaya icimani.*"

"*Okoblaya icimani,* Maikoda," Indy responded lightly as she shut the door to the cabin.

Neither one of them noticed the figure standing under the tree near the road watching them.

Chapter 7

Jonathan had been furious as he turned the mules around to head back to the ranch house. He couldn't believe that Indy had said she wouldn't marry him if he was the last man on earth! Then why the hell was she on his ranch?

It wouldn't have been the first time one desperate mother or father had thought to try to trap him or Jacob into marriage by throwing their daughter at them. Damnation, he was going to haul her butt into Meeteetse tomorrow if it was the last thing he did and find out who sent her. Then, he was going to find the preacher and have him marry them right then and there. She had been on his ranch with nothing but males for the past four weeks.

Her reputation would be ruined if I didn't marry her, he thought savagely. *No respectable man would touch her if they found out she had been alone on a ranch with nothing but men. Hell,* he thought ruefully knowing his and his brother's reputations. *No respectable man would touch her once they found out she had been alone with me or Jacob.*

Once they were married, he was going to make love to her as soon as they got far enough out of town he knew they could have some privacy. He desperately needed to relieve the damn pressure in the front of his pants since he first laid eyes on her. He wouldn't give her a chance to argue about it either.

He knew she wanted him as much as he wanted her. The fire in her kiss had damn near melted him with its intensity. After he had satisfied the ache they were both feeling, he would return to Meeteetse alone and beat the hell out of the ones responsible for putting her in such danger! He didn't care who the hell they were. She should never have been placed in such a position.

Jonathan was so busy picturing all the ways he wanted to beat the shit out of the person or persons responsible for endangering Indy that he didn't even realize that they were back at the house. He jerked back to the present when Jacob touched his arm. He looked at his brother with a dark scowl of fury.

"So, do you want to tell me what that was about?" Jacob asked cautiously, not sure of the darkening look on his brother's face.

"About what?" Jonathan snarled, tossing the reins to Carl, who came out of the barn to take care of mule team when they pulled up in front of the homestead.

"You could start with the 'Jacob please leave the cabin'. That would be good or the 'I'm going to marry you' would be even better," Jacob said, hopping down off the seat onto the hard ground while keeping his brother in his sight.

Jonathan jumped down on the opposite side and stared tersely at his twin. Taking a deep breath, he finally answered. "I can't share her, Jacob," Jonathan replied quietly, looking down at the ground. "I can't share her with anyone," he added looking up at his brother. "She's mine. I don't know what the hell happened or why, but I feel like I would kill anyone who touched her, even you."

Jacob looked at his twin brother and nodded in agreement. "I'm okay with that. She's off limits. Though I have to tell you if I see her wearing what she was wearing today I am going to be doing some serious looking," he added with a wicked grin.

Jonathan tossed his head in aggravation. "She'd better not be wearing what she was wearing today ever again. Except for me, that is," he grumbled quietly.

Jacob laughed as he slapped his hand on his slightly older brother's shoulder in support. "So, what was this about marrying?" He asked with a raised eyebrow.

"I told her I would marry her," Jonathan admitted ruefully. "All she needed to do was tell me who sent her. It won't matter, I'm going to marry her anyway. I wanted to know if whoever sent her wanted money for her or just the prestige of her being married to a Tucker," he added with a frustrated shake of his head.

"And from her response I gather she wasn't very impressed with your proposal?" Jacob probed gently.

Jonathan stopped, staring blindly at the house where he was raised. He released a deep sigh before he walked slowly up the steps into the house. "She said it would be a cold day in hell before she told me who she was and where she came from. You also heard her say she wouldn't marry me if I was the last man on earth. Just who in the hell does she think she is?" He asked his brother in annoyance. "We have to fight to get the women off of us. I tell her I'll marry her and she turns me down," he muttered, running his hand through his hair in frustration and looking in confusion at his brother. "I don't want to take a chance on any of the men finding out about her. I'm going to pack a bed roll and head back down to the cabin in a little while. I don't want her there alone," he added gruffly.

It was true, he was afraid the other men would find out about her and might try something, but the biggest reason was he didn't want to be that far away from her. The kiss they had shared had done something to him. He didn't even attempt to understand it. He had kissed his share of women over the years. Hell, he had fucked his share of women and more over the years, but with her it was different. He didn't want to fuck her. He wanted to keep her safe. He wanted to hold her. He wanted to make love to her.

Jonathan smiled grimly at Jacob when his brother patted his shoulder again before he headed upstairs to change and pack a bedroll and supplies for the night. He double-checked his guns, making sure he had plenty of ammunition. He would shoot any son-of-a-bitch who tried to hurt Indy. Grabbing his coat, he headed back downstairs to the kitchen. Jacob was sitting at the table drinking a cup of coffee while Wally packed up a pail of food for Jonathan.

"Ed should be here sometime tomorrow with the horses. We'll keep them in the east pasture near the house until we can divide them up and begin training," Jacob said as he watched Jonathan take a sip of the hot coffee Wally handed him.

Jonathan nodded, setting down the empty coffee cup and picking up the food Wally had packed. "I won't be back until probably the day after tomorrow at the earliest depending on what I find out in Meeteetse once I come back for the buckboard in the morning," Jonathan said with a nod of appreciation to Wally for his help.

"It's hard to think of you as being a married man," Jacob said with a wide grin. "There are going to be a lot of unhappy momma's and papa's out there, not to mention their darling daughters."

"Mr. Jonathan is married?" Wally exclaimed, looking back and forth puzzled. "When did Mr. Jonathan get married?" He asked in confusion, wondering how he missed one of the boss men getting married.

"I'm not married yet, but I plan to be by tomorrow if all goes well," Jonathan said sliding his bedroll over his shoulder.

"Yeah, he just has to convince the bride to marry him first," Jacob joked ducking when Jonathan reached out his hand to slap him upside his head.

"Oh, she'll marry me. I don't plan on giving her any choice in the matter," Jonathan said with a determined grin suddenly feeling excited about the idea.

"Who is the lucky lady who does not want to marry Mr. Jonathan?" Wally asked curiously.

"It's the kid who saved Jake and Cal's asses out on the range," Jacob replied with a grin.

"Mr. Jonathan is to marry a boy? Wally does not think that is possible," Wally said with a frown.

"Indy is not a boy. Indy is a very stubborn, very frustrating, very...." Jonathan growled out.

"Beautiful," Jacob added.

"Very beautiful woman," Jonathan finished. He was growing hard again just thinking about her lush curves, her mouth, and those long legs. Groaning, he pulled the door open and slammed his hat on his head. "I'll be back first thing tomorrow morning to get the buckboard."

Jacob grinned as his brother left the house. Things were going to be getting very interesting over the next few weeks. He couldn't believe his brother had been bitten by the 'love' bug. He had to admit, he was going to enjoy watching his soon to be sister-in-law ruffle his normally calm brother's feathers. Yes, life was most definitely going to be getting very interesting.

* * *

Several hours later, Jonathan rode down the narrow road to the cabin letting the moonlight guide his way. Luckily it was almost full. He decided he needed to take care of a few things before he and Indy went to town.

Running a spread as large as the one he and his brother were took a lot of time and energy, not to mention manpower. That was something they were always short of even two years after the war ended.

More and more people were starting over by moving west, but it was still almost impossible to find good, dependable help.

He got off his horse when he got close enough to see the light shining from the front window of the cabin. Dismounting, he was just about to unsaddle his horse when the door to the cabin opened, spilling light from the interior. A moment later, a tall Lakota brave walked out onto the small covered porch. Jonathan's breath froze in his lungs and he reached for his gun.

Soft feminine laughter carried over the wind as Indy appeared next to the brave. She was wearing the same clothes from earlier and seemed perfectly comfortable being near the Indian. The brave said something and Indy laughed again before replying. She let out a big yawn and shook her head.

Jonathan was too far away to hear what they were saying, but it was obvious Indy was not in the least bit afraid of the Indian. He didn't care whether Indy was afraid or not when he saw the Indian slide his hand down her cheek. He was ready to shoot him just for daring to touch her. When Indy called out a goodbye and shut the door, Jonathan sank back into the shadows in relief.

* * *

Maikoda realized they were not alone when the dogs kept looking over towards the woods near the front of the cabin. Concerned for Indy's safety, he wanted to make sure she was tucked safely inside with her dogs before he slipped around to see who was hiding in the dark. If it was someone who meant to harm the delicate white woman he would slit their throat and disappear before anyone knew he was there.

Jonathan watched as the tall Lakota brave walked around the back of the cabin and disappeared towards the river. Moving closer to the cabin, Jonathan stepped around the side of it so he could peer through the kitchen window. He wanted to make sure Indy was safe before he made camp for the night. Just as he was about to look inside, he felt the cold blade of steel pressing into his lower back.

"What is your business here, white man?" A deep voice growled close to his ear.

Jonathan froze, his hand on the gun at his waist. "I came to make sure she was safe," he replied coolly.

"Then we wish the same," Maikoda said, moving the blade away and stepping back.

It had taken a few moments for Maikoda to recognize the man who had slipped out from the shadows surrounding the cabin. Up close, he was able to recognize the face of the twin brother named Jonathan. He knew the white woman cared for this man, even if she would not admit it.

"Come, we must talk," Maikoda said, moving toward the trees where Jonathan's horse was tied.

Jonathan stared after the retreating figure of the Lakota brave his brother had nursed back to health several years before. He had met Maikoda only once before when the brave had mistaken him for his brother. He had been out on the range and had come across the brave passing through. He had been impressed with the man's quiet confidence and lack of fear. They had talked briefly before going their own way.

Now, he followed Maikoda back to where he had tied his horse wondering what the brave had to say. If he thought to move in on Indy he was about to learn that Jonathan had a mean streak in him. He was not about to stand back for any man, red or white.

Standing under the shadow of the trees, both men looked toward the light flowing from the front window of the cabin. Indy had shut the shutter so only streams of it peeked out from the cracks in the wood. Jonathan stared at the cabin for a moment before turning to study the brave who was intently watching him.

"What will you do with the white woman?" Maikoda asked quietly, trying to study the emotions flashing across Jonathan's face.

"I mean to marry her, tomorrow if I can," Jonathan replied in a soft, steady voice.

Maikoda grinned. "She does not look like she will make it easy for you to do this. She is a fierce one. I saw her stand up to you. She is not afraid," he replied amused.

Jonathan ran his hand over the back of his neck glancing at the cabin again. "You can say that again. I don't plan on giving her a choice in the matter though. She's been on this ranch for over four weeks with nothing but men. Her reputation is ruined," he responded tersely.

Make-do looked at the cabin, then back at Jonathan. "I do not think she will care what others think. She is not like the women of our world, red or white. She is…. Different," he added, deciding not to share the unusual things he had seen on the strange silver and black box she had. It was better for the man to discover just how different the white woman was on his own.

Jonathan nodded his head in agreement, even as a rueful smile twisted his lips. "Well, whether she cares or not isn't going to matter. The women folk in town will make her life pure hell if I don't make an honest woman out of her."

Maikoda stared hard at Jonathan before asking. "You will protect her?"

"Yes, with my life if necessary. She is different. She is mine," came the soft, firm reply.

Maikoda was quiet for a moment before he nodded. He understood what the white man was saying. He could hear the confusion in his voice at the strong feelings the female brought out in him.

Maikoda understood because he had felt the same way when he had looked at the image of Aleaha in the magic silver box. Turning to look toward the mountains, he decided he would travel to the other side of the mountain to find this Aleaha. He needed to return to his tribe first to relay the information he had discovered first, but as soon as it was delivered, he would travel through the Pass little sister told him about.

Jonathan turned to remove the saddle from his horse wondering if the Indian would tell him what he and Indy had been doing in the cabin. He decided he would go ahead and ask, but when he turned around, he found he was alone. *That damn Indian was quiet when he moved,* Jonathan thought, staring into the dark. It was a good thing they were on the same side.

* * *

Indy was dead tired from all the work she had done over the last two days. Even so, she was determined to take a bath to wash the dirt and sweat off of her tired body. Besides, she decided, the warm water would help her sleep better.

Closing the wood shutters on the inside, she removed her clothes. Maikoda had checked out the wood stove for her while she made dinner to make sure it was safe to use and built a small fire in it to take the chill out of the cabin. Now, the cabin was nice and warm.

Indy had found a big pot and an old wash tub big enough to use as a bathtub behind the lean-to. She filled the big pot with water heating up enough to fill the big wash tub. It would be a tight fit, but it was better than nothing.

She left the pot on the stove to heat more water for in the morning. It would be nice to have warm instead of frigid water to wash her face in the morning. Now she had enough to bathe and to wash her clothes out.

She would get up early in the morning and pack up what was left of her supplies. There were some hard decisions that needed to be made. She would need to do some hunting and foraging or head back to Sam's ranch to restock sooner than she wanted or go hungry.

She had only been gone a couple of months and knew as stubborn as Hayden was, he wouldn't have given up yet so it would be dangerous to head to Sam's place. One thing Indy knew for certain about Hayden, he did not like to lose - to anyone.

Standing naked in front of the wood stove, Indy poured the hot water into the big tub adding just enough cold water to take the edge off. Once the tub was filled half way, she stepped into it and sank down, pulling her knees up so she could slide down until the water lapped around her neck. Pulling her hair up and knotting it on top of her head, she laid her head back against the rim of the tub.

God, it felt so good, she thought tiredly. If she would have had the strength to be mad at her brothers at that moment she would have castrated all three of them for driving her away from her nice cozy bedroom and big bathtub.

A tear coursed down her cheek as she realized she would never be allowed to walk through the big ranch house which had been her home. She was technically homeless. Laying her arm across her eyes, she tried not to cry, but the tears kept coming. She hadn't had a chance to really grieve for her grandfather or the loss of her home. Now, in the middle of an old cabin, in a pint-size bathtub, she broke down, crying until she could barely breathe.

* * *

Jonathan had finished eating the food Wally had packed for him and cleaned up the mess. It was going to be a cold night from the clarity of the night sky. The stars were brilliant.

Deciding to take a quick peek in on Indy to make sure she was alright before he bundled up for the night in his bedroll, Jonathan moved quietly up to the cabin. Looking through the cracks in the window Jonathan's breath rushed out of him as he saw her standing nude in front of the wood burning stove.

He knew he should move away, but he couldn't have torn himself away from the view if his life depended on it. His gaze moved over her figure taking in the curves of her hips and round ass, her narrow waist, and her long legs. He fisted his hand into his mouth to keep the groan from escaping as she turned to pour water into a huge wash tub.

He watched as her full breasts swayed and her nipples peaked in the cooler air of the cabin. As his gaze moved lower he was stunned to see she was bare between her legs. He had never seen a woman without hair between her legs before and the sight that greeted him had him, clutching his growing cock at the idea of how sweet and soft she would taste.

Unable to stand the pressure in his pants any longer, Jonathan removed the glove on his right hand and fumbled with the fastening holding his pants, closed so he could release his throbbing cock into the cold air in a hope it would help him relieve the pressure. He pulled his cock out and into his hand feeling the straining flesh.

His cock didn't seem to realize it was cold outside as it continued to grow and pulse as Jonathan watched Indy step into the tub and sink down. He stroked his cock back and forth as Indy raised her arms to pile her hair onto the top of her head. The movement caused her breasts to rise up and Jonathan could see her big, dark rose-colored nipples pointing at him as if begging for his attention.

Jonathan pumped his cock faster, squeezing it harder as his breathing increased as he felt the pressure build up. Stumbling backwards, he moved to the side of the cabin groaning out softly as he felt the explosion of his climax shooting out into the dirt. Grabbing the bandana from around his neck, he pulled it loose and used it to clean himself. Never in his life had he ever lost control like that - never.

He closed his pants with a shaking hand. If just seeing her nude did this to him, he couldn't imagine what would happen when he finally made love to her. Afraid to see her again and ashamed of himself for watching her without her being aware of it, Jonathan moved back to his lonely, cold spot under the trees. Tonight was going to be one of the longest and loneliest nights of his life.

Chapter 8

It was amazing what a good cry could do to help you put things in perspective. Indy had cried her eyes out last night in the big old wash tub. Then, she had pulled herself back together.

She had gotten ready for bed, washed her dirty clothes and hung them in front of the wood stove to dry, poured the water out the back door and gone to bed to sleep like the dead. Unfortunately, that also meant she was running late this morning. She had been startled when Jonathan had banged on the door to the cabin at first light. Mumbling expletives under her breath about people who got up too damn early in the morning, Indy had opened the door to see a very rumpled and cold looking Jonathan standing on her doorstep.

"What the hell do you want?" Indy muttered darkly, pushing her long hair out of her eyes. Chester and Tweed jumped around behind her trying to get past, so they could go outside and do their business. Indy stood to one side and motioned for them to go. She watched as they tore off down the steps and into the woods sniffing and marking everything in sight. She rolled her eyes, thinking males were the same no matter what species they were. "Well, did you want something or did you just want to piss me off first thing this morning?" She asked grumpily leaning one slender hip against the doorframe.

Jonathan looked at Indy trying to get his brain to function. She looked so damn beautiful standing there in a long flannel shirt that went almost to her knees and a thick pair of socks with her hair all disheveled as it flowed down her back in wild abandon. He was remembering what she looked like naked last night and wanted to groan in frustration. He wanted more than anything in the world to slide his hand up under her nightshirt to see if she was wearing anything underneath it. He had a feeling all he would feel would be smooth, silky skin.

Trying to focus, Jonathan cleared his throat, which had suddenly gone dry. "I told you to be ready to go first thing this morning. I'm taking you to Meeteetse to find out who sent you," he said gruffly.

Indy's eyes flashed at the mention of him trying to find Hayden. "And I told you when hell freezes over, if I remember correctly. I'll be up to the ranch house in an hour to collect my pay," she bit out glaring at him with daggers in her eyes.

Indy was furious he would wake her up just to insult her by telling her he was taking her back to her greedy brothers! She let out a loud whistle for the dogs to come back in. She waited silently fuming until they charged by her before stepping back into the cabin and slamming the door in his face.

She couldn't believe he had the nerve to wake her up at the crack of dawn to tell her he was taking her back. That was so not going to happen. Once she collected her pay she was heading back to the mountains.

She would lose herself so far in them, she wouldn't even know where the hell she was. Moving over to the warm pan of water, she dished some into the washbowl and washed her face. She quickly changed into her jeans and a flannel shirt before braiding her hair. She grabbed one of the breakfast bars she had to give her enough energy to get through to lunch. She was almost done packing when another knock sounded at the door.

Growling under her breath, she swung the door to the cabin open yelling in frustration. "What the hell is your problem? I told you I would be up to the damn ranch house in an hour..." Her voice faded as she saw Jake standing before her, not Jonathan.

"Oh, Jake. Sorry about that. Come on in," Indy muttered, moving aside so Jake could enter.

"Indy? You're the naked woman?" Jake stuttered out turning red.

"Naked woman?" Indy looked at Jake for a moment before shaking her head. "Forget it. I really don't think I want to know. Did you need something? As you can tell I'm a little busy right now," she said, waving her hand toward the table where she had her saddlebags, sleeping bag, and other items in various stages of packing.

Jake looked puzzled as he watched Indy pack her stuff up. "You going somewhere?"

"Yeah. The boss man fired me so I turned around and quit. Guess he doesn't like the idea of a woman working as a cowpuncher on his ranch. That's okay. I have other places I can go to anyway," she said with a dismissive shrug.

"Where you going to go? You heading to Meeteetse?" Jake asked as Indy pushed more items into one of her saddlebags.

She shook her head, trying to decide how much she wanted to tell her old friend. "No, I figured I'd head back toward the mountains. I know them pretty well. That's where I was living before I came across you and Cal. With winter moving on it will be a little easier. I can build a primitive shelter and hunt for food for the boys and me." Indy figured telling Jake she was headed to the mountains couldn't be too dangerous considering there were a lot of mountains around. She didn't have to tell him anything specific.

"The mountains? That's damn dangerous, even for a man. You could get yourself killed up there," Jake said looking at Indy with a puzzled look on his face. "You still afraid those men are looking for you?" He asked shrewdly.

Indy looked up sharply, surprised that he remembered. "I know they are. One of them will never give up, not as long as I'm alive," she replied bitterly, thinking of the look Hayden had given her before she stormed out of the den.

"Why would they want you dead?" Jake asked looking intently at Indy.

He couldn't imagine anyone wanting to hurt her. Even when he thought Indy was a boy he couldn't imagine anyone wanting to hurt someone so nice. A dark thought crossed his mind at the same time as Indy spoke the words out loud that he was thinking.

"They don't want me dead necessarily, although what they want to do to me would kill me eventually," Indy said shortly thinking about how her older brother wanted to force her to give up her animals and move her to a big city.

Shaking her head, she looked at Jake with tears in her eyes at the thought of being forced to live the kind of life Hayden wanted her to. She knew the first thing he would do is sell her off to the highest bidder that would benefit him both financially and politically. That was probably one of the reasons he was trying to force her to move. He never did anything unless it benefited him in some way. Indy couldn't hide the shudder that coursed through her at the thought of being some uptight lawyer's trophy wife.

"I can't let them catch me, Jake. It would be a fate worse than death. I'd be better off dead than living the life they would force on me," Indy whispered, brushing away a stray tear that had escaped with trembling fingers.

Jake just stared at Indy as he took in what she was saying. He could tell that she had been hurt by the men chasing her and she was damned scared at the idea of them catching her. He had to let the boss men know she was in danger. She had saved his and Cal's life that day on the range and he would do anything he could to protect her.

Jake stayed for a little while longer before telling Indy he had to get back to work. He joked with her about how he had wanted to come meet the woman Indy had working on the roof of the cabin. They laughed about the confusion it had caused when it turned out to be her instead.

Jake blushed a bright red when Indy gave him a big hug and kissed one of his wrinkled cheeks, telling him she had really enjoyed meeting him and would miss him when she was gone. Waving goodbye to him, she turned and finished packing everything before moving outside to get the horses ready for the long journey she had to make.

* * *

Jake made it back to the ranch house in record time. He had to talk to the boss men. He had to tell them about the danger to Indy before they decided to do something stupid like turn her over to the men looking for her. Seeing Jonathan getting the buckboard ready, he walked over to him and stood waiting for him to finish talking to one of the other ranch hands.

"Boss, can I talk to you a minute?" Jake asked, nervously twisting his hat around in his hands. "Alone," he added gruffly looking at Carl, who was standing nearby.

Jonathan nodded tiredly. He jerked his head, motioning for Carl to step away. He waited until Carl had moved back toward the barn before he glanced at Jake.

"What do you want, Jake?" Jonathan asked, exhausted from his sleepless night. He was not in the mood to deal with ranch problems right now, but Jacob had ridden out to meet up with Ed so he figured he didn't have much choice.

"I went to see Indy this morning," Jake began haltingly when Jonathan swung around staring at him with narrowed eyes. Jake cleared his throat. "I thought to ask about the woman who was helping him. I was a might surprised when I discovered they were one and the same," he added with a wry grin.

Jonathan's eyes turned even colder at the mention of Jake seeing Indy in so little clothing. "I'm taking Indy to Meeteetse this morning to find out who sent her out here." He figured he didn't have to add he was marrying her while he was there. The men on the ranch would find out soon enough.

"I don't think that is such a good idea, boss," Jake said softly, looking at the dark expression on Jonathan's face.

"And why is that?" Jonathan asked in a suspicious voice.

"She's in danger. She don't want to say anything, but she let slip three men are looking for her. She was crying when she talked about them catching her. Said that what they wanted to do to her was a fate worse than death. Boss, she's mighty scared of 'em. She said she would rather be dead than let them get a hold of her." Jake rushed through what he had learned from his earlier conversation with Indy.

He was getting more nervous as he spoke due to the cold, hard look that came into Jonathan's eyes when he mentioned Indy being in danger. He knew the bosses were good men and wouldn't let nothing happen to a defenseless woman.

"Damn it, why didn't she say anything to me?" Jonathan bit out savagely.

"She told me a little the day I met her. I asked her if she was wanted by the law. She said maybe, but she didn't lie, steal, or hurt other people. She had been living in the mountains hiding from the men. She says she is going back there," Jake responded.

Jonathan stared down the road towards the cabin feeling frustrated as hell. She should have told him she was in danger. He and Jacob would do everything in their power to protect her.

Had those men treated her so badly she felt like she couldn't trust them? What had those men done to her that would drive a fragile, beautiful woman like her to live in the mountains all alone? Hell, he would have a hell of a time surviving up there and he was a man. How had she done it with just two dogs and two horses? He admired her courage, but it didn't change his plans on marrying her. If anything, it made him even more determined as she would have the protection of him, his brother, and all the ranch hands.

Making a quick decision, he called Carl over. He spoke rapidly, giving Carl his orders and told him to make haste. He watched Carl nod in understanding before the cowpuncher quickly climbed up onto the buckboard and swiftly pulled away. Staring thoughtfully at the departing wagon, Jonathan decided he had his work cut out for him. With luck, he would be enjoying the life of a married man in a few short hours and Indy would be safe from whoever was after her.

* * *

Indy finished packing her remaining supplies on Kahlua and saddled Midnight. She double-checked to make sure she hadn't forgotten anything. She also made sure the fire was totally out of the wood stove before reluctantly shutting the door to the cabin. It was hard to believe she had only stayed there two days. It didn't even look like the same place.

Settling her hat on her head, she whistled for Chester and Tweed. Mounting Midnight, she gave the order for the dogs to move out ahead of her. She would collect her paycheck, though she didn't have a clue as to when or where she would cash it, and head for the mountains.

If she was smart, she would just head for the mountains and skip the paycheck. She would have if she didn't have the overwhelming need to see Jonathan Tucker one last time, not that she would ever admit that to him. The kiss they had shared yesterday had her thinking things she had never thought before. Things like, how sweet he would taste elsewhere? Things like what she would do if she ever got him naked.

Groaning, she tried to push her errant thoughts away. She had read enough romance novels and had even watched a couple of soft porn movies with Sam's girls one night to see what could happen between a man and a woman. She blushed when she thought of what she would like to do to Jonathan if it had been him and her naked together.

Dreams, that is all they would ever be, Indy thought bleakly, *nothing but dreams.*

Indy was surprised to see Jake come out of the barn when she reached the ranch house. She had thought he meant he had work, elsewhere on the ranch. She really was going to miss the old cowpuncher. In some ways, he reminded her a lot of her granddad.

"Indy, boss man said for you to go to his study to get your pay. It's the last door down the hall on your left. I'll take the horses and dogs for you while you're in there," Jake said before calling out to Chester and Tweed.

Indy was surprised, but figured maybe Jonathan didn't want the dogs in the house. Some people didn't like having animals in their home. It surprised her because she didn't get the feeling Jonathan would mind all that much.

Taking the steps two at a time up to the front porch, Indy admired the beauty and size of the house. Knocking loudly on the front door, she opened it enough so she could poke her head inside and called out. A little Asian man came scurrying out of the kitchen. He was talking so fast Indy wasn't sure what he was saying.

"Mr. Tucker," Indy said slowly to the man. "He told me to meet him in his office."

"Yes. Yes. You follow Wally," Wally said, looking and grinning at Indy. "You not a boy. That is good you are not a boy."

Indy let out a small chuckle. "Yes, I guess so," she responded, taking off her gloves and shoving them into the pocket of her jacket before she reached up and removed her hat. She twisted the dark brown Stetson nervously between suddenly sweaty palms.

Indy followed the him down the long hallway, stopping to wait as Wally knocked on the door and introduced her. Wally turned and ushered Indy into the room, bowing as he left saying it was a good thing she wasn't a boy again. Indy looked bemused at the little man and thanked him for his help.

"Is he always like that?" Indy asked with a small smile as the door closed behind her.

"Yes. It can be quite entertaining at times," Jonathan said, standing rigidly behind the desk.

He looked Indy over carefully. For the first time, he paid really close attention to the way she was dressed. She was wearing dark blue trousers covered by a pair of finely made leather chaps. He couldn't see what she was wearing under her coat, but the coat itself was made of very high quality material. It was stitched like he had never seen before.

It was obvious she probably had it for a while, but it was in excellent condition. She had removed her gloves, which were sticking out of one pocket while she held her hat tightly with both hands. He could tell by the way she was twisting it that she was nervous, as if she was waiting for him to say something else.

He let his gaze run over her neatly braided hair before noticing she was wearing what appeared to be large diamond studs in her earlobes. Everything about her screamed she came from money yet she appeared unaware of it.

"Indy, where are you from?" Jonathan asked quietly watching her expression harden as soon as the words were out of his mouth.

Indy stiffened at his question. "Since I am no longer employed by you I think that is a moot point. If you have my paycheck ready I'll take it and leave," Indy said, trying to keep the tremor out of her voice.

She couldn't help but think in the back of her mind that she would have been better just heading to the mountains instead of giving in to her own desires. *God, he was so damn good looking it hurt to look at him. Not in a pretty boy way, but in a real man way. Why did he have to ruin my last few minutes with him by asking questions I can't answer?* She thought in despair.

"Who are you running from? Why are those men looking for you?" Jonathan asked point blank.

Indy jerked back a step as if she had been hit, paling. "Who told…. Jake," Indy took a deep breath before replying. "It doesn't matter. As soon as you give me my pay I'm out of your hair and off your ranch. You don't have to worry about anyone coming to bother you," she assured him coolly.

Jonathan watched the fear flash through Indy's eyes and her face turned a deathly white at his questions. Jake had been telling the truth when he said she was afraid of the men looking for her.

Jonathan felt a rush of fury at the men who would cause her such distress.

Moving around his desk, Jonathan walked over until he stood in front of her. He gently raised her chin, softly asking her to tell him the information he needed to know. "Tell me who they are, Indy. What do they want with you? Who are they to you?" He pressed, refusing to let her look away from him.

Indy tried to jerk her chin away from Jonathan's grasp, but he refused to let her. Her eyes filled with tears at the thought he might betray her to Hayden, Gus, and Matt. Firming her lips, she stubbornly shook her head.

"I don't know what you are talking about," she insisted.

Jonathan's fingers tightened on her chin at the blatant lie. "I'll find out sooner or later. I won't let them hurt you, Indy," he quietly promised her.

"Why should you give a damn? If you would just give me my paycheck I'll be out of your hair and you won't have to worry about what happens to me," Indy declared huskily, silently begging him to let the subject die.

"I'll pay you when you answer my question. Who are the men who are after you and why do they want you?" Jonathan demanded again roughly.

Indy jerked away from Jonathan and moved several steps back to put some distance between them. She had a hard time thinking straight when he was touching her. She stood staring at him for several long minutes. What could she say? Her oldest brother wanted total control over every aspect of her life? Her other two brothers just wanted the money? That they had taken almost everything she had ever loved away from her and would if they ever caught her?

Shaking her head back and forth, a silent tear slid a path down her cheek. Indy looked up into Jonathan's eyes in resignation. There was nothing to say just - goodbye.

"Keep your money, where I'm going I won't need it anyway," she responded in a quiet, firm voice. Slamming her hat back on her head, she turned and started to yank the door to the office open. "Goodbye, boss man," she muttered hoarsely.

Jonathan was stunned by the look of utter hopelessness that flashed through Indy's eyes. A fierce anger swept through him. Striding over, he slammed his hand on the door, shutting it with a loud bang. Indy turned, startled only to find herself trapped between Jonathan's hard body and the door. Jonathan slid his other hand up, removing Indy's hat and tossing it towards the long sofa sitting across the room near a fireplace. Running his hand along her jaw, he murmured something she didn't quite catch before he claimed her lips with his own.

Indy was lost. She was drowning in his kiss. Never had she felt the emotions swirling through her like they did when he was close to her. She kissed him back with a passion she never knew she had inside her.

She didn't fight as he carefully slid her thick coat off her shoulders and let it fall to the floor at their feet.

Her body felt like it was too warm all of a sudden and she relished the feel of her breasts pressing up against his broad chest. She raised her arms and wrapped them around his neck, moaning as she arched into his hard body.

Jonathan had no intention of ever letting Indy go. Right now he was fighting the urge to take her right there on the floor of his office, claiming her forever as his. The only thing stopping him was the knowledge she deserved better and she would be his legal wife before the night was over. Wrapping his large hands around her wrists, he pulled them down so he could hold them in one hand. He quickly wrapped a soft rope around them, tying them together.

"What are you doing?" Indy asked huskily, staring at her wrists in confusion as he tied them.

She was so lost in the aftermath of his kiss, it didn't register he was tying her hands together until she felt him jerk the rope tighter. Pulling back, she tried to push him away from her. She began to panic when he jerked her closer and pulled on the rope to make sure it was tight.

"What are you doing?" Indy repeated, panicking. She began struggling against him in earnest. "Stop it. Let me go. You have no right to do this," her voice rose as she felt his hands tighten on her.

Jonathan's mouth firmed to a straight line as he finished tying the rope. Picking her up, he had to hold on to her tightly as she began hitting him with her fists. Indy began crying as she wiggled, trying to get out of his arms.

When he laid her on the sofa, she tried to roll off only to find him holding her down by pressing one hand into her chest while he pulled another length of rope out of his pocket. Kicking her feet, she found herself turned over onto her stomach and a knee in the center of her back. Jonathan caught her flailing feet in his large hands. He quickly tied them, effectively keeping her from escaping. He turned her over gently and brushed her hair out of her eyes.

Indy jerked her head away from his touch, flinching. She glared at him before forcing out the words that were choking her. "I hope you enjoy the money you'll get for me. Hayden must have offered you a large amount for turning me over. You are just as underhanded and devious as he is. I hope you both rot in hell."

"Who is Hayden?" Jonathan asked softly. He could tell Indy was trying to hide her fear behind a mask of anger.

She just turned her head into the back of the sofa and closed her eyes. Jonathan ran his hand over her face again ignoring the way she shrank away from his touch. Once he had risen, Indy rolled over onto her side and tried to curl up into as small a ball as she could on the long sofa.

Jonathan watched as her small shoulders shook with the force of her silent tears. It was tearing him apart watching her. He needed to tell Jake to put her horses in the paddock away from the ranch house and to keep the dogs with him in the bunkhouse for a couple of days.

He didn't want to take a chance of her escaping or setting the dogs on him. He wasn't about to leave her alone for long. He had discovered she was very resourceful. He had a feeling if he took his eyes off her, she would be gone in a heartbeat and he would never find her.

Opening the door to the office, Jonathan yelled for Wally. He ignored Wally's wide eyes as the little Chinaman took in Indy's tied condition. He told him to get Jake immediately.

Shutting the door, he walked over to where Indy was lying on the sofa. Kneeling down next to it, he ran his hand over her hair again. It hurt like hell the way she tried to jerk away from his touch.

"Indy, I'm doing this for your own good," Jonathan began. Indy's shoulders just shook harder as she cried. She could no longer keep the sobs quiet.

A soft knock on the door sounded and Jonathan let out a sigh as he rose to answer it. Opening the door, he saw Jake standing there nervously twisting his old hat.

"You wanted to see me, boss?" Jake asked. His eyes widened in concern when he saw Indy's tied up body lying on the sofa. His gaze jerked back up to Jonathan, silently questioning him.

Jonathan nodded for Jake to move back out the door. Closing the door to the office, Jonathan turned to Jake before answering him. He didn't want Indy to know where her animals were to be taken. He had a feeling she wouldn't leave without them. If it meant using them to keep her here, he would.

"Jake, I want you to unsaddle Indy's two horses and take them to the east paddock away from the ranch house. I don't want Indy to be able to see them or call for them. Put the dogs in the bunkhouse and keep them there until I give you further instructions," Jonathan ordered briskly.

"Boss, you ain't going to turn Indy over to those men, are you?" Jake asked suddenly worried he had made a mistake telling Jonathan about Indy's troubles.

"Rest easy, Jake. I mean to marry Indy today. I sent Carl for the preacher and his wife to come to the ranch. They should be here by shortly. I plan to marry her to keep her safe. She won't tell me anything, but I have a feeling if she gets loose, she'll disappear faster than a fox from the hen house," Jonathan assured the old cowpuncher. "Jacob should be back anytime with Ed and the others. Let him know I'm in the office."

"Sure thing, boss," Jake said relieved.

He liked that Indy was marrying one of the Tucker boys. They would keep her safe. Putting his hat back on, Jake touched it and headed out to do the boss' orders. He felt better already.

* * *

Indy waited until she heard the door close. As soon as the door clicked, she grabbed for the knife she had tucked inside her boot. Sawing as fast as she could, she quickly cut through the rope around her ankles.

She flipped the knife around, holding it between her knees and cut through the rope around her wrists.

Rolling, she sat up and grabbed her hat off the floor while impatiently wiping at her damp cheeks. She moved as fast as she could to the window of the office and pushed it open. She was half way through it when the door to the office started opening behind her.

"Shit!" Jonathan exclaimed as his glance went from the empty sofa to Indy's backside disappearing through the window. "Damn it, get back here," he yelled, rushing to the open window.

Indy flung herself out the window, landing hard on the ground. She lay for a second, looking up into Jonathan's furious face before rolling over and jumping to her feet. She was running as fast as she could across the yard whistling frantically.

She could hear the dogs barking and Midnight neighing. Rounding the house, she slid to a stop as she watched Jake and another man fighting with Kahlua and Midnight. Kahlua was moving around and around in circles kicking out her back legs while Midnight was rearing up kicking out with his front legs trying to get away from the grip the men had on their reins. Tweed and Chester were fighting against ropes around their necks where they were tied to a post.

"No!" Indy screamed in horror. She was afraid one of her four-legged friends would get hurt in all the commotion. "Leave them alone. Don't you touch them!" She cried out as she ran toward the dogs.

Jonathan burst out the front of the house just as Indy rounded it. He jumped off the porch tackling her before she could get to the dogs, knocking her down to the ground. Indy threw a punch, hitting Jonathan in the chin and knocking him backwards giving her a chance to roll out from under him.

Jonathan grabbed her by the ankle as she tried to get back up, pulling her down again. Indy brought her booted foot up to kick Jonathan in the jaw, but missed as he rolled to the side where she hit his shoulder instead. She heard a grunt of pain as he worked his way up her body, trying to trap her.

He blocked another punch grabbing her wrist in his large hand while trying to protect his lower body from her knee. They ended up rolling over and over as Jonathan tried to get high enough up her body to hold her still. He ended up taking a blow to the nose when she head-butted him.

"Damnation, that hurt! Will you stop?" Jonathan bellowed out.

"Never!" Indy panted, struggling to break free. "I'll fight you all the way to hell and back if I have to!"

With all the commotion going on between the dogs barking, the horses fighting the men, and Jonathan and Indy yelling, no one heard the riders coming in until Jacob yelled above all the noise. He pulled his horse up and stared in disbelief as his older brother by two minutes fought with a woman. This was not what he expected to see when he rode in.

"What the hell is going on?" Jacob yelled loudly, looking at the chaos with disbelief.

Ed Rawlings looked down with amusement as the little filly under Jonathan took advantage of his distraction to head butt him again, this time hitting him in the mouth. Jacob had told him a little about what was going on but he never expected to come back to the ranch house to find the boss getting his butt kicked by someone half his size.

"Damn it! Will you stop that? I think you've busted both my nose and my lip now," Jonathan growled down at Indy.

"Yeah, well, move half an inch to the right and I'll include your balls with that!" Indy snarled, still fighting.

The sound of laughter echoed around the yard as the other men who had ridden in heard Indy's reply. This was the best entertainment they'd had in the last six weeks. They watched in amusement as Jonathan tried to keep a grip on the female who was just as determined to get away from him. This was something none of them had ever seen, as it was usually the other way around.

"Jacob, will you get your ass down here with some rope and help me? Ed, help Jake with the horses and someone shut those damn dogs up!" Jonathan snarled out.

"You leave my horses and dogs alone, you asshole. I'll skin your scrawny ass if you hurt them! Do you hear me? I'll...," Indy yelled out as she struggled to break free from Jonathan's determined grip.

Jonathan didn't wait to hear what else Indy was going to do to him. He shut her up the only way he could think of - by kissing her. He held her firmly against him, refusing to let her get away. Her arms were stretched high over her head and his body pinned her to the ground under him.

Jacob chuckled as he got down off his horse and pulled out some rope. He knew life was going to be interesting. He just hadn't expected it to be quite this entertaining. Coughing lightly, he leaned down looking at his brother who was kissing the very feisty, furious female.

"The rope?" Jacob said.

Jonathan pulled back just far enough to mutter swift instructions out to his brother. "Tie her damn hands, then her feet. If I get off her…. Damn it! Stop that…. She'll run," he bit out, nursing another bruise on his jaw when Indy head butted him again. He grabbed her forehead, holding it to the ground as Jacob took over her arms.

"Jacob, I'll castrate you for this!" Indy threatened, her voice thick with tears of frustration, anger and hurt. "I'll use the rustiest knife I have to cut your balls off and I'll hang them on the trailer hitch of my pickup truck so everyone will know. You'll never have kids by the time I get done with either of you," she promised hoarsely as she felt the tug on her wrists when Jacob tightened the rope.

Jacob winced. "I sure hope you know what you're doing, brother. You might want to tie her to your bed tonight while you sleep," he advised trying not to laugh.

"I'll be long gone by tonight. I don't work for you anymore. You can't hold me against my will. This is kidnapping!" Indy said, kicking as much as she could when Jacob moved down to tie her feet.

"No you won't," Jonathan said, sitting up and straddling Indy who was tied up again. "Where's the knife?"

"Go to hell," Indy snarled out savagely.

Jonathan was just about to search Indy when the sound of the buckboard returning drew his attention. It was Carl with the preacher and his wife. He would have to give Carl a bonus, he had made the trip in record time. The preacher and his wife were staring at him in horror, taking in Jonathan's rumpled figure, Indy's tied one, and the men still fighting with the horses and dogs.

Jonathan glared at Ed. "Will you get those damn horses out of here? I told Jake where to put them." Ed grinned and called out to several of the men, telling them to get the horses moved out.

"Indy, tell the dogs to stand down now. If they attack any of the men, I'll put a bullet in them," Jonathan demanded coldly.

Indy looked up at Jonathan with pure hatred in her gaze. Tightening her lips, she let out a sharp whistle followed by a movement of her hands. Both dogs immediately calmed down. They were panting and their eyes never left Indy, but they were at least finally quiet.

"Mr. Tucker, may I inquire as to what is going on? I was under the impression you wanted me to perform a marriage?" The preacher asked, helping his wife down off the wagon.

Indy's eyes widened as she stared up, startled at Jonathan. Marriage? This was a hell of a time for someone to get married.

"Yes, I do, Mr. Blackburn," Jonathan said, sitting on a now quiet Indy.

"And who, may I ask, is getting married?" Mr. Blackburn asked, looking at Jonathan's bloody nose and lip, then down on a dust covered Indy lying tied up under him.

"I am," Jonathan said slowly getting up and pulling Indy up with him as he stood. Tossing her over his shoulder, he started moving toward the front porch of the ranch house.

"And who will you be marrying?" Mr. Blackburn asked, trying to keep the twitch of laughter from escaping.

"Why, this here filly I've caught," Jonathan replied calmly as he moved up the stairs and into the house.

Indy had had enough of the jokes. She looked up at the preacher and his wife ready to scream for help when she stopped and stared in disbelief at what the woman was wearing. She had never seen a dress like what the woman had on except in an old western movie. Shaking her head, she tried to prop herself up far enough to glare at Jacob and the preacher.

"I'm not marrying anyone! I told you I wouldn't marry you if you were the last man on earth! Mister, you've got to help me. I just came for my paycheck. Tell him he's making a mistake and needs to let me go. I'll be gone so fast..." Indy's voice faded off as she saw the preacher shaking his head. His wife looked horrified at her appearance.

Moving into the office, Jonathan sat Indy down on the sofa holding her there with a hand to her shoulder.

"Wally!" Jonathan yelled out.

"Yes, Mr. Jonathan?" Wally scuttled into the office.

"Get a hot bath set up in my room upstairs," Jonathan said. "Also, get the trunk that belonged to my mother out and moved into it," he ordered briskly.

Jacob walked in grinning as he looked at Indy's determined face set in mute defiance. He had a feeling fireworks were going to fly before the night was over. For a moment he felt a wave of envy wash through him. If Indy was as passionate in bed as she was out of it, she would drive a man to distraction. He hoped he could find a girl like her one day.

"Mr. Blackburn, please begin," Jonathan said, tightening his hold on Indy's shoulder when she started to move.

"Now?" Mr. Blackburn stammered out looking at the two of them. He had attended a number of shotgun weddings where the men were tied up. He had never been in the position where the woman was the one fighting the wedding.

"Yes, now. Miss…" Jonathan stopped suddenly as he realized he didn't even know Indy's full name. "What is your name?"

"You don't even know her name?" Mrs. Blackburn gasped, her eyes huge in her otherwise plain face.

"It's go-to-hell," Indy said through clenched teeth. "That's Ms. to you," she added with a hiss, staring daggers at Jonathan.

Jonathan looked at Indy for a moment before kneeling in front of her. He grabbed the back of her neck and kissed her deeply, ignoring the outraged gasp from Mrs. Blackburn and the discrete cough Mr. Blackburn tried to give at such improprieties.

Pulling back slightly, Jonathan stared into Indy's darkened eyes. "What is your name? I plan to marry you with or without it," he asked softly.

Indy stared deeply into Jonathan's soft, concerned eyes. "Indy…. Indiana Wild," she whispered suddenly feeling very, very confused by what was happening.

Her eyes darted around taking in the strangely dressed couple, Jacob's sympathetic smile, Jonathan's determined face and the antique furniture in the room. She hadn't paid attention to it when she had come in earlier, but now everything seemed to be overwhelming her. Something was off and she couldn't figure it out. She looked back into Jonathan's soft eyes again.

Gently running his hand down her cheek, he leaned in and kissed her tenderly again before standing. Turning to the preacher and his wife,

Jonathan nodded for him to continue. Indy sat in a daze as the preacher began the wedding. She vaguely heard Jonathan say, "I, Jonathan Ryan Tucker, do take…"

Indy didn't even remember saying 'I do' when the preacher asked, but she must have because the last thing she heard was him saying 'You may kiss the bride' and Jonathan bending and kissing her again.

I really do have such a hard time thinking straight when he kisses me, Indy thought vaguely.

Jonathan and the preacher walked over to the desk so the preacher could fill out the paperwork proving he had married them. She could hear them talking quietly but everything seemed surreal. She focused on the preacher's wife as she walked over to sit next to her on the long couch.

Patting Indy on the knee, Mrs. Blackburn spoke sternly. "I must say, Mrs. Tucker, this has to be one of the most unusual weddings I've ever attended. I hope you realize it was extremely nice of Mr. Tucker to marry you to save your reputation. I can't imagine living alone for over a month with nothing but men. My, but if he hadn't married you, I can't imagine any man wanting you. You know many women are going to be very upset you took one of the Tucker men out of the marriage pool. Why women for over a hundred miles have been trying to catch one of those boys," Mrs. Blackburn continued to rattle on.

Indy finally looked at her and said the first thing she could think of. "Why are you dressed so funny?" She asked quietly.

Mrs. Blackburn gasped, putting her hand to her throat. "Why this is the latest fashion," she said wth a huff of her breath.

"Yeah, if you live in the 1800's maybe," Indy muttered, looking up at the preacher approached her.

The preacher cleared his throat as he stood in front of her. "Mrs. Tucker, can you sign this with your hands tied?" He asked hesitantly.

Indy looked down at her hands, then at the paper, nodding slowly. When the preacher handed her an old fashioned quill, looked at it with a puzzled expression. They wanted her to sign her wedding certificate with a quill?

"If you can't spell, you can put an X on the line and I'll write your name in," the preacher said gently.

Indy looked up with a frown. "Of course I can write. I have a college education. I've just never used a quill before. Don't you have a regular pen?" Indy asked, confused.

"Just sign the paper, Indy," Jonathan said impatiently.

He wanted to get this done and over with so there could be no doubt that she belonged to him. Once she signed, there would be no going back. She would be his and he already had plans to make sure there was no denying she belonged to him once he got her upstairs.

Indy signed the paper, pausing at the date. Her eyes widened when she saw Jonathan and the preacher had both dated the paper May 3, 1867. What the hell? Indy's eyes flew up to the top of the marriage certificate. It also said in the year of our Lord, May 3, 1867.

Indy's eyes searched Jonathan's face to see if this was all a joke. It must be, the way the preacher's wife was dressed, the wagon they had ridden in on, and the marriage certificate. It was just a fake. For the life of her she couldn't figure out why but she felt a sense of relief that this was just some weird joke.

Shrugging her shoulders, she signed it the same date as the others had. As far as she was concerned, she wasn't really married. As soon as Jonathan untied her, she would wish him happiness for the future and head for the mountains as fast as she could once she got Midnight, Kahlua, and the dogs.

Jonathan let out a sigh of relief as Indy handed the paper back to the preacher who said he would file a copy of it with the local territorial courts. Pulling a few coins out, he thanked the preacher and his wife for their assistance and told them he would have Carl return them to town. The preacher's wife leaned toward Indy and awkwardly gave her a brief peck on the cheek, wishing her congratulations on her marriage.

Jacob smiled at Indy as he watched Jonathan call for Wally to escort the preacher and his wife out.

"Well, I guess I get to kiss the new bride now, don't I?" Jacob said coming over to where Indy was sitting on the sofa still.

She gave a short, stressed, laugh at his comment. "Give me a break! That wasn't a real marriage!" She exclaimed, looking back and forth between Jonathan and Jacob with raised eyebrows.

"Of course it was real. The preacher married us, we had witnesses, and the preacher is going to file the paperwork with the territorial authorities," Jonathan said growing frustrated that Indy was still fighting him.

"Yeah, right. Did you see the date on the stupid marriage certificate?" She asked impatiently, getting tired of the whole charade.

She had a long way to ride today if she was going to get close enough to the mountains to hide before Hayden found her. Now that everyone knew her real name, it wouldn't take long before the local law showed up to take her in. She needed to get moving as soon as possible.

"Yes, May 3, 1867," Jonathan said, wondering what date Indy thought it was.

"Duh! The preacher and his wife might have been dressed like the old west, but I hardly think a marriage like this would be considered legal in today's time. Now, will you please untie these damn ropes?" Indy asked, impatiently holding out her hands.

"What do you mean by the 'old west'?" Jacob asked curiously, studying Indy's face carefully.

Indy rolled her eyes at Jacob's question. "Come on, Jacob. Do you really expect me to believe the year is 1867?" She asked, staring at the two brothers like they had lost their minds.

Jonathan felt his stomach clench unexpectedly. He studied Indy's face intently for several long moments as he let her question roll through his mind. He had a bad feeling that the answer she gave was going to be something beyond what he was expecting. He also had a feeling it would explain some of the missing pieces about Indy that would explain why she was so different from any woman he had ever met.

"What year do you think it is, Indy?" Jonathan asked quietly, coming up to kneel on one knee in front of her.

Indy nervously used her tied hands to push a strand of long hair that had come loose back behind her ear. "Everyone knows it's 2013," Indy said with a nervous laugh, watching as shock flashed across both men's faces. "Come on. Are you seriously trying to tell me you two think it's really 1867?" She asked in disbelief, looking back and forth between Jacob and Jonathan's face.

Jonathan's face darkened with anger. "Indy, if you think acting deranged will get you out of this marriage it won't. You are mine," Jonathan said tightly.

Indy shook her head. "I'm not the one who is deranged. It is May 3, 2013. I was born August 12, 1991. I'll be twenty-two years old in a few months. I have a pickup truck, a bachelor's degree in nursing from Northwestern University, and..." Indy's voice trailed off as she saw confusion and unease flash across both men's faces again.

Suddenly, an old story Sam told her flashed through her mind. He said when he had traveled through Spirit Pass it had taken him to another world. A world where red man and white man didn't get along.

The more Indy thought about it, the more scared she became. The rustlers, the fact she hadn't seen or heard a car, truck or airplane since she came, the way the men reacted to her clothing yesterday, and Maikoda's surprise at her lack of fear of being near an Indian, not to mention, the preacher, his wife, and the wagon.

She looked at Jonathan as her body began to tremble with fear. "Holy shit. It really is 1867, isn't it?" She choked out in a voice barely above a whisper.

Both men nodded slowly, gazing at Indy with a stunned look. Jonathan gently ran his fingers along her pale cheek. "You really didn't know that?" He asked it more as a statement than a question.

Both of them turned to look at Jacob when he suddenly started laughing. "Damn, Jonathan. When you finally find a girl, you really find one!" Jacob said, slapping his brother on his shoulder.

Indy looked down at her hands again. "Could you please untie me?" She whispered softly before looking back up at Jonathan with a look of horror on her face. "Oh God! Does this mean we really got married?" Indy whispered, turning even paler than before.

Jacob choked back a laugh. "I think I'll let you deal with this on your own. Congratulations on your marriage, brother. You have a truly beautiful and unique bride," Jacob stated before he leaned over and brushed his lips across Indy's chilled cheek.

Both Indy and Jonathan watched as Jacob stood up and walked out the door, leaving them alone. Jonathan stared down into Indy's big green eyes, wondering what the hell he was going to do now. He was married to a woman he didn't even know was a woman until yesterday, found out she thought she was from the future, and now had to figure out a way to make sure she truly didn't disappear to a place he would never be able to find her.

Chapter 9

Indy hadn't known what to do when Jonathan had gently picked her up and walked up the stairs with her. She vaguely realized she was in shock. She could tell by the uncontrollable tremors shaking her body. Of course, being slightly wet, dirty and cold from the wrestling match earlier didn't help.

She stood frozen in the middle of a large bedroom staring at a huge copper bathtub filled with steaming water. She couldn't move since she was still tied up. Instead, she remained standing in the spot where Jonathan had set her back on her feet and watched him move about the room.

Her eyes widened when he removed his gun belt, laying it down on a table near the bed. A very, very big bed as far as Indy was concerned. She began shivering even more as she wondered what he was planning to do next.

A gasp escaped her when he slowly began taking his clothes off. She tried to protest when he pulled his shirt and undershirt off, but the only thing that came out was a squeak. She licked her lips as she studied his broad chest. It was much more defined than she had imagined.

He had muscles on top of muscles due to years of hard work. He only had a light coating of hair on his chest tapering off as it disappeared under the waist of his pants. Jerking her eyes up to his face again, she saw him fighting a grin as he realized she was as affected by what was happening as he was. He pulled his boots and socks off setting them next to the dresser.

"What... what are you doing?" Indy asked hoarsely, licking her lips again.

"I'm undressing. When I'm done undressing, I'm going to undress you and then we are going to bathe together. Both of us are filthy from our tumble in the yard," Jonathan explained calmly as his fingers moved to the buttons on the front of his pants.

Indy drew in a deep breath as she watched his long, hard cock emerge from the trapping of his pants. It was obvious he was turned on. She stumbled backwards, falling as her tied legs refused to let her move. Jonathan caught her before she hit the floor, laying her down gently before standing back up to remove his pants the rest of the way. Indy was panting nervously as she studied his hard, aroused body standing over her.

"You... you go ahead. I really don't need one.... one.... one right now," Indy whispered, her eyes glued to his hard, throbbing length.

Jonathan could feel his cock pulsing up and down the longer Indy stared at him. He would be lucky not to come like a boy in front of her if she continued to stare at him like she was. Kneeling next to her, he carefully untied the ropes around her ankles, holding onto her leg and giving her a warning look before gently removing her boots and socks.

"What are you doing?" Indy asked hesitantly, trying to look into his eyes to see what he was thinking.

Jonathan smiled tenderly back at the slender figure laying on the floor. He could tell she was nervous, perhaps even frightened. He needed to treat her much like he did a newborn foal trying to discover what strange new world it had been born into. He let his hands caress her slender feet and ankles.

"I'm undressing my wife. Then I am going to bathe her. Then, I am going to make love to her all night long," Jonathan responded quietly.

"Oh," Indy said stupidly. "Okay."

Jonathan smiled as a look of innocent confusion crossed Indy's face. If he didn't know any better, he would think she had never been with a man before. The idea of Indy with another man, regardless of what century, sent a flash of jealousy through him. He didn't care if she was a virgin or not, she was his now and he would do everything in his power to keep her safe.

He frowned as he undid the fastenings on her pants, marveling at the zipper. When he grabbed the top and slowly pulled them down her long legs, his breath caught at the undergarment she was wearing.

He reached out and gently touched the black lace with the tips of his trembling fingers. "What the hell is this?" He asked hoarsely, eyeing the scrap of black lace that barely covered her. It was a tiny bit of a triangle with two small lace straps over her hips.

Indy looked down at her black lace thong. At first she didn't think she would but after letting Allie talk her into wearing them, she had found them to be very comfortable. Indy had made a few concessions to her feminine side. She had pierced her belly button, liked sexy underwear, and liked to wear earrings in her ears - even out on the range.

"Untie my hands and I'll show you," Indy said huskily.

She was burning to find out what Jonathan had in mind for her. If seeing her in her underwear turned him on then she was more than willing to show him. She knew she had a nice figure. She worked too damn hard not to have one. She was nervous as hell, but she was also very curious. And, even though she had seen plenty of naked males while she was in nursing school, none of them had turned her on or fascinated her the way he did.

Jonathan looked up from the spec of black lace between her legs trying to decide if he could trust her. The burning heat in her gaze told him she wanted him as badly as he wanted her. He quickly untied her wrists and stepped back, watching as she gracefully stood up.

When her hands went to the buttons of her shirt, he almost groaned out loud. In his state of undress it was impossible to hide his rampant arousal. His cock bounced eagerly up and down with every button she undid. When she finally let her shirt fall to the ground, his eyes were glazed with unrestrained desire as he soaked in her beauty.

Indy reached up pulling her long braid up so she could undo it. The movement caused her breasts to strain against the black lace covering her breasts.

Running her fingers through her long hair, she let the silky strands fall in a shimmering wave down her back. She turned around so Jonathan could see her from the back. She looked over her shoulder with a small smile and winked. A heady sense of power pulsed through her as she realized he was not immune to what he was seeing.

She ran one slender hand over the cheek of her ass. "This is called a thong. This is the type of undergarments a lot of girls wear in my time," Indy explained. "Sometimes we even wear things like this to go swimming in," she added, her eyes lighting up with mischief when she heard his breathing become uneven as his eyes followed her hand.

"Holy shit!" Jonathan breathed out.

His eyes were glued to the globes of her ass and the black lace there. He could feel the bead of pre-cum beginning to drip from his cock. A slight tremor ran through his body as he fought for control. Moving quickly to her side, he turned her around and pulled her against his hard, throbbing body.

"How do you take it off?" He muttered hoarsely, staring down at her bra.

Indy chuckled as she reached up and showed him how to undo the latch on the front of her bra. Her groan quickly filled the air as Jonathan took one of her big, rose colored nipples into his mouth and sucked on it hard. The shock of the warmth and pressure startled her, pulling a loud moan out of her as she arched into him. She wrapped her arms around his head trying to pull him even closer as the tugging on her breast caused an equally fierce reaction between her legs.

"Jonathan!" Indy breathed out sharply. "Oh!" She moaned again as her legs started to give out from under her.

Jonathan's hands moved down to the thin straps holding the black thong onto Indy's hips. Pushing them down, he ran his callused palms down the sides of her hips and around to her womanhood. He had to know if she was as soft and silky as he had imagined last night when he had seen her standing naked before the wood stove. Cupping her bare mound in his hot hand, he ran his fingers gently over her smooth, wet lips.

"Jonathan!" Indy cried out his name again as the feel of his callused fingers running over the sensitive lips of her clitoris sent shockwaves through her.

A deep growled of need escaped Jonathan as he felt how wet and swollen she already was for him. He wasn't going to make it to the bath. Sweeping Indy off her feet, he moved over to the bed and laid her down. He wanted to taste her. Ripping the black lace the rest of the way down her legs, he pulled her thighs apart, staring down at the pale, pink mound before burying his face in her wet sweetness.

Indy smothered a scream as he buried his mouth between her legs. She had never expected to feel anything so amazing. She threaded her fingers through his hair, pulling him even closer as wave after delicious wave of ecstasy washed through her at the feel of his tongue and teeth on her swollen nub.

Spreading her legs wider, she whimpered as she felt his tongue lapping at her clit. The heat inside her increased to the point it hurt. She tried to close her legs as the pressure inside her belt, but his strong hands, held them open to his feasting mouth. She began kneading her fingers through his hair as the pressure increased to unbearable levels.

"Please!" Indy whimpered as her whole body began to shake. "Please," she choked out hoarsely.

Releasing her clit for a moment, Jonathan raised up to look at Indy. "What do you want?" He asked in a strangled voice.

"You," Indy begged, staring back at him as if in a drug induced haze of passion. "I want you to fuck me!"

Jonathan's body jerked at her demand. He was beyond being gentle, at least for this first time. Pushing his fingers into her deeply to see if she was ready for him, he was surprised to find a barrier preventing him from going any further. His gaze jerked up to meet hers as she moaned at the feel of his fingers inside her tight, slick vaginal channel. She was his, only his.

With a growl, he pulled her legs apart fitting his throbbing cock between her legs. "Indiana Tucker, you are mine. I'll never let you go," he vowed harshly as he pressed his cock into her. He heard her whimper as he stretched her. He paused, cursing under his breath. "It will only hurt for a moment. I promise," he choked out looking down at the beautiful woman spread out beneath him.

When he saw her open her eyes to look at him, trust glowing from them, he pushed forward in one quick thrust. He broke through the barrier, burying himself all the way to his balls inside her. He knew at that moment he was in love with her. It was as if his heart and soul were buried deep inside her along with his body. He would do everything in his power to take care of and protect her for the rest of his life. He closed his eyes and gritted his teeth trying to hold still. He wanted to give her time to adjust to his invasion. He knew he was big and she felt so damn small lying under him.

He opened his eyes and stared down at her flushed face. Her eyes were closed and a single tear coursed down the side of her face from the corner of her eye. Leaning over, he licked the tear before he began to slowly move in and out of her.

A groan of pleasure escaped her lips as she began rocking her hips to match his movements. Grasping one of her nipples in between his lips, he sucked on it as he continued his slow rhythm of movement in and out of her tight sheath. She seemed to fist him as he rocked, grasping his cock in a hold so tight it felt as if they were one.

Jonathan couldn't contain the groan as he felt the pressure build inside of him. His balls drew up into hard sacks as he felt his orgasm build to a point he knew he was going to explode. Indy suddenly jerked upwards, crying out as she came. Jonathan felt her vaginal walls clamp down on him, pushing him over the edge. Pushing as deeply as he could into Indy, he let his seed pump deep into her womb straining as he felt his release sweep through his body. A hoarse cry ripped from his throat as powerful feelings overwhelmed him.

Indy had heard about orgasms and had even tried to bring herself to one once before, but had never been able to. If she had known it was going to feel so damn good she would have tried harder. It had hurt when Jonathan had taken her virginity, but only for a moment.

When he had begun moving inside her, she had been overwhelmed with the feelings rushing through her both mentally and physically. She felt like she was finally home; finally safe. Indy gave herself totally to him, wanting everything he had to give. When she felt the orgasm building she had let go and felt like she was flying.

Jonathan collapsed on top of her pulling her tight against his body. He was still buried deep inside her. He wanted to stay there forever. He had never felt so satisfied. He pressed a kiss to her bare shoulder. He had not been very gentle with her. He should have taken more care, especially as it had been her first time. Pulling away to look down at her, he smiled at the look of satisfaction she had on her face.

He leaned down and pressed a tender kiss to her lips. "You are so beautiful," he murmured.

Smiling, she kissed him back. "You were pretty incredible," she responded. Wrapping her arms around his neck she pulled him down, kissing him again deeply this time. "I enjoyed that. I wouldn't mind doing it again," she admitted with a blush.

Jonathan chuckled. "It will be my pleasure. I just don't want you to get sore," he said reluctantly before looking over his shoulder at the huge copper tub sitting near the fireplace. "The water won't be as hot as it was but if we are lucky it might still be warm enough it won't be too bad. Let me bathe you like I planned."

She couldn't contain the soft moan that escaped her as he pulled out. She blushed as he helped her up off the bed. There was a little blood on the inside of her thighs, but luckily it didn't look like any got on the bedspread.

Jonathan held Indy's hand and guided her over to the huge copper bathtub. Fortunately, the water was still warm. Wally must have realized it might take a while before they made it in and had heated up the water to near boiling. It felt delicious as Indy sank into it with Jonathan sliding in behind her.

He pushed his legs out so Indy was sitting on them with his cock tucked firmly between the cheeks of her ass. She flushed as she felt his cock brushing against her. He pulled her back, wrapping his arms around her and gently washing her bare, ultra-sensitive mound. Groaning, she moved up and down on his hand.

"How is it you have no hair here?" Jonathan asked huskily in her ear.

"Do you mind?" Indy asked, not sure of the protocols of such things in this time period.

It was still hard for her to believe that she had somehow traveled back in time. Her mind shied away from having to deal with the reality of it yet. So much had happened in such a short time that she felt like she was on overload. She could only deal with the here and now at this precise moment. She would worry about the rest of it later. Hell, finding herself married was enough of a shock! She jerked back to Jonathan's question when he nipped her neck to get her attention.

"Not at all. I find it extremely arousing," Jonathan groaned, rubbing against her so she could feel his cock growing hard again under her ass.

"When I was in nursing school Sam's girls, Aleaha and Allie, came to visit. We talked about doing something wild and sexy. Since none of us wanted to get a tattoo we decided we could get a Hollywood wax done. I liked it so much I learned how to do it myself so I don't have to go anywhere. Since I have extremely fine hair on my body, it doesn't grow back very quickly," Indy said, enjoying how his fingers rubbed against her clit. Her body heated at his touch and from the feel of his thick cock which was pulsing under her he was ready for round two. She slid forward enough that she could turn until she was facing him. "Now it's my turn to wash you," she murmured huskily.

Raising up enough so that she could straddle him, she picked up the soap and lathered it in her hands before sliding them down his chest. Jonathan's eyes darkened as he watched Indy's face light up as she moved her hands over his chest and stomach.

He moved his hands up to cup her breasts playing with her nipples. He enjoyed watching them grow at his touch. He jerked in surprise when her hands wrapped around his cock which had hardened again at her innocent yet seductive touch.

Indy leaned over running her lips along his jaw before kissing his mouth. Jonathan felt the air sucked out of him as she rose up just enough to slide his cock under her. He let a groan escape into her mouth as she impaled herself on him. She continued rising and slowly lowering herself on him, riding his cock as she let her breasts rub against his chest. He slid his hands around her before gripping her hips tightly between his large palms.

As she began to ride him a little harder he let his hands slide over the cheeks of her ass wondering how she would feel about him touching her so intimately. Only once before had he tried to touch a woman there and she had not appreciated it when he had tried to experiment. He groaned at the idea of taking Indy in such a possessive way.

Indy felt his hands move, pulling her ass cheeks apart as she rode him. She leaned into him, giving him better access to explore her body. She let her own hands move down to cup his ass, pulling him tighter to her. When she let her fingers slide along the crack he jerked and groaned deeply into her mouth, a moment later Indy felt one of his thick fingers pressing against her tight ring pushing for entrance.

With a moan, she leaned into him raising her ass higher. "Yes," she breathed.

Jonathan froze when he heard her breathy moan. Pulling her cheeks further apart, he rose up burying his cock all the way in her pussy as he pressed his finger into her anus. Indy hissed at the burning before she shuddered at the feeling of fullness. She had seen anal sex being performed on the videos her, Allie, and Aleaha had watched and having been in nursing, she knew it could be another way of having satisfying sex.

She had never been sure whether she would want to try it or not, but with Jonathan she felt like she wanted to try every way imaginable. Right now she was so hot she would try anything once to feel the satisfaction she had felt after she'd had her first orgasm. She decided she could become addicted to them.

"More," Indy groaned, pushing back against his hand.

Jonathan felt the tremble course through his body at the thought of finally finding a woman who could satisfy his needs. Pushing another finger, then another into her, he worked at stretching her. Would she allow him the ultimate prize of taking her from behind? The thought of watching as his cock disappeared into her ass had him, letting out a growl as his body jerked and he filled her again.

He pushed his fingers in and out of her as his cock jerked deep inside her, causing her to shudder as waves of heat flooded her. She bit down on his shoulder and let out a smothered scream as she came hard. He could feel her clamping down on both his cock and his fingers.

Slowly pulling his fingers out of her, he wrapped his arms around her as she laid her head on his chest. They didn't move until the water became so cool they both began to shiver. Lifting her up into his arms, he set her gently down on the rug in front of the fire before getting out himself. Picking up a towel, he dried her first then himself. They didn't say anything until they both stood there looking at each other wondering what to do next.

"I mean for you to stay, Indy. I can't let you go," Jonathan said gruffly.

She bit her lip, looking up at him for a moment before turning to gaze at the fire. "I promised Sam I would be back in the spring to check in and let him know I was okay. I don't know how long I can stay here. If I go back, I don't know if I can return," Indy said softly, trying to wrap her mind around the fact she had traveled through time.

"You don't understand, Indy. I won't let you go," Jonathan said, gripping her arms tightly for a moment. "I don't care who this Sam is but you need to understand you are my wife now. Your home is here with me," he bit out forcefully, terrified at the thought of losing her just when he found her.

Indy's head jerked around at the forceful tone in his voice. "I have to go back sometime. I have to at least let Sam and Claire know I'm still alive. That I'm okay," she insisted.

Jonathan just shook his head, his lips firming into a straight line of determination. "I won't allow you off the ranch. I won't take a chance on you disappearing on me. Do you know how you got here?" He asked suddenly.

Indy didn't say anything but he could see that she knew by the look on her face. He wanted…. needed to know that she was safe. If he had to, he would tie her ass up until she gave up the thought of leaving.

I won't let her out of my sigh if that's what it takes, he thought as a shiver of fear and dread coursed through him at the thought of losing her.

Whatever it took, he would make sure she stayed. Turning away from her, he moved over to the dresser and started pulling out clean clothes. Indy watched him for a moment before walking over to where her clothes were lying on the floor. Before she could pick them up, Jonathan grabbed her arm in a gently, but firm grip.

"You won't be needing those anymore. I had Wally bring some of my mother's dresses in here for you. You can wear those until I can get you to town to get some made if you don't know how to sew," he said pulling Indy's jeans and shirt into his arms.

Indy jerked her arm loose as his words sunk in. "What?" She asked in disbelief. "You don't honestly expect me to wear dresses all the time, do you? I had maybe one dress if I was lucky at home. I never wear dresses!" She said, clenching her fists as her temper began to burn.

"Not only do I expect you to wear them all the time, but I expect you to learn how to be a proper wife," he replied looking at Indy standing in front of him completely nude.

She didn't seem to even be aware of it as she crossed her arms over her breasts. He had to bite back a groan as he saw her nipples peeking out at him. He cursed silently as his wayward cock tried to respond again. She was going to be the death of him! Between her independent attitude, her innocent sex appeal, and her comfort at wearing virtually nothing, he was going to be hard pressed to get anything done.

Indy looked pointedly at her new 'husband'. "Jonathan, this is not a good way to start a marriage. If you know what is good for you, you will drop my clothes right now and forget the he-man attitude," Indy said calmly, placing her hands on her hips and looking at him in warning.

"I don't know anything about a he-man attitude, but it is well within my rights as your husband to make sure you are dressed properly," Jonathan said weakly wondering if he was making the right decision based on the look she was giving him. He nodded toward the trunk at the foot of the bed. "There are plenty of dresses in there. You are about the same size as our mother was so they should fit for the most part," he added in what he hoped was a firm voice.

"Is that your final answer?" Indy asked with a sarcastic smile.

"Yes," Jonathan said looking worriedly at her, as if he was unsure of whether he should answer her.

"You are sure?" Indy asked again taking a step closer to him.

"Yes," Jonathan replied hoarsely running his eyes over her. "I have to check in with Jacob to see when he plans on starting the training for the Mustangs. I'll see you later this evening," he muttered hoarsely before turning and hurrying out of the bedroom with her clothes still clutched tightly in his hands.

Indy smiled sweetly to his departing back. "Of course, darling. I'll see you later. Have a nice time at work."

Jonathan glanced over his shoulder, relieved that Indy acquiesced to his demands. Maybe being married and teaching her how to fit into his world would be easier than he thought. She seemed to understand he was the boss and she should do as he said. The problem was if she ever discovered the power she held over his heart, she would know that she was the one really in charge.

* * *

As soon as Jonathan left the room, Indy dropped the sweet smile. That bozo really thought she was going to give in that easy? He obviously needed a lesson in twenty-first century women!

She had discovered from her dealings with Gus, Matt, and Hayden when to pick her battles. This was one battle she was determined to win. Jonathan was about to discover that she didn't bow or take orders from anyone, including him. There was more than one way to fight.

Moving to the chest, Indy opened it with a smile. Oh, she would wear a dress alright. And yes, she could sew thanks to Claire's insistence. Let's see how he liked the modifications she made to the dresses. She had a feeling she wouldn't be wearing them for very long though.

Chapter 10

Jonathan spent the rest of the afternoon out in the eastern pasture looking over the Mustang's Jacob had brought in. He knew getting away from the house was the only way he would be able to keep his hands off of Indy. A warmth spread over him at the thought of being married to such a passionate, interesting, feisty woman. He knew he would never get tired of being around her – mentally or physically.

He just nodded his head to Jacob when his brother started in surprise to see him so soon. When Jacob asked him how married life was, Jonathan couldn't keep the satisfied grin off his face. He couldn't remember his body ever feeling this relaxed or sated before.

Jacob felt a flash of envy race through him again at the contented look on his twin brother's face. He was about to explode with curiosity as well. He would never admit it to Jonathan, but it had taken everything decent inside of him to stand back and not compete for Indy's attention.

He knew she was one filly neither one of them would have let escape without a fight. He was glad his brother was happy. He would always support him no matter how much he wished it had been him instead of Jonathan who had found Indy first.

Shifting in his saddle, he finally couldn't contain his curiosity any longer. "So, is she as passionate in bed as she is out of it?" Jacob asked with a sheepish grin.

"More," Jonathan said, not elaborating.

Jacob released a loud groan of frustration. "I'm surprised you made it out of the bedroom, then," he said, studying his brother. "If it was me, I would still be in bed with those long legs wrapped…" he grounded out trying to get a response from his uncooperative brother.

Jonathan turned in his saddle to glare a warning. "She's mine, Jacob," he growled shortly before releasing his breath at his brother's mischievous grin. "Besides, I didn't want to hurt her. She was an innocent. I knew if I stayed in the same room as her I wouldn't be able to keep my hands off her. Hell, I can't imagine being in the same house without making love to her again and again. That is why I'm here and not back at the homestead. At least this way she can have a little bit of a rest before tonight. I also need time to deal with everything we've learned about her. She isn't used to this way of life, at least how the women of this time act," he said, thinking it strange that he could accept that Indy was from a world he couldn't even imagine. "I'm worried, Jacob," he admitted reluctantly. "I'm scared of losing her."

Jacob just shook his head. Jonathan seemed to have all the luck. A beautiful woman who was passionate in bed and who was smart to boot. He wondered what her world was like before she came here. It must have been bad to cause her to run the way she did. He had gotten bits and pieces from Jake as to what had happened. Jake told him Indy was afraid of some men who had hurt her. He figured if those men decided to come over to their side of the world, he and Jonathan could show them what happened to men who wanted to hurt a delicate, beautiful woman like Indy. Jacob halfway wondered if there might be another woman out there for him. He let his eyes scan the surrounding mountains before turning his attention back to his brother who was deep in his own thoughts.

"What are you worried about? Those men chasing her or Indy? We can show those men what happens to a man who wants to hurt a defenseless woman. As far as Indy is concerned, I have to admit I'm a bit surprised. I expected her to resist you more," Jacob said. "She sure as hell was madder than a rabid fox earlier."

"I thought so too, but once I got her clothes off her it was like lightning on kindling, we both just went up in flames," Jonathan admitted with a small grin. "Shit, Jacob, she was wearing these undergarments…" He moved in his saddle as his cock grew hard again at just the memory of her standing there in them.

"Well?" Jacob asked impatiently. "You can't just start a statement like that and not finish it," he grumbled in annoyance.

"She said the women in her time wear them. The top is this lacy thing that only covers her breasts and is so sheer you can see right through it. Hell, I could suck on her nipples through it. It was solid black with these little pink bows on the straps. Her bottom, damn, I can't think about it without getting hard. The bottom was this little bit of lace that was cut into a triangle and barely covered her womanhood. It had two thin straps over her hips and there wasn't anything in the back just a thin strip of lace between her buttocks. She called it a thong." God, he was hard as a rock again. "She said the women even wore stuff like that to swim in."

Jacob shifted in his saddle again. "Ah shit, Jonathan. You're killing me here," he cursed out not even trying to hide his envy this time.

Jonathan chuckled. He was killing himself just thinking about it. It was going to be damn painful riding in the condition he was fast finding himself.

"She also…" Jonathan started before wondering if he wanted to tell his brother about her not having any hair covering her womanhood or not.

"She what? Damn it, Jonathan. She what?" Jacob demanded hoarsely shifting uncomfortably in his saddle.

Jonathan looked out over the herd of horses, but his eyes were seeing something entirely different. "She doesn't have any hair over her womanhood. She said she likes it bare," he whispered. "It was incredible."

Groaning, Jacob turned from his brother. "You sure about not being able to share her?" He asked in a tight voice.

Jonathan let out an expletive, shooting his brother a heated look. "I'll kill any man who tries to touch her. I need to know I can trust you, Jacob," he said grimly.

Jacob stared at Jonathan for a moment before replying. "You can trust me," he promised, letting out a deep sigh. "But damn, how did you get so lucky?" He asked gruffly.

Jonathan laughed as the tension melted out of his shoulders at his brother's promise. "Maybe she has a friend," he speculated thoughtfully.

"If only I could be so lucky," Jacob muttered darkly.

They spent another two hours out with the horses talking about how they were going to get them ready in time before calling it a night. They were going to meet up with some of the men at dinner tonight to discuss the training. Wally was fixing a feast for the men who had just come in since they had been living on range food for the last six weeks.

Jonathan was anxious to see Indy again. He couldn't believe he was now a married man. Damn, if it didn't feel good too! He had thought she would have been more upset about him insisting she wear dresses, and was glad she would be decently attired for company around the men. He felt bad she had to wear his and Jacob's mother's dresses, but it would just be until he was able to take her to town to get material to make some.

Riding back to the ranch house with Jacob and Ed, he was glad to be back. He had only been gone a few hours, but he found he already missed Indy. Taking care of his horse, he was walking up to the porch when Wally opened the door.

"Welcome home, Mr. Jonathan, Mr. Jacob, Mr. Ed. Welcome, welcome," Wally said, bowing. "Wally has dinner ready. Other men have come. They are in the living room."

"Where's Mrs. Tucker?" Jonathan asked, taking his hat off and hanging it on the hat rack next to the door.

A choked cough was his only warning before he turned to see his new wife walking down the stairs with a welcoming smile on her face. Jonathan thought his heart had stopped beating for a minute as he stared wide-eyed at his wife. She was absolutely gorgeous. She was absolutely dead.

* * *

Indy had pulled out the dresses and grabbing a pair of scissors, she had started to work on all of them so he couldn't find one to push her into. She modified most of them to look like the short cowgirl dresses the girls wore to the bar she hung out at on the weekends with Allie. She cut each of them until they were just a couple of inches above the knee. She made sure it showed off her long legs.

Modifying the top of the one she had chosen to wear that night had been a little tricky on such short notice. She liked the dresses with a type of vest. She quickly cut the sleeves to make most of them short sleeve.

For the number she was going to wear tonight, she had left the sleeves long, but had removed most of the material on the bosom so only the bottom part was left. She had left the first four buttons undone so she had plenty of cleavage showing. It was a dark green and would show off her eyes.

The cut was perfect for showing off her large breasts and narrow waist. She actually liked the high top shoes she found in the trunk. They were kind-of sexy and made her legs look longer than they really were with the slight heel on them.

Pulling on her thong and bra, she looked like she was going out with Aleaha, Allie, and the boys on a Saturday night. She didn't have any make-up, but the afternoon of love making had put a rosy glow on her face. She piled her hair up in a funky, sexy knot, leaving strands of autumn colored hair flowing down her back and over her shoulders. She looked like she was ready to go dancing – in 2013.

"Hi Jonathan, did you get a chance to check out the horses this afternoon?" Indy asked as she did her best impression of a beauty queen walking down the staircase of a Miss Universe Beauty Pageant. She walked up to the men who were staring at her in a daze, giving them a huge smile before she leaned up and placed a light kiss on Jonathan's cheek. "How was the rest of your day, Jonathan?" She asked with a satisfied twinkle in her eyes as she turned to give Jacob a kiss as well.

Let him chew on this, she thought silently.

"What...?" Jonathan choked out looking at Indy as she lifted one, very well defined leg up as she kissed Jacob on the cheek. "What are you wearing?" He asked hoarsely.

"Why, don't you recognize it? It's your mother's dress. You did say you wanted me to wear dresses, didn't you?" Indy asked innocently.

Jacob choked back a laugh. "I don't ever remember mother wearing that one. Wait a minute, now I do. I think she wore that one to church on Sundays." Jacob couldn't help but burst out laughing. Yes, maybe he didn't need to be envious of his brother after all. He had a feeling his brother had met his match.

"You look absolutely beautiful, Indy. I really like what you've done to the dress. I have to say it never looked that good on our mother," Jacob said grinning down at her.

Indy laughed, twirling around. The movement caused the skirt to fly up dangerously high. All the men groaned as it settled back down in fluttering waves just above her knees.

"Do you really? I'm glad because I modified *all* the dresses so they would fit me just like this one," Indy said, emphasizing the word 'all' so Jonathan would understand she was not about to be told what to do *or* what to wear.

"Indiana, my office now," Jonathan choked out in a low voice.

She raised her eyebrow at him in challenge. "But, what about dinner? You can't just leave your guests standing around," she pointed out as she crossed her arms in front of her and looked pointedly at the men standing around in the living room. Not a one of them looked like they were the least bit interested in eating dinner, at least not the dinner Wally had to offer.

"To hell with dinner," Jonathan growled out through clenched teeth. He gripped Indy's elbow in a firm grasp wishing it was her neck. "My office.... Now!"

Indy smiled in triumph at seeing Jonathan lose his cool even as a shiver ran down her spine at the heated look in his eyes. His look was nothing like the ones Hayden gave her.

She waved to the dazed men watching the scene unfolding before them in bemusement. Jacob was grinning like an idiot, his eyes glued to Indy's legs and ass. All he could think about was if she was wearing the undergarments Jonathan had told him about under her dress or not? Groaning, he looked at the other men staring after Jonathan and Indy before heading for the decanter sitting on the low table.

"I don't know about you gentlemen, but I could really use a drink," Jacob said to a chorus of agreement.

* * *

Jonathan barely made it through the door before he pushed Indy up against it and crushed her lips with his. It had taken every bit of self discipline he had to make it as far as his office. When he saw her coming down the staircase, her long legs bare for all to see and her hair flowing down her back like he had just made love to her, he had felt ready to explode. Damned if he could look at her without getting hard, especially now that he knew what she was like when he made love to her.

Reaching up under the short dress, he felt her mound. He couldn't hold back the groan when he found it was hot and swollen. He impatiently pushed the material from her lacy panties to one side so he could slide his finger into her to see if she was ready for him.

Finding her wet and slick, he moaned softly as he buried his finger as deep as it would go into her hot vaginal channel. He knew he was going to take her hard and fast again. The last thing he wanted to do was hurt her.

Indy muttered incoherently as she felt him pulling her panties aside and pushing his thick finger into her. She fumbled with the front of his pants, unable to stand the idea of not being able to touch him as he was touching her. As mad as she was at him earlier for forcing her to wear a dress, she had no complaints right now.

Finally getting the buttons of his pants undone, she pushed his pants down as far as she could before grabbing his throbbing cock in her hand. God, he was so thick. She could barely wrap her fingers around him.

"Lift me up," Indy whispered as she ran little kisses up and down his jaw. Wrapping her arms around his neck, she repeated her demand in a voice that was a little more desperate than before. "Lift me up now, Jonathan."

Jonathan groaned again as he pressed Indy into the door of his office. Lifting her up by the waist, he shuddered as she wrapped her long legs around his waist and reached down to guide him to her hot, slick mound. Neither one of them could suppress the shuddering groan that escaped as she slid down onto his hard length.

"Shit Indy," Jonathan moaned softly. He thrust his hips up hard impaling her as she clung to him. Thrusting up over and over, he breathed in the scent of their arousal. It was enough to make him grow even harder.

"Jonathan," Indy whimpered, clutching his shoulders as she rose up and then dropped down onto his thick cock as he thrust upward.

"You are fucking mine!" Jonathan grunted out as he pushed harder and faster into her. He gripped her hips, his fingers holding her steady as he felt the burning start deep down and begin to build with a relentless pressure.

Indy held on as he pounded into her with a savage need that scorched her from the inside out. She felt her own climax surge through her as he rose up, pushing deeply into her body. Letting out a soft, long cry, she jerked as her body shattered. She arched back against the door as her orgasm swept through her body, leaving her shaking from the intensity. Her fingers dug into his shoulders as she tried to hang on as the fierce surge of the release sucked every ounce of her strength from her.

Jonathan heard Indy's cry a moment before he felt the hot walls of her vagina clamp down around him. He fought against his own urge to come. He wanted her. He wanted all of her.

He pushed one hand against the door as he kicked off the pants around his ankles. He wound his arms tightly around her, carrying her over to his desk as she lay draped against him. Clenching his teeth together, he lifted her off of his hard cock, ignoring her startled cry of dismay as he did. Setting her down, he had to hold her as her knees gave out.

Jonathan wasn't done yet. As far as he was concerned, he had just started. He swept one arm out knocking items off the desk so he could bend her over it.

Turning her around so her back was to him, Jonathan spoke hoarsely. "Bend over the desk. Now, Indy," he begged in a deep, desperate voice.

Indy was still dazed from her climax. Unsure of what was happening, but wanting to feel the utopia only he could bring her, she did as he asked. Bending over the desk, she held the top part of her body up by her elbows while she looked at him over her shoulder. A weak, satisfied smile curved her lips as her head drooped.

Jonathan grabbed the short dress by the hem and lifted it up so it draped across Indy's back. His breath caught in his throat as he looked at her bare ass. He looked at Indy again. He wanted her and he planned on taking her.

"Mine," he said as he rubbed the pale globes of her ass.

Indy groaned and pushed up against his hand. "Yours. Fuck me, Jonathan, make me yours," she whispered huskily.

Jonathan's eyes flared with passion at the raw words coming out of her mouth. He gripped her hips again and thrust into her without warning, pushing her tight against the edge of his desk. He knew he should probably take it slower. He should give her more time to adjust to the demands he wanted to make on her and her body but he couldn't. He needed her too much. He had never felt this way before. He was thrusting into her hard, pushing as deep as he could go. Indy lowered her head, gripping the desk as Jonathan took her.

"I want you so badly, Indy. I don't want to hurt you. But, I want to fuck you," Jonathan said through gritted teeth. "I need you so much," he admitted. "You make me feel things that I don't understand, but I need you."

The waves of heat caused by his words and the rhythm of his body sliding in and out of hers was causing her own body to react. "I don't understand this either, but I need you too," Indy whimpered.

She tightened her grip along the edges of the desk, thankful for its support because there was no way she could have held herself up. She dropped her forehead down onto the desk and cried out loudly as her body tightened around his again as the friction between them became unbearable. The orgasm that gripped her was pulled from the depths of her soul and she sobbed as it exploded.

Jonathan thrust one more time into her, letting his orgasm take over as he spilled his seed deep into her womb. He held himself still, his eyes closed, as he pulsed deeply into her body. It was only when his shaking legs couldn't hold him up straight anymore that he bent over, folding his long length over her smaller one.

"I love you, Indiana," he murmured, pressing a soft kiss against the side of her neck.

* * *

Folding his arms around her, Jonathan slowly straightened. He carefully pulled out of her, afraid he had been too demanding. He ran a brief kiss over her shoulder as she whimpered. Picking her up in his arms, he walked over to the long sofa on shaky legs. Was it only this morning he had tied her up so he could marry her? It was hard to believe so much had happened in such a short amount of time. He felt like she had always been a part of his life.

Indy ran her hand up under Jonathan's shirt loving the feel of his strong, broad chest under her hands. She skimmed her fingers through the light coating of hair, enjoying the feeling of it as much as just being held by him. In his arms, she didn't worry about Hayden or the future. She felt safe.

"So, do you like the dress?" Indy murmured, brushing a kiss along his throat.

Jonathan shook his head and chuckled. "Too much. You know I can't allow you to wear one like this. I'd have to kill every man who looked at you in it, including my own brother."

Indy sighed deeply. "Well, if you make me wear one this is what it is going to be like. I'll cut every damn one this short or shorter. I told you, I don't wear dresses," she said, snuggling even closer as the chill in the room mixed with the damp sweat from their lovemaking.

He pulled her closer against his warm body. He was still trying to wrap his brain around how to handle the wild spirit that was his little wife. If she was from the future, and he was beginning to believe she had to be as he had never met another woman like her, then he was going to have to figure out how to work and live with her because there was no way he was ever going to let her go.

Indy pulled away and looked up at him with a mischievous grin. "You have to admit shorter dresses make it easier to fool around. Who knows, I could wear them with nothing underneath and you could come up behind me like you just did and we could..." she never got a chance to finish what she was saying.

Jonathan groaned and crushed her lips under his even as his cock jerked to attention again. She was definitely going to be the death of him at this rate. The idea of being able to come up at any time, lift her dress, and take her from behind had his imagination going into overdrive.

He reluctantly pulled back so he could rest his forehead against hers. "What am I going to do with you?" He groaned softly.

She pulled her head back far enough so she could study his face for a moment. "Jonathan, I won't be told what to do or be controlled. As long as I'm here we have to be partners. I was born on a ranch and it is all I know. Let me be who I am. If you don't, you will be no different than Hayden," Indy said softly, pressing her hand against his cheek and looking deeply into his eyes.

A shiver ran down his spine at her words. "What do you mean as long as you're here? Where the hell do you think you would be going? And who in the hell is Hayden? Why are you afraid of him finding you?" Jonathan asked with a dark frown, pulling up so he could sit on the sofa.

Indy scooted back and sat up as well. She pulled her dress down around her and bit her lower lip, trying to think about how she could reply to his questions. She owed him the truth. If she was truly in the past, surely there was no way Hayden could touch her. She was finally safe.

Relaxing into the corner of the couch, she watched Jonathan as he rose and walk over to where his pants lay crumpled on the floor near the door. Her eyes followed his every movement, enjoying the view of his tight ass as he bent over and the taut muscles of his strong legs. She didn't even remember him taking his boots off.

She wondered how he managed that little feat during the time they were making love. She flushed when he turned around and stared at her, a small knowing smile curving his lips. She drew in a deep breath and slowly began explaining how she had come to be on the Twin Rivers Ranch.

Folding her hands tightly together in her lap, she sighed as she thought about her brothers. "I have three older brothers. Hayden is the oldest, followed by Gus and Matthew. They are all over twenty years older than I am. I was a surprise to my parents. Anyway, I was born and spent my life up until a couple months ago on the Wild Ranch in the state of Montana. The ranch belonged to my grandparents. It was to go to my parents then my brothers and me. Ten years ago my grandmother and parents were killed in a car accident." Indy noticed Jonathan's frown at the mention of the word 'car'.

Sighing again, Indy briefly tried to explain. "We get around using a machine called an automobile. It is like your wagons only it has an engine and four wheels so you don't need horses," she said, wishing there was an easier way to help him understand what she was saying. Jonathan frowned as he tried to picture what she was saying. She shook her own head. "I have pictures of them on my iPod. When you return my belongings to me from wherever you put them, I can show you one plus some other things that might help you understand what my life was like before I came here," she explained.

Jonathan walked over and sat down next to her on the couch. Lifting her slender fingers in his hands, he noticed they were trembling. He tugged gently on her hand, letting her know that he wanted to hold her close as she told him more.

Indy rose up far enough that he could slide under her. She released a shuddering breath as she felt his strong, warm arms circle her shivering body. He pulled her close, running his hand up and down her back tenderly.

"Go on," he encouraged quietly.

She relaxed back against him, laying her head on his chest. "My grandfather raised me after that. It was just the two of us. We were very close. Almost a year ago, my grandfather had a stroke. Hayden flew out for a couple of weeks. It was the first time since our parents died that he returned to the ranch. I didn't realize he had an ulterior motive for coming." She paused as she remembered the feeling of betrayal. A tear slid down her cheek as she remembered sitting day and night next to her vibrant grandfather and watching the spark slowly fade from him. "Hayden is a high power attorney out in California. He had my grandfather sign a letter giving him Power of Attorney over his assets. When grandpa died, Hayden sold the ranch out from under me." She turned her face into Jonathan's chest, breathing in his familiar scent while she tried to get her emotions back under control.

Jonathan felt the quivers shaking Indy's fragile frame and a burning anger flared. How could her own family betray her like this? He could hear the grief in her voice. He had a feeling there was more to the story and that he wasn't going to like it anymore than the one he was picturing now.

"What did he do that would drive you to such desperate measures?" He asked brushing his hand along her hair.

"The ranch sold for millions," Indy replied. "Hayden shouldn't need the money. He is rich, but my other two brothers need it. Matt is a gambler, he'll be broke in a year or less. Gus and his wife have two sons that have just started college. Gus never made much and his wife never worked. Hayden wasn't very happy with me, I'm afraid. I wasn't very nice when I found out what they had done behind my back. I don't know how he was able to convince a judge that I wasn't capable of taking care of myself mentally, physically, or financially, but Hayden got a court order giving him guardianship of me and control over my share of the ranch. He was going to force me to give up Chester, Tweed, Kahlua, and Midnight and move to Los Angeles," she shuddered, pulling back far enough to look up into Jonathan's eyes. "It is a huge city in California. It is very crowded. I would die being cooped up without the wide open spaces."

Jonathan ran his fingers down along her cheek, a smile curving his lips. "Well, that is not likely to happen now. You are my wife and there are no cities like you describe, except maybe over in England or France. I've heard there are big cities there. The biggest city I've ever been to was back East, and it doesn't sound like it is as big as what you are describing," he assured her. "Why would your brother try to force you to live in such a place?"

Indy bit her lip again before she turned troubled eyes up to him. "Hayden never does anything that doesn't benefit him in some way. If he thought he could get an extra dollar or opened a door for political gain he wouldn't think twice of doing whatever he had to do to get it. I just never expected him to be this ruthless. I think he is trying to use me to sweeten some deal he has in the works. He wants to move into politics and has been rubbing elbows with some really powerful people. I found a letter he wrote my last semester of college to my grandpa asking for him to send me to live with him as soon as I graduated. He mentioned he had some very influential men he wanted to introduce me to. He told my grandpa it was in my best interest to marry someone who could take care of me," she snorted in disgust. "Like I need someone taking care of me! If any of those jackasses ever got held up they would probably shit in their pants before they fainted."

Jonathan's arms tightened around her at the thought of her brother selling her off to the highest bidder. If anything, he was more determined than ever that he keep her here with him. A shiver of fear swept through him at the idea of losing her to some unknown force.

"Indy, how did you get here?" He asked gruffly. "Is it possible for you to go back?"

Indy frowned, thinking about his questions. "I think it has to do with Spirit Pass. Sam told me about it when I was younger, but I never thought much about it. I figured he was just telling me another of one of his tales," she said thoughtfully. "I guess it would be possible to go back through it to get back home. Sam did it. He said he traveled through the Pass and found himself in a strange world. He found Claire and her brother and brought them back home. Neither Claire nor William ever said much about where they were from, but I remember thinking Claire acted a little old fashioned about some things."

Jonathan tilted her chin up so she could see the seriousness in his eyes. "I don't want to lose you," he said. "I won't let you go back through that Pass. I want your promise you won't try to return to your old home."

Indy smiled and reached up to trail her fingers lightly over his cheek. "You work with me, accept me for who I am, and let me be not only your wife, but your partner and I promise to stick around," she promised. "But, if you try giving me any more ridiculous commands...." She paused to make sure she had his attention. "I promise to make your life a living hell," she vowed with a tender brush of her lips against his.

Jonathan chuckled at her veiled threat. "If you cutting up my mother's dress is an example of the hell you are going to give me, I might just have to do it every now and then to see what happens," he suggested before covering her mouth with his in another breathless kiss.

Chapter 11

"What have you found?" Hayden Wild asked coldly as he rested his hands on the desk in front of him. "It has been over four months. There is no way she could have just disappeared! I'm paying you a small fortune to produce and you have yet to do anything but give me lame excuses."

Alexander Gent leaned back in his seat and shifted uncomfortably. He was one of the best private investigators in the country. He never failed a client. If a person went missing, he could find them. There was no way in today's time that a person could totally disappear off the map. Especially someone as naïve and unsophisticated as the young woman he had been hired to find and deliver. He frowned down at the documents in his hands.

"The last reported sighting of her was of her heading into the mountains. You sent out search teams. They found a scattering of trails, but they all disappeared under the snow that fell. I've been tracking all her bank accounts, including credit cards, and there has been no activity. I've had men watching the Whitewater ranch as well and she hasn't been there either. It is possible she didn't survive," Alex stated in a calm voice.

Hayden was already shaking his head. "She's alive. She is too good and too stubborn not to be. I need her here by the end of the month. I have someone who is getting very impatient to meet her. It is in both of our best interests that she is here for that meeting," Hayden added with a dark warning in his voice.

Alex's mouth tightened at the veiled threat. "I have a new person in place working on the Whitewater ranch," he replied in an equally cool voice. "If you say your sister is as close to Sam and Claire Whitewater and their family as you seem to think, it only makes sense that she will contact them sooner or later. Do I have permission to use whatever means is necessary to bring her back?" He asked.

Hayden's mouth curved into an ugly smile. "You can tie her ass up if you have to, just get her to Los Angeles before the end of the month."

Alex stood up. "She'll be there," he promised before nodding his head in acknowledgement that the meeting was over.

Hayden watched as the ex-military investigator walked out of his office. He turned his chair to stare out at the glittering lights of Los Angeles. His fists clenched as he thought of how much aggravation his little sister was causing him.

He had set plans in motion for her the moment he had seen her when he had returned for the funeral of their parents and grandmother. He realized even as young as she was that she was going to be a beauty when she grew up. That kind of beauty, matched with the money she would inherit from the sale of the ranch, would make her a very valuable tool.

He already had an offer that promised him a chance of election to the U. S. Senate. He just needed to deliver his sister and her millions to the proper hands. She was still young enough to be molded into the type of wife that would make any man happy to have her on his arm. Once she was under Hammock's control it would be his problem in teaching Indiana how to behave as she should. He needed Hammock's support and contacts if he was going to win the seat he wanted. He looked at the picture of his little sister staring up at him from the folder he had on her. She had a huge grin on her face as she sat with the two dogs she loved curled up next to her.

Yes, she would make Hammock very, very happy, Hayden thought in satisfaction as he closed the folder and put it away in the drawer of his desk. *And, she will make me a very, very happy Senator.*

* * *

Three days later, Alexander Gent released his breath and grinned. Finally, a break in the case. He had worked to get one of his agents into the Whitewater house when they had hired a crew in to cater a party. The agent had placed listening devices throughout the house. It had finally paid off when Sam Whitewater and his wife were talking late last night after the function. Now, he just needed to find a local who knew the area to take him to the prize.

He walked out of the little local motel and looked around. The night air was chilly and he shivered as the wind cut through the thin black leather jacket he was wearing. His eyes narrowed on the flashing light of the local bar. He had been to it several times during his stay near the Whitewater ranch. All the locals hung out there and he had learned Indiana liked to go there occasionally.

He had hoped to hear someone mention her, but there had been no talk at all except of what a bastard her brothers were for screwing her over the way they did. It was none of Alex's business how the brothers treated their sister. He had been hired to do a job and that was what he would do.

Shoving his cold hands into his pocket, he looked both ways before jogging across the street to the bar. Money was a powerful tool and right now he had an open account. He was sure he could find someone desperate enough to take him where he wanted to go and look the other way when he did what he needed to do. There was always someone out there that would sell a little bit of their soul for some of the green stuff. He knew because he was one of them.

* * *

Indy smacked the tightly coiled rope against her dusty pant leg watching as the Mustang turned as she did. She kept getting closer and closer with each circle, controlling the beautiful brown and white horse's movements. She ignored everything but the horse, giving it her undivided attention.

"She's incredible," Jacob said, leaning against the fence next to his brother.

Jonathan smiled at his brother's simple statement. Incredible didn't even begin to describe her. Oh, there had been some rough patches over the last few weeks. He found she had strong opinions about certain things and could be very stubborn when she felt she was in the right.

The morning after their marriage he had returned her belongings to her, including her animals. She had quietly thanked him for trusting her. He had watched as she shyly unpacked her bags in the bedroom they would share.

He had moved his clothes to give her room. He had picked up numerous items in fascination. She took the time to stop and explain what they were and how they worked. The small silver box she had shook him. He had turned it over and over in wonder. When she had put the little plugs in his ear, he had damn near jumped out of his skin. He had insisted she explain what each picture was, how the device worked, and yet he still couldn't believe what he was seeing.

If he'd had any doubt before about her story, it had disappeared when she unpacked her things. He cautioned her not to show some of the items she had, including the little silver box, to anyone except maybe Jacob. He didn't trust anyone else. Indy reluctantly admitted she had shown Maikoda the device before she knew that she had traveled back in time.

"He didn't say anything," she assured him. "I don't think he was upset by it."

"Indians are different from white folks. They accept things that are strange or unusual," Jonathan explained. "Jacob knows about you but no one else does. It is for your own safety, Indy. Promise me you won't show anyone else the things you have shown me," he insisted, concerned for her safety.

"I promise," she said, looking at him with understanding. "Only you and Jacob should know about my past." Jonathan had then shown her where she could hide the items under the floorboards for safe keeping.

Things had fallen into a routine over the few weeks after that. Both of them were learning how to compromise. It wasn't always easy, but they were trying. He discovered she had a wicked sense of humor, was interested in the current political state of the country, and concerned about the changes that she knew would happen.

Her compassion for the Indians in the region was evident as she talked about the atrocities done to them by the government. She had rebelled at first when she found out he and Jacob had entered into a contract with the government to supply horses to Fort Shaw, a new fort being built to protect the major supply line to Fort Benton.

He had to swear he would never harm any Native Americans or help in any way that would cause them harm. "I may not be able to change history by stopping what will happen, but I sure as hell am not going to be part of it," she had sworn vehemently.

Now, as Jonathan gazed out at Indy, he couldn't help but admire her skills as the horse she was working with came to a stop and she slowly approached it. His heart was in his mouth as he watched the horse lower its head at her touch. She stood next to it, stroking its chin and whispering in its ear.

"Yes, she truly is incredible," he replied in a thick voice. "She makes me happy, Jacob."

Jacob glanced at his brother and smiled. "I'm happy for you, brother. You deserve it," he said before turning back to study Indy. "She knows how to handle a horse. I've never seen training the way she does it. It is like she can talk to them and they understand her. We've been able to break more horses than I expected. I have to admit I like the way she does it. The horses keep their spirit and they handle better."

Jonathan nodded. "She says it is important to build their trust. If you have their trust, they will do anything you want."

"Not unlike your wife," Jacob observed.

"Not unlike my Indy," Jonathan agreed with a smile.

Both men watched as Indy took off the bridle and gently rubbed the horse down before she released it back into the paddock with the other horses. The moment the horse was out of the corral, Chester and Tweed ducked under the fencing and excitedly raced to her side.

She laughed as she played with the two dogs. She looked over and started in surprise when she saw Jonathan and Jacob watching her. Jonathan grinned at the soft blush that tinted her cheeks.

"I think I'll go see how Ed is doing," Jacob said with a chuckle, slapping his brother on the shoulder.

"Thanks," Jonathan nodded absently, not taking his eyes off his wife.

* * *

"Hi, I thought you guys were over in the Eastern paddock working with the horses there," she said as she walked over to the fence.

"We were but Ed and the other men have it under control," Jonathan said. "I missed you," he added, a faint red tinting his own cheeks at the admission.

Indy chuckled and leaned over the fence to give him a quick kiss. "You saw me just a few hours ago," she reminded him with a raised eyebrow and a knowing grin.

Jonathan shook his head and laughed. "I don't know if I'll ever get used to you being so forward," he commented.

Indy paused in the process of climbing over the fence. She had swung one leg over, but stopped at his comment, biting her lip in concern. Jonathan had reluctantly given in to her demand about not wearing dresses. It had taken a while for the other men to get used to seeing a woman in pants, but after a few days none of them appeared to mind anymore. She looked down at him with a serious expression on her face.

"Does it bother you? Me saying things like that.... speaking my mind?" She asked, bringing her other leg over and sitting on the top of the fence looking down at him.

Jonathan reached up and wrapped his big hands around her slender waist. He wondered what it would feel like when she was swollen with their child. Just the thought of Indy being rounded brought a sharp pang of desire sweeping through him. Hell, if he wasn't feeling about as horny as a stallion watching his favorite mare.

"No, I like it," he murmured, making sure her body slid down the length of his. "I like it a lot," he added huskily.

Indy sighed and wrapped her arms around his neck. "I'm glad because I have to tell you, I probably wouldn't be able to change even if I wanted to. Grandpa always said it was important to speak your mind so others would understand who you are and where you are coming from. He was a wise man and I miss him," she said sadly.

Jonathan's arms tightened around her. "Do you miss your life from before?" He asked hesitantly, not realizing he was holding his breath as he waited for her response.

She leaned back so she could look into his eyes. "I miss some things. Mostly Sam, Claire and their kids. They are the closest thing I have left to having a family. I miss my big bathroom as well," she admitted with a twinkle in her eye. "I had a huge tub and shower and the toilet as well."

"Do you want to go back?" He asked with a sinking feeling.

She shook her head immediately. "And give up all of this? Not on your life! You're stuck with me, Jonathan. You might as well just get used to my mouth," she said with a grin.

His eyes lit up at her passionate response. "I don't think I'll ever get tired of it," he murmured, remembering how she had used that delectable mouth on him last night.

A light pink bloomed on her cheeks as she laughed softly. "I hope not," she teased meeting him halfway as he bent to kiss her.

Chapter 12

"Boss," Carl called out riding up as Jonathan headed toward the barn the next morning. "We've got problems."

Jonathan frowned up at Carl as he jumped down off his horse. "What seems to be the matter?"

Carl removed his hat and ran his hand through his hair. "Last night something spooked the horses. It sounded like wolves. The funny thing is we didn't find no tracks. Whatever it was, it stirred the horses up and about twenty-five of them got loose. I've got some of the boys tracking them," Carl explained.

It wasn't unusual for a pack of wolves to come around, but they normally stayed clear of a herd of horses and the campfires the men had burning. Jonathan muttered a curse before he nodded his head at Carl. He knew Jacob was going to be pissed if they lost any of the horses they had spent so much time breaking.

"I'll let Jacob know and we'll meet you out there in a little bit," he told Carl. "See if you can find the tracks for the wolves. We need to make sure they don't come back once we get the horses rounded up. We'll need to bring the horses closer to the ranch house if we can't find the wolf pack."

"Sure thing, boss," Carl replied.

Jonathan watched as Carl climbed back up on his horse and rode off. He turned as the door to the house opened. Jacob was coming out, talking to Wally. He met them at the bottom of the stairs.

"Jacob, we have a problem. Some wolves scared the horses out in the Eastern paddock. Twenty-five Mustangs got loose. Carl has some men tracking them and I told him to see if he can track the wolves. I think we should bring the ones that are left closer to the house and the others too once they are rounded up," he explained.

"Damn, I should have expected something like this," Jacob said in disgust slamming his hat on his head in irritation.

"Wally, can you let Indy know we might not be back tonight?" Jonathan asked just as the front door opened.

"Do you need any help? I can be ready to go in just a couple of minutes," Indy said as she stepped out onto the front porch.

Jonathan's eyes darkened at how beautiful she looked this morning. Hell, she looked beautiful all the time. The thought of her being around a bunch of rough cowpunchers who hadn't been with a woman in God knew how long had him adamantly shaking his head.

"No, we can handle it. I think it would be better if you stayed close to the ranch house. Jake will be here if you need anything," Jonathan responded.

"Wally too," Wally said with a grin. "Wally help protect Mrs. Indy."

Indy laughed and wrapped her arm around the Chinaman who had become a dear friend since she came to live in the big ranch house. He had patiently shown her how to use the huge cook stove and a

Dutch oven, as well as shared many of his recipes with her. She gave him a kiss on the cheek, drawing a huge grin from Wally and a low growl of disapproval from Jonathan.

"I'll be fine," Indy assured her overprotective husband. "I can continue working with the horses here and I may take a ride out to the Western pasture. Midnight and Kahlua could use the exercise. I've been so focused on training the new horses I haven't spent much time with them lately."

Jonathan frowned at the thought of her traveling so far from the ranch house without him. "I would prefer it if you stayed closer to the ranch," he said.

"Oh come on. Jake can go with me." Indy smiled persuasively with a small pout. "I haven't been out to see Cal since I've come in. I'd like to see how he is doing."

She knew she would go with or without his permission, but it was fun seeing if he fell for the pout. Her grandpa and Sam never could resist it. She had gotten her way or out of trouble more than once with a flutter of her eyelashes and that tiny pout. She figured a girl had to use whatever weapons she had when it came to keeping the peace.

"Alright," Jonathan agreed reluctantly. "Just make sure you take Jake with you. I don't want you riding alone."

He didn't have the heart to turn her down, especially with the way her bottom lip slid out so seductively begging him to nibble on it. Damned if he could tell her no even as everything inside him wanted to. It was an effort to pull his eyes away from the temptation and focus on the situation at hand.

"I promise," she said, skipping down the stairs so she could brush a kiss across his lips. "You just be careful. I'm going to miss you tonight," she whispered in his ear.

Jonathan wrapped his arms around her slender form, holding her tight and breathing in her fresh scent. "I'll miss you as well," he said tenderly. "We shouldn't be more than a day, two at the most."

Indy nodded. "You need to remember I was raised on a working ranch," she reminded him gently. "I understand when things like this happen. I'll see you when you get back."

"Jonathan," Jacob began uncomfortably. "You could stay. The boys and I can handle this."

Jonathan took a reluctant step back, releasing Indy. He shook his head. He had left enough to his brother over the last few weeks. He knew Jacob was doing it so he could spend more time with Indy and appreciated it, but as Indy said, she had been raised on a working ranch and understood the responsibilities involved.

"No, I'm riding with you," he said firmly.

* * *

Several hours later, Indy sighed with joy at the feel of Midnight's huge body under her. They moved as one as they galloped across the uneven terrain. Chester and Tweed loped off to the sides and Kahlua kicked up her heels every once in a while as she followed.

"You have quite the animals, Indy," Jake laughed as he watched the two dogs racing around each other with an overabundance of energy. "Do they ever get tired?"

"They will be by the time we get home tonight," Indy grinned back at her old friend. "They are enjoying getting out as much as I am."

They slowed to a slow trot to give the dogs a chance to rest and to make it easier to talk. They rode in silence for several minutes before Jake spoke up again. He cleared his throat loudly before he spit to the side.

"I'm glad you came, Indy," Jake started out gruffly. "Not only did you save me and Cal that day, you've been good for the boss. I don't remember him looking so happy and content," he added in his deep, gruff voice.

Indy leaned over and patted Midnight's neck when he jumped a little when the dogs got a little too close. She thought about everything that had happened since she left Sam's ranch over four months ago. It was hard to believe her life could change so much in such a short time, especially through an unusual glitch caused by some strange natural phenomenon.

"He's not the only one who is happy," she admitted with a blush. "I love him something fierce, Jake."

Jake chuckled and nodded. "I can tell," he responded in a teasing voice. "You start glowing the minute he walks up. And I swear, he has been walking around with his head in the clouds ever since he met you."

Indy ducked her head to hide the pleased smile Jake's words brought to her face. Jonathan had only said he loved her the one time, after the time they made love in his office. Her face warmed as she remembered it. She had thought he had said it in a moment of passion. She had been afraid to open herself up by telling him how she felt.

She and her grandpa had loved each other, but her grandpa had been a gruff old rancher like Jake and didn't express his feelings in words. He always told her actions spoke louder than words. He said some of the best examples were the people who said they cared about you while stealing you blind. Her brothers were a perfect example of that. She had never spent much time around them and really didn't know them except by what they did by selling the ranch without consulting her about it.

No, she thought sadly, *the only ones who ever showed they really cared about me besides grandpa was Sam, Claire, and their kids.* Indy made up her mind she was going to tell Jonathan just how much she loved him when he got back tomorrow, before she lost her nerve.

"Looks like Cal has left some coffee brewing for us," Jake said with a relieved groan as he shifted in his saddle. "I sure could use a cup."

Indy grinned as she saw the young cowpuncher riding slowly around the outside of the herd of grazing cattle. "I'll join you in a little bit. Come on, boys. Let's go say hello to Cal," she said before she let out a loud whistle and motioned with her hand for the boys to head for the cattle.

Both dogs took off like bullets. Indy kicked her heels into Midnight and leaned low over his neck. Kahlua took off beside them, whinnying and nipping at Midnight who kicked up his back legs briefly. Indy laughed in joy at the playfulness of her creature friends. They needed this time out.

Cal waved in greeting as she rode up, a big smile plastered on his face. "Hey Indy!" He called out.

"Hi Cal," Indy said as she brought Midnight up to a stop near him and turned him so she could watch the herd. "You haven't been out here all this time have you? I thought Jonathan and Jacob only let you guys stay out a few weeks at a time?"

Cal grinned and nodded his head. "They do. My ma and pa have a small place in town. I go there and help out when I'm not here," he said. "One day I want to have a spread like this. We came out here when I was little, about the time the war started. My pa is a peaceful man and didn't believe in fighting so he moved ma and me out here. He opened the trading post and they run it. My pa wants me to follow after him, but I like being out in the open."

"Well, I think you are doing a great job," she assured him. "So, you haven't had any more problems with those rustlers, have you?"

"No, ma'am," he said. "The one I shot showed up at Doc's in town. Turned out he was wanted for deserting the Army and they came and got him. The other two with him took off. No one has seen them. Pa heard the men from the fort say they think the other two may have been deserters too. The Army has sent a couple of scouts out looking for them, but it looks like they headed back East."

Indy sat and chatted with Cal until his watch was over. They rode back over to where Jake was chatting with another cowpuncher Indy hadn't met yet. She nodded to the man as he stared at her with undisguised interest, his eyes roaming over her figure. She raised an eyebrow and stared back with a tight, grim expression on her face.

"Ma'am," the cowpuncher finally murmured before he tossed the remaining coffee in his cup into the fire where it hissed. "Nice talking with you, Jake," the man said, standing up and tipping his hat again to Indy before he walked away.

"Who was that?" Indy asked, watching the man suspiciously. There was something about him that made her uneasy.

Jake shrugged. "We get men heading west, passing through all the time. Some stop and work for a while, others just keep on going. This one came around a few days ago. He needed a job and we were down a couple men who decided to move on without telling us first," he explained. He nodded his head toward the pot of coffee. "He makes a mean pot of coffee. Just made a pot if you want some."

Cal rubbed his hands together. "I sure could use some," he said with a grin. "Indy, do you want any?"

Indy was still watching the man as he rode out toward the cattle. She shook her head, frowning. There was something off about him. The hair on the back of her neck was practically standing on end.

"No, I think I'll pass," she murmured.

"Is it true, Indy? I heard you married Jonathan Tucker," Cal said as he blew on his coffee before taking a deep drink of it. "The talk in town is he had you tied up tighter than a calf at branding and made the preacher marry you right on the spot."

"Shut up, boy," Jake growled out as he watched Indy sink down on the log across the fire from them in shock.

"Really?" Indy whispered before she began giggling. "I bet that gave the old ladies in town something to entertain them for a while! So, our marriage is the talk of the town, is it?"

Cal had the decency to look embarrassed and drank the rest of his coffee in a couple of quick gulps. "We don't get much excitement out here," he muttered shifting uncomfortably. "If it helps, there were more than a few tears from some of the women in town, their ma's, and more than one widow," he said with a small smile.

Indy raised her eyebrow in inquiry. "More than one widow?" She asked in interest.

Jake elbowed Cal and gave him a stern look before a huge yawn broke across his grizzled face. "Damn, didn't realize how tired I was," he said with a frown.

Cal yawned at the same time. "You aren't the only one, Jake. I sure feel funny all the sudden," Cal said in a slurred voice. "I thought coffee was supposed to help me keep alert."

Indy looked at both men as they slid down off the log they were sitting on onto the ground, the empty cups in their hands falling to the ground as they fell back unconscious. She jerked up startled, looking at both of them laying propped up against each other with their mouths open.

"Jake, Cal?" Indy called out to both of them in concern. "Come on, guys. This isn't funny," she said, getting nervous as she moved around the fire to them.

Indy checked Cal's pulse. It was strong and steady. She opened his eyelids and saw they were slightly dilated. She did the same thing to Jake. She looked around suspiciously, trying to see what could have caused both of them to pass out.

Her eyes fell on the coffee cups lying on the ground beside them. She picked one of them up and looked inside the cup. There were a few black coffee grounds, but mixed in with it was a white residue.

Indy ran her finger along the bottom, holding it up so she could see it better in the late afternoon light. Rubbing the mixture between her fingers, she sniffed it before touching it with her tongue. A bitter taste, different from the coffee, washed over her taste buds. She dropped the cup in horror as she realized the coffee had been drugged.

She looked around frantically trying to think who would have the resources and a reason to try to drug them. She turned when a movement from behind a small group of trees to her left answered her question as the man who had been sitting by the fire stepped out from behind the trees. She stumbled back when two more men came out, one stood next to him while the other stayed in the shadows.

"Who are you?" She asked, straightening her shoulders and flexing her fingers to alert Chester and Tweed that there was danger.

"I wouldn't do that if I were you, Ms. Wild," a tall, lean man wearing a dark leather jacket said.

Indy signaled for the dogs to lie down. She gasped when the man standing toward the back stepped closer so she could see him. She recognized him immediately from back home.

"Billy, what are you doing here? How did you....?" She asked frightened.

"I'm sorry, Indy. I needed the money. Rosalie is expecting again and I got laid off down at the plant," Billy Cloudrunner said. "She's been real sick with this one and we couldn't afford the medicine she needed," he added looking at the two men carefully. "I was only asked to guide them through the mountains. I didn't know they were after you until it was too late. I wouldn't have helped otherwise."

Indy swallowed over the lump in her throat. She knew how fragile Rosalie was and how much Billy loved his little wife and kids. The current economy had hit many of them hard in the area, especially out on the reservation. Her eyes slid to the other two men. They were the ones she had to worry about.

"What do you want with me?" She asked coldly, raising her chin up defiantly.

"You have a choice," the lean man said as he stepped forward. "You can come peacefully or you can come fighting, but I promise you, we will be taking you back to your brother. He has paid a substantial amount for your return and really doesn't care how we get you back," the man smiled before he nodded toward the two dogs who were laying slightly behind Indy growling menacingly. "If they so much as twitch, Rodgers will put a bullet in both of their heads. He is an ex-ranger and won't miss."

Indy trembled with rage and took a step forward. "I'll cut your balls off and feed them to the wolves if you harm one hair on my dogs," she snarled out in a low voice. She motioned with her hand and both dogs reluctantly rose. "Go find Jonathan," she ordered before giving the dogs the 'go find' signal she had taught them recently.

Alex cursed as his face darkened in anger. "Kill them," he ordered sharply.

Rodgers quickly raised his arm to fire at the retreating dogs. Indy and Billy both moved at the same time. Alex grabbed Indy as she flew in front of Rodgers' raised arm at the same time that Billy gripped Rodgers' arm, pulling it upward. The gun fired harmlessly into the air. Rodgers reacted violently, turning and jamming his elbow into Billy's face, knocking him out.

"Let me go," Indy screamed in anger and terror. "You have no right to do this! Hayden has no control over me. I'm an adult and have the right to make my own decisions," she cried out in frustration when Alex's arms tightened until she could barely breathe.

"Knock her out," Alex ordered Rodgers coldly. "We are already behind schedule. I want to get out of this western nightmare. I'm sick of sleeping outside." He squeezed Indy tighter as she fought to get free.

Rodgers nodded as he pulled a small vial and a needle out of his coat pocket. He pulled the cover off the needle with his teeth and spit it out on the ground. Filling the syringe, he stepped closer to Indy's struggling body.

"You are a feisty little thing, aren't you?" Rodgers murmured as he pressed the needle into her arm. "A very beautiful one."

Indy immediately felt the drug coursing through her body. It didn't matter how much she fought against it. Her legs sagged, no longer capable of supporting her. Her head rolled back and she fought to keep her eyes opened.

"You bastards," she whispered in a slurred voice. "I hope you rot in hell," she choked out before everything turned dark.

"What about him?" Rodgers asked, nodding toward Billy even as he lifted Indy's slight figure in his arms. "Want me to kill him?"

"No, leave him," Alex said, pulling his gloves on. "We'll be long gone by the time he comes to. We've got what we came for, let's get out of here."

Rodgers looked down at the pale face of the girl in his arms. He felt a twinge of regret that she was nothing more than a pawn in a very complicated game of chess. He wouldn't have minded spending time with her otherwise.

He looked up at Gent and nodded. He carried Indy over to his horse. Holding her partially over his shoulder, he mounted. Once he was settled, he slid her down and positioned her until she was straddling the horse in front of him and pressed back against his broad chest.

Yes, he thought with regret, smelling the clean scent of her hair. *If only we had met under different circumstances.*

He kicked his heels into the dark brown gelding enjoying the power of the beast under him. He couldn't help but think he should have been born two hundred years before. He would have fit in better in the old west than he ever would in present day America.

Chapter 13

Jonathan rubbed his knuckles from the blow he had delivered to the man lying in the dirt at his feet. He had returned early that the next morning in a panic. In the middle of the night, Chester and Tweed had shown up at his camp. Both dogs were exhausted, stumbling as they walked up to lay next to him panting and whining. What startled him even more was when Wally had come stumbling in behind them. It had taken a while to get the Chinaman calmed down enough to understand what he was trying to say.

Wally had explained that the dogs had shown up just before dark barking and carrying on. When he had tried to come out to see what was going on, they had run into the house searching it frantically before running back to the door and scratching like crazy to get out. He was worried because Indy and Jake had not returned when they had promised.

He had mounted one of the horses left by another cowpuncher and followed the dogs. They had led him to Jonathan. It was too dark to risk returning and they had to wait until dawn. As soon as it was safe to head back to the ranch, Jonathan, Jacob, Carl, Wally, and the dogs had headed out. Jonathan became concerned when the dogs went right by the house and continued toward the western pasture.

Jonathan ordered Wally to remain at the house and to send one of the men if Indy or Jake returned. He, Jacob, and Carl continued on at a gallop. They made it to the western pasture by late morning. As they rode up, they saw Cal and Jake standing over a man who was sitting tied up on the ground near the fire.

Jonathan slid out of his saddle before he had even brought his horse to a complete stop. Jacob and Carl were right behind him. His face darkened when he didn't recognize the man who sat with his knees drawn up in front of him and his head down. He did recognize two distinctive details about the man though. First, he was an Indian, or Native American as Indy liked to call refer to them as, and second, he was wearing clothes like Indy did. His stomach clenched as he absorbed the last detail.

"Where's Indy?" Jonathan demanded in a harsh voice.

"That's what we're trying to find out, boss" Jake said, spitting into the dirt near the man who slowly raised his head to look at Jonathan.

A large bruise darkened his skin just below his left eye."I didn't know what they wanted. If I had, I never would have helped them," the man said in a low voice.

A red haze covered Jonathan's mind as his worst fear came to life. He jerked the man up and struck him hard in the jaw, knocking him over the log and onto his back in the dirt. Taking a step toward him, he was about to go after him again when he felt Jacob's hand on his shoulder.

"Find out what happened before you kill him," Jacob suggested quietly.

Billy struggled to sit up, wiping the blood from his busted lip on the sleeve of his shirt. "I'm telling you, man, I had no idea they were after Indy. I wouldn't have led them to her if I had known. Everyone is pissed at what her brothers did to her. She and her grandfather were respected by everyone in town. Hell, Indy has helped Rosalie and me on more than one occasion when one of the kids got sick or Rosalie was having a hard time. They just said they needed a guide who knew the mountains," Billy insisted.

"Do you know where they took her?" Jonathan gritted out.

Billy nodded his head. "I think so. Or at least I have an idea. I know that her oldest brother has been looking for her for months now. He had men all over the place for a while. I thought he had given up. I've been working in Anaconda for the past couple of months until I got laid off a couple weeks back. My wife is expecting again and she's having a hard time. I've got her and the kids to think of. This man, said his name was Alex Gent, came into the bar in town a week or so ago asking for a guide who knew the mountains. He was offering a huge amount for a back country trip. I needed the money and thought it would be an easy trip up and back," Billy explained.

Jonathan took a step closer to Billy, shrugging off his brother's restraining hand. "That's not what I asked you. I asked if you knew where they took her?"

Billy looked at the dark faces looking down at him and swallowed. "Yeah, they took her back to her brother. I overheard Gent say they were going to grab her and get back as fast as they could," he said looking warily from one to the other. "I swear I didn't know until they saw her. They were going to shoot her dogs and I stopped them. Rodgers, he's one scary son-of-a-bitch, he hit me in the face and knocked me out."

Jonathan drew his gun out of the holster at his side and checked the rounds before aiming it at Billy. Billy jerked back, trying to scoot back across the ground. His face turned white and his eyes grew huge as he stared down the barrel of the gun aimed at him. A trickle of sweat slid down from the edge of his hairline as he looked death in the face.

"Jonathan," Jacob said, coming to stand next to his brother. He laid his hand on Jonathan's outstretched arm. "He could lead us to her. We can still get her back."

Jonathan's finger trembled on the trigger of the gun as he drew in a sharp breath. Was it possible? Could they travel back the way Indy had come, to her world and find her? He drew in a deep breath before he slowly lowered the gun back to his side. He still gripped it as he weighed the possibilities. If the man could travel through from his world to theirs and the other men had returned with Indy there was no reason why they shouldn't be able to follow.

Jonathan turned to stare at his brother before he nodded. "Jake, I want you and Carl to watch over things until we get back. Cal, can you handle being out here alone until they can send a couple of men to help you out?" He asked, looking at the boy who had seemed to turn into a man before his eyes.

"Sure thing, boss," Cal said confidently.

"I'll get the horses ready for you, boss," Carl said.

Jake spit again and rubbed the whiskers on his jaw, nodding. "Wally and I'll make sure everything is running smoothly for you, boss. You just bring Indy back home where she belongs. She told me she loves you something fierce. I don't think she is going to take kindly to being taken away."

Jonathan's heart clenched painfully in his chest at Jake's words. He had only told her that he loved her once. He should have been telling her it every damn time he saw her. He wouldn't make that mistake again.

"You are going to take us to her," Jonathan growled out, reaching down and grabbing Billy by the front of his shirt and pulling him up. "What is your name?"

"Billy," Billy replied looking relieved that he didn't have a bullet between his eyes. "Billy Cloudrunner. I'll take you to Sam. He'll know where Indy's brother lives."

"You better not try anything or I'll be the one shooting you," Jacob growled out. "Jonathan, let him ride your horse. You can ride Midnight," he said, grabbing Billy by the arm and pulling him behind him to the horses.

Jonathan quickly removed his rifle and rope from his horse and transferred them to Midnight who shivered with nervous energy. Within minutes, the three men were heading up into the mountains. Jonathan couldn't help but feel a shiver of apprehension at the thought of what they would encounter. He only hoped Indy would not want to remain there once he found her.

* * *

Rodgers shifted Indy slightly, easing the pressure on his arm where he had been holding her. He knew she was awake. She had woken several minutes before, but tried to keep her breathing stable, making it appear she was still unconscious. He had to hand it to her, most people would have tried to fight. That would have ended badly for her because he would have to dope her up again.

"If you don't fight anymore, I won't drug you again," he murmured in her ear.

Indy drew in a deep breath and opened her eyes. Her head ached from whatever he had given her and her arms and legs felt shaky. When she woke a few minutes ago, she hoped to learn more about their plans so she could try to escape. It would appear it was not going to be as easy as she had hoped.

"Why are you doing this?" She hissed out angrily. "All I want is to be left alone. And for crying out loud, don't hold me so tight!"

Rodgers shrugged and pulled her closer to his body when she stiffened. He chuckled when she tried to elbow him in the gut. Instead of loosing his hold, he leaned in and drew in a deep breath, letting his lips brush the skin of her neck. She immediately stiffened.

"Don't," he said in warning, squeezing her. "We should be to where the truck is parked by late this afternoon."

"How long have I been out?" Indy asked fearfully.

"Almost twenty-four hours," Rodgers replied calmly.

Indy looked down at the handcuffs clasped around her wrists. Her mind was quickly trying to calculate the distance they had traveled and the amount of time it might have taken for the dogs to alert Jonathan that something was wrong. She frowned when she tried to figure out how they had gotten so far. They must have traveled through the night.

"We did," Rodgers said, answering her soft question. "Night vision goggles are wonderful tools."

"Hayden must want me pretty bad if you are willing to risk your neck to travel through the mountains at night to get me back," she responded bitterly. "You know it won't do you any good. As soon as I get in front of a judge they are going to have to release me. There is no way he can prove I can't take care of myself."

"Oh, I don't think you will be going before any judge," Rodgers said in a low voice, keeping his eyes on the horse in front of him to make sure their conversation couldn't be overheard. "What do you know of your brother's plans for you?" He asked curiously.

Indy frowned and tilted her head back far enough so that she could look into his eyes. "Why?" She asked suspiciously. "Do you know something I don't?"

Rodgers shrugged, enjoying the feel of his chest, brushing against her back. "Just asking," he replied before going silent again.

Indy looked back at the man riding in front of them. It was weird that she was more afraid of the slender man in front of her than the one who looked like he could snap her in two without getting winded. She thought about her older brother. What did she really know about him? He was rich, greedy, even. He liked to live in luxury. He was smart, aggressive, but had a way of making people agree with him. He was also very ambitious. She shook her head as another thought came to her as she remembered the letter he had sent to her grandpa that she had found.

"He can't use me that way," she muttered under her breath.

"He can't use you how?" Rodgers asked, guiding the horse down the narrow path. He adjusted his weight, leaning back and pulling her with him as the horse stumbled a little on the rocky surface. "How do you think he wants to use you?"

Indy sighed and decided it didn't matter if the man knew about the letter or not. "I found a letter in my grandpa's things as I was packing up. I didn't read it until I was on the trail. Hayden mentioned he wanted me to come live with him as soon as I graduated from college. To my face, he acted like he wanted me to continue on with my education but in the letter he told my grandfather he wanted to introduce me to some men. He felt I needed to be 'married' to the right man who could take care of me," she snorted. "I don't need any man taking care of me. I need a man who is my partner. A man who loves me. A man like…." Her voice faded away as her throat tightened with tears at the thought of never seeing Jonathan again.

"Like…." Rodgers asked in disappointment when she didn't immediately finish her sentence.

Indy straightened her shoulders in determination. "Like my husband," she said defiantly. "He'll come after me. He won't stop until he finds me."

Rodgers bit back a silent curse. There had been nothing in the reports that said anything about Indiana Wild being married. Having a husband in the equation was going to complicate things, especially if he showed up too soon.

His eyes narrowed on the man in front of him. He would bet his paycheck that Gent had no idea that Indiana was married. Hell, he doubted the man would give a damn. As long as he got his money, Gent didn't give a rat's ass about anyone or anything. The man worked just this side of the law. He never strayed far enough to get out of the gray, at least from what he had been able to discover. He thought to the information he had on Hayden Wild and Jerry Hammock. Neither man would be pleased to find out their prize wasn't as 'available' as they thought.

Neither one of them said anything after that, lost in their own thoughts. The skies were just beginning to darken when they broke off the narrow trail onto a logging road. A short distance down it, Indy could see a dark black truck and horse trailer.

Panic began to set in as she realized that if they got her in the truck, she might truly never see Jonathan again. She erupted into a fury of violence, slamming her head back into Rodgers' face and throwing her leg up and over the horse's neck. She hit the ground hard and rolled as dark curses filled the air around her. Struggling to her feet, she had only taken a few steps before she was gripped from behind.

"No!" She cried out, turning to swing her fists up at the man trying to stop her from escaping. "No!" She whimpered as he pushed her face down into the dirt road.

She looked up at the way they had come, searching the darkness for a familiar face. She gasped at the prick of the needle as it was pushed into her thigh. She fought against the drug as long as she could, wishing desperately that she could see Jonathan's face.

"Jonathan," she whispered before her head sunk down and darkness overcame her.

Chapter 14

Jonathan looked around as they slowly made their way through the narrow cut in the rocks. The moment they passed the entrance, the temperature appeared to drop twenty degrees. Even the horses were tossing their heads and looking around.

Chester and Tweed trotted next to them. Both dogs' heads were bent and their tails tucked under them as if they were trying to appear as small as possible. Jacob looked over his shoulder and nodded silently. He felt the change as well. Something was definitely unusual about the Pass they were riding through.

Small rocks rained down periodically, echoing loudly. He looked up toward the top of the rocks and shuddered. Thick swirls of mist covered the opening above them with only an occasional glimpse of the sky peeking through.

"How much further?" He called out quietly to Billy, who was in the lead.

Billy turned in his seat and grinned. "Not much. It's spooky, isn't it?" He asked. "I nearly shit my pants the first time my father brought me up here when I was a boy. I was supposed to go through to the other side and bring back a hawk's feather," he said turning back around.

Jacob waited impatiently. "Well, what happened? Did you get it?" He asked, kicking his horse so he could get a little closer.

"Nah, I found one a couple weeks before and stuffed it down my pants. I only made it far enough inside the Pass that my dad couldn't see me. I hung out for about an hour and then ran out waving my feather," Billy responded lightly. "He knew, of course. The only reason he didn't say anything was because he had done the same thing."

Jacob stared at Billy while Jonathan just grunted. He couldn't blame Billy. He wanted to get the hell out of there as well. The place had goosebumps rising all over his body. He breathed a sigh of relief when he saw the mist surrounding them getting thinner. He ignored the hard, cold lump in his throat and stomach at what might lie on the other side. The only thing he cared about was finding Indy. If he had to travel to the depths of hell and back to find her he would.

They burst through the narrow cut one at a time, each pulling in a deep breath of relief. Jonathan turned to look at the entrance and was amazed to see it was almost invisible to the eye. He turned back in his saddle to look at Billy, who was grinning at both of them.

"No one would ever find it unless they had been shown. The elders don't talk much about it except to scare the young braves who are going through the right of passage to become a warrior," he commented with a small shake of his head. "Not that there is much need for warriors anymore. Just trying to support a family is hard enough. I'd hate to have to go through what my ancestors went through. I probably wouldn't have lasted a day."

Jonathan nudged Midnight closer to Billy. "Where to now?" He asked.

This was taking longer than he anticipated. He had thought they would have caught up with the men who had taken Indy by now. They had ridden hard yesterday, pushing the horses, dogs and themselves before having to make camp for the night when they could no longer see in front of them.

The horses and dogs needed to rest. Instead, they had not found any trace of a fire where the men would have camped. Billy said the men had some type of thing they placed over their eyes so they could see at night. He called them 'night vision goggles'.

Neither Jonathan or Jacob could conceive such a thing, but Billy had sworn that it was true. He said that must have been how they were able to continue in the dark. They had left their camp at dawn, foregoing anything to eat except the hardtack of biscuits and jerky that they carried.

"We head downhill toward the south. There is an old logging trail where I parked my truck and the horse trailer. If we are lucky, it will still be there. If not, we are on the backside of Sam Whitewater's ranch. We'll head to his place on horseback. It will take about another three hours to reach it that way, less than an hour if the truck is still there," Billy explained, turning the horse he was riding slightly to the right and heading off in a southerly direction.

Jacob pulled back until he was even with Jonathan. "Did you understand half of what he just said?" He asked quietly.

Jonathan nodded. "Indy showed me images of some of the things he mentioned. I don't understand how one can make the time shorter, but right now I don't care. All I want is Indy back at my side and to get back through that damn Pass in one piece," he muttered moving ahead of Jacob.

Jacob frowned at his brother's retreating back. Damn, if he wasn't going to have to ask Indy to show him some of those images. He would like to at least understand what he was getting into before he got wherever in the hell they were going. He fingered the gun at his waist, finding comfort in the familiar grip. He had to agree with his brother, though, he just wanted to get Indy back so they could go home.

* * *

Two hours later, Billy was cussing up a storm as he stomped back and forth along the long, narrow road they had come out on. Jonathan could see the unusual tracks in the dirt. He had no idea what could create them. They looked similar to what a wagon would do, but were much wider and had strange wiggly lines in them. Jonathan called out at the same time as the ground beneath them began to rumble.

"Earthquake?" Jacob asked, looking around nervously and trying to hold his horse under control.

Jonathan's horse danced around Billy, who was trying to calm him down while Midnight just shifted from one foot to the other. He looked down the road and saw a huge, black beast slowly approaching them. He jerked back on the reins hard in alarm causing Midnight to raise his head and whinny. His hand went for the gun on his hip and he drew it, aiming at the creature as it approached.

He would have fired on it if not for the fact Billy was waving his hands up in the air. The huge creature lumbered to a slow, growling stop about twenty-five feet from them. Jacob pulled back on the reins of his horse until he was even with Jonathan as a huge puff of smoke belched from a long, narrow silver pipe sticking out of its head before it went silent. A moment later, the side of the beast opened and a skinny man in his twenties jumped out of its stomach.

"Hey Billy, Watcha' doing up here?" Ansel called out, pulling his bright red baseball cap around to shade his eyes from the sun. "I thought I saw your truck in town earlier."

"Hey Ansel," Billy said, walking up and gripping his arm in greeting. "You happen to have a cell phone on you? Mine's dead. I need to call Sam and see if he can come pick us up," Billy asked in relief.

"Hell, I can do better than that. I just heard Aleaha and Allie were headed this way. They have Allie's pickup and horse trailer. Cole called in to say the beauties were on their way back. You know he's had a crush on Allie since the second grade. They were passing mile marker 125 about ten minutes ago. If you ride down to the cutoff at the highway you'll probably get there about the same time as they do. I'll radio Allie and let her know to stop and pick you up," Ansel said with a grin as he turned back toward the cab of the truck.

Billy called out his thanks and told Ansel he would see him at the bar tomorrow night for a game of pool and an ice cold beer. Ansel waved his hand at

Jonathan and Jacob before he climbed back into the stomach of the beast and closed the door. They could see him talking into a small black box. After a few minutes he leaned his head out the window and grinned down at Billy.

"Allie says to get your ass down there. She's tired and pissed. She said if you don't hurry your ass is going to be eating her dust. Aleaha says to tell you hi and wants to talk to you about how Rosalie and the kids are doing," Ansel chuckled out.

Billy slid his foot into the stirrup and pulled himself into the saddle with a groan. "Right now my ass is sore from riding. I'm looking forward to sitting it on a nice plush seat. I just hope Allie doesn't make me ride in the back like she did the last time she picked me up," Billy groaned, shifting as he tried to find a place that wasn't hurting.

Ansel waved as he started up the huge truck again. He waited until Billy, Jonathan and Jacob rode by before he put the huge diesel into gear and headed up the logging road. Jonathan watched nervously as he rode by, reaching out to touch it with the tips of his fingers. They were about ten feet behind it when the 'truck' as Indy called it pulled away. Jonathan grinned when Jacob almost landed in his lap when the huge metal beast made a loud roar.

Jacob slid back into his saddle with a shake of his head. "What in the hell is that thing?" He whispered. "Where the hell are we?"

Jonathan grinned at his brother and shook his head. "That is what Indy called a 'truck'. In the images she showed me they didn't look as big. This is the world Indy came from," he said as the grin faded. "I hope she doesn't miss it," he muttered, looking back over his shoulder at the cloud of dust left by the huge truck.

"You aren't the only one," Jacob cursed as he kicked his heels into the side of his horse so he could catch up with Billy. Jonathan whistled for Chester, and Tweed, who had finished sniffing the nearby trees, to follow them.

The journey down the road proved to be the easiest so far. The ground was compacted from the huge truck and was wide enough that they could trot. They came out along a long hard black surface road the likes Jonathan and Jacob had never seen. It went as far as they could see in both directions. A moment later, a large silver truck, similar to the one in the images Indy had shown him, came into view. It slowed down before a light began blinking on and off and it pulled up just past them onto the gravel.

Jonathan nodded to Jacob and they dismounted, holding the leads tightly in their fists as they watched the doors open. Jonathan glanced at Jacob when he heard him draw in a sharp breath. He turned his head to see what had startled his brother and watched as a small, dark haired woman wearing the dark blue trousers that Indy liked so much walked toward them. The difference was she was wearing a top that clung to her slim figure and left her arms and midriff bare. Her hair was short and fanned out around her face, highlighting her startling blue eyes.

"Hey Allie, thanks for the lift," Billy called out as he walked toward her.

"Who the hell did you get into a fight with? You look like shit," Allie said, walking around to the back of the empty horse trailer. "You're lucky I had the trailer with me. Boseman is on my shit list. The asshole was supposed to have the horses we requested ready, but he didn't. I've wasted my whole day driving to St. Mary's and back," she added, dropping the ramp down so they could load the horses. "I have two mares expecting anytime."

"Hi Billy," Aleaha said coming from around the passenger side of the trailer to help load the horses. "Oh my, what happened to your face?" She asked in concern coming to take a closer look.

Billy glanced over to where Jonathan and Jacob were standing. Aleaha's eyes narrowed as she took in the two cowboys standing side by side. She turned her attention back to look at Billy, who was trying to skirt around her.

"Ah Aleaha, it's nothing. Just walked into a wall is all," he muttered, turning red as she jerked his chin around so she could examine it.

"More like a fist," she snapped, glaring at the two men standing silently while Allie loaded Billy's horse. Her eyes widened as she took in the horse Jonathan was holding. "Allie," she whispered slowly taking a step back from Billy, suddenly nervous.

"What?" Allie snapped looking over to where Aleaha was staring in horror. "Son of a bitch, where did you get Indy's horse!" She snarled taking a step toward Jonathan and Jacob with her fist clenched. "So help me, if you've harmed one hair on her head, I'll kill you!" She jerked to a halt when Chester and Tweed suddenly came running out of the woods up to her whining for attention.

The two dogs had been waiting on the edge of the woods for Jonathan's signal to come. He wanted to make sure of their situation before he had the dogs come out into the open just in case Billy tried anything. He felt fairly confident that the Lakota Indian was being upfront with them, but he was in a strange world and didn't want to take any chances.

"Allie, Aleaha," Billy began. "It's not what you think. They need your dad's help. Indy's in trouble."

"Why does he have her horse?" Allie asked suspiciously, kneeling and putting her arm around both excited dogs. "She would never leave Midnight, Chester, and Tweed. What have you done to her?"

"We haven't done anything to her," Jonathan stated coolly, staring into Allie's furious eyes. "We are looking for her."

"Why are you looking for her?" Aleaha asked huskily keeping her eyes on both men. "Can't you guys just leave her alone! She hasn't done anything to you."

Jonathan took a step closer to Aleaha. Allie stood up and moved a step closer to her sister only to find her path suddenly blocked by the silent cowboy who had been standing next to him. Jacob jerked his head at Billy, who nodded and took the reins to both of their horses and started loading them.

"Move or be moved, cowboy," Allie growled out in a low voice.

"Listen to him. We don't want to hurt Indy," Jacob said in an equally low voice. "She's in danger."

"Why should you care if she is in danger or not?" Allie asked, ignoring Jacob's narrowed eyes as she pushed him so she could walk by him. "What is she to you?"

"She's my wife," Jonathan replied calmly.

Chapter 15

Jonathan ignored the dark looks Allie was throwing at him in the mirror. After he dropped his little 'bombshell' as Billy called it, both women had erupted into a flood of furious questions. It was only after Billy suggested that they could talk and drive at the same time that the women reluctantly walked back to the front of the metal wagon.

Jonathan had taken the same side as Aleaha while Jacob had followed closely behind Allie. Billy had grunted in resignation when Allie snapped at him to get in the back of the silver wagon. He had grumbled as he climbed over the back of it and settled on a stack of horse feed with Chester and Tweed.

"Why should we believe that you are Indy's husband?" Allie asked, glancing in the mirror again.

Jonathan would have loved to tell her he was not going anywhere and to please keep her eyes on the black road in front of her. He had a death grip on the 'armrest'. He didn't know why it was called that. At the speed they were traveling, he would have called it a 'lifegrip' or something else.

He swallowed when the vehicle crossed over the center of the line and another metal wagon coming toward them honked. Allie stuck her hand out the window and raised her middle finger as they passed in response to the other person's gesture. He wondered if that was the way people waved to each other in this time.

"I don't care if you believe me or not," he forced out over the lump in his throat as she swerved back onto her side of the road. "Indy and I are legally married. She is my wife and I mean to get her back from the men who took her or from her brother. I don't care how I do it. If I have to kill them, all the better."

Allie turned her head and suddenly grinned at him. "You might be likable yet," she said.

"Will you please look at where you are going before you kill us!" Jacob suddenly snapped out as the truck weaved across the line again.

Allie turned to face forward again, but she was glaring at Jacob in the mirror this time. She opened her mouth to say something, but Aleaha put her hand on her sister's arm to quiet her. Allie glanced at her older twin and rolled her eyes before she reached over and picked up a pair of sunglasses on the dashboard and slipped them on.

"Great!" Jacob muttered darkly. "Now she covers her eyes so she can't see at all! We'll all be dead before we get to this Sam for help."

Allie snorted and sped up a little in retaliation to Jacob's comment. Billy's loud curses and the thump of his fist on the back window caused her to ease her foot off the gas a bit as she remembered she had a full trailer instead of an empty one behind her now. She stuck her hand back out the window to let him know she heard him.

"Why didn't Indy ever mention you?" Aleaha asked, turning in her seat. "She tells us everything."

Jonathan looked deeply into Aleaha's soft concerned eyes considering how much he should tell her. "Our marriage was a little unexpected, but I promise you it was every bit legal. The preacher and his wife both signed as witnesses," he assured her. "My biggest concern is finding her and taking her back home where she belongs."

Aleaha studied him carefully before she nodded her head. "Papa will know where she is," she murmured and turned back around as Allie slowed down as they came into the city limits.

None of them talked as Allie pulled into a dirt parking lot filled with metal wagons of all different shapes, colors, and sizes. Jonathan and Jacob looked on in amazement at everything around them. Allie stopped the truck and Billy climbed out of the back with a mumbled thanks.

"Billy, you get home and take care of Rosalie," Aleaha admonished as he came up to her side of the truck. "I saw her today. She is doing better, but she still has some swelling. You need to help her with the little ones for a while."

"I will, Aleaha," Billy said with a grin before he turned to look at Jonathan.

He waited until Allie pressed the button for the window to slide down. Jonathan jerked back in surprise as the clear glass disappeared into the door. Billy leaned in and nodded to Jacob, who was staring stonily at the back of Allie's head.

"Good luck," Billy said quietly. "I'm sorry for what happened. I want you to know I really like Indy. She is a good woman."

"Thank you," Jonathan replied just before Allie pressed the button on the window again and impatiently pulled away.

He watched as Billy ran over to a large black truck and climbed in. He glanced back as they pulled away. It was starting to get dark out and bright colors of light were beginning to light the buildings as if by magic. He shivered as the world around him changed again.

"This isn't right," he heard Jacob muttering.

"We'll be home before you know it, Jacob," Jonathan murmured. "We just need to find Indy first." Jacob didn't say anything. He just continued to stare at the bizarre world they had found themselves in.

* * *

Almost an hour later, Sam and Claire Whitewater sat at the table in their dining room looking at the two men sitting across from them. They had never told their children the full story of how they met. William, Claire's younger brother, was the only one that knew and he had remained quiet after Sam had brought them to live on his ranch.

William had told Sam when he was fifteen that it was as if his life before he came had been a dream. He was happy that he and Claire were safe and that was all he really cared about. William was now an engineer working over in Germany. It looked like now their two daughters were about to discover their secret.

"Can you help me?" Jonathan asked as he sat on the edge of the chair and rested his forearms on the table. "Indy was terrified of her brother. I need to find her before he hurts her."

Sam squeezed Claire's hand in comfort when she made a distressed sound. "Yes, I can help you. Hayden lives in Los Angeles. He is a powerful and ambitious man. I have always worried that he had plans to use Indiana. Hugh was concerned with Hayden's sudden interest in Indiana as she got older. It was at Hayden's insistence that she completed her degree in nursing, telling her it would help their grandfather as he got older. She didn't want to go into it, but she would do whatever she could to care for her grandfather. Hugh showed me some of the letters Hayden sent as her graduation came closer. He wanted Hugh to send her to him to live with him as soon as possible. Hugh knew it would kill Indiana to leave the ranch."

Claire smiled at Jonathan and Jacob. "She came home at every opportunity. She hated being away. She was born to ranch-life, unlike her brothers who couldn't wait to leave. Much like our Allie," she said softly.

"Ah mom, they don't care if I prefer horses and cows to living the high life in some concrete jungle," Allie snorted out throwing a seething look at Jacob that dared him to say something negative. "Does anyone want something to drink?" She asked, getting up from the table.

"Would you mind making a pot of coffee, Allie?" Sam asked.

"Sure, Papa," Allie said, giving her dad an affectionate grin as she turned toward the kitchen area.

"I'll help you," Aleaha said, getting up to follow her sister.

Sam waited until both of his daughters had gone into the kitchen before he continued. "Neither one knows about Spirit Pass. I never took them or our boys up there. I knew what could happen and how dangerous your world is, especially for a half-breed."

"Sam," Claire admonished gently before she explained in more detail. "We both decided our children did not need to experience the trial of going through the Pass to prove their worth. Many have agreed that it may be too dangerous and the elders have decided to no longer allow it after the last ceremony this past spring."

Both Jonathan and Jacob nodded in understanding, there was a huge difference between the past and the present worlds. "You were telling us about Hayden and his plans for Indy," Jonathan reminded them. "How can I find him?"

"Hugh believed Hayden had promised Indiana as a prize for support in his upcoming race for the Senate. He told me a few days before he had his stroke that he wanted to keep Indiana as far away from her brothers as possible and was worried about what would happen to her if something should happen to him. He had an appointment to change his will, giving her the ranch. I'm not sure if he was able to finalize it before his stroke," Sam said with a heavy sigh.

Jonathan sat back, his jaw tightening in anger. "What do you mean as a prize?" He bit out.

Sam looked at him sadly. "Some powerful men like to have a sweet, young beauty on their arm. The men Hayden is dealing with play what is known as 'hardball'. Indiana has everything they want, beauty, money, and connections."

"Yeah, but she'll eat them up and spit them out like yesterday's chewing tobacco," Allie said carrying a tray loaded with cups and a huge pot. Aleaha followed with another tray containing milk, cream, and sugar. "She won't let Hayden use her."

"I worry she won't be given a choice," Sam responded to his daughter's statement.

Allie set the tray down and put her hands on her hips. "And, why do you think that?" She asked with a raised eyebrow.

"Hayden is a desperate, hungry man. He wants the Senate seat and he has made a lot of promises he has to fulfill if he gets it," Sam explained patiently. "The men he owes are no different. If they want Indiana, they will use whatever means they have to in order to control her, including drugging her or using physical violence."

Allie sank down in the chair next to Jacob, unaware that he slid his arm around her when she turned pale. She raised a shaking hand to push the short, dark silky strands of her hair behind her ear.

Jacob reached under the table when her hand fell back into her lap and cupped her slender palm with his own.

"How could he do that to her? He's never had a thing to do with her when she was growing up," Allie said hotly. "You have to help her, Papa!"

"I will, Allie. Or should I say, you will," Sam promised her before turning his attention back to Jonathan. "Allie will fly you to Los Angeles. I will have someone I know meet you at the airport. You can trust him. Hayden is not the only one who has powerful friends," he added with a smile.

Jonathan leaned forward again and nodded. "When do we leave?"

"First thing in the morning," Sam said rising. "I have some phone calls to make. Allie and Aleaha will show you where you can get cleaned up and rest."

Claire rose to follow her husband. She paused for a moment before turning back. Smiling, her gaze softened when she saw Jacob's arm draped behind her youngest daughter's chair. It was obvious Allie wasn't thinking straight or she would have realized it and lit into him.

"This world is very different from ours, but in many ways things have not changed," she said quietly. "Men are still greedy and the world is still a dangerous place. If….," she paused and drew in a tearful breath, shaking her head. "No, when you find Indy just love her with all your heart. I know she would be happier in your world than here," she added quietly before turning and hurrying out of the room.

Aleaha frowned as she followed her mother with worried eyes. "What did she mean by 'your' world?" She asked puzzled.

Jonathan stood up and glanced at his brother with a light shake of his head. He snapped his fingers for Chester and Tweed, who were lying on the rug in the living room. Both dogs scrambled to his side. He touched his fingers to their heads. There was something about them that helped remind him that Indy was real.

"You must have misunderstood her," Jacob responded, standing up next to Allie's chair.

He ignored the way she rubbed the hand he had been holding on her pant leg and how she moved to get up on the opposite side of the chair from him. She could resist all she wanted. He already knew when he, Jonathan and Indy returned through the Pass they would not be alone. Allie Whitewater was his and he was going to make sure she knew it!

* * *

An hour later, Jonathan walked out of the bathroom that separated the bedrooms they had been given. Aleaha had given them both a brief tour of the rooms and the bathroom. Each bedroom was done in a different color.

His was done in bold burgundy, copper, and beige while Jacob's room was done in softer whites, yellows, and blues. They had remained silent until after the women left before bolting to the bathroom again to explore it. It had taken them a good ten minutes to figure out what everything was. They just shook their heads as they flipped the switch for the lights on and off in amazement before discovering how the sink, toilet and shower worked.

Jonathan threw the soft, plush towel he had been using to dry his hair on the end of Jacob's bed. His brother was leaning against the headboard of the bed looking at a flat box mounted to the wall. Images flashed across it as he pushed on the small black box Allie had handed him before walking out the door.

"This world is too strange," Jacob commented as he watched the images. "People on the wall, lights without fire, water out of the walls. Why would Indy or anyone else for that matter want to give it up to live back in the past?" He asked glumly pausing to stare at a group of beautiful young women wearing, or he should say not wearing, much clothing.

"Would you want to live here?" Jonathan asked. "The only thing I've found that I think I would miss is the bathroom. Indy was right about that being the only thing she would want to change at the ranch house. Maybe we could figure out a way to build one in the house."

Jacob turned off the television and set the remote on the bedside table before sitting up and running his hand through his hair. "I would live here if I had to but there is something missing. Hell, I don't know," he grumbled.

Jonathan studied his brother for a moment before he leaned back against the door jam. "What's wrong?"

Jonathan asked bluntly. "You normally would be enjoying an adventure like this, but something is off. I know it isn't just about Indy or all the unusual things we've seen."

Jacob glanced at his brother before looking back down at the floor. "It's Allie," he admitted quietly. "I want to get to know her better."

"Allie?" Jonathan said, shocked, before he frowned in concern. "Jacob, we aren't going to be here for long. I don't want to be here for long. I like our place. We would be lost here. Back home, we have something.... something we made with our own two hands, a place our folks cut out through sweat and blood. A place we understand," he added soberly.

Jacob stood up in aggravation and went to stand at the window, gripping the edge of the windowsill tightly. He stared moodily out over the modern ranch below him. There were huge metal machines in the distance that he didn't have a clue what they were. Wires wove from post longer and thicker than the telegraph wires and the area was lit up like the early dawn hours back home. No, he liked an adventure, but he also liked knowing he was in control. Here, why would a woman like Allie need a man like him when she could obviously take care of herself with all the fancy machines available to her.

He turned around with a resigned expression on his face. "Let's concentrate on getting your wife back," he said changing the subject. "Did you understand what Sam was talking about when he said Allie would 'fly' us to where Indy was? You don't think they can actually fly in this time, do you?" He asked with a wry grin.

"God, I hope not! Give me a horse any day. If man was meant to fly God would have given him a pair of wings. I'm sure it was just a figure of speech. Hell, I'm still trying to figure out what language they are speaking half the time. I know it's English, but damned if I can figure it out," Jonathan said, relieved to see his brother acting more like his old self. "Let's get some rest. If we are lucky, we'll have Indy back with us by tomorrow and can head home where we belong."

Jacob nodded and looked around the plush bedroom again. "They have more comforts here than a King would have. I can't complain about having a soft bed to sleep in," he said as Jonathan turned to head back to his room on the other side of the bathroom. A sudden thought came to him and he called out to his brother as he started to leave. "Jonathan, you're right, you know. We need to see if we can't figure out how to build a couple of those indoor bathhouses at the ranch house. Maybe then the women won't mind living there so much."

Jonathan opened his mouth, then closed it, just nodding in agreement. He wasn't going to question his brother's use of the word 'women'. Whatever his brother had up his sleeve was fine with him as long as it made him happy. He would do what he could to support him, even if it meant what he thought his twin had in mind.

"See you in the morning, Jacob," Jonathan said with a sudden grin, feeling lighter than he had since Indy had been kidnapped.

"Good night," Jacob called out before turning off the light with a shake of his head, wondering what other surprises this world had for them.

* * *

Indy stood in the middle of her brother's home office at his townhouse in Los Angeles and glared at him. She folded her arms across her chest and raised her eyebrow with a smirk. Hayden was doing his usual act of trying to intimidate her. It wasn't working.

She'd had enough of her brother's attitude. She was ready to fight him tooth and nail if need be. He had gone over the line when he had sent men to kidnap her. Not only that, she had something very important to fight for now- getting home to Jonathan.

"If you know what is good for you, Hayden, you'll just let me walk away," she said in a low voice. "I am over the age of eighteen and perfectly capable of making my own decisions in life. One of those decisions is to forget that you, Matt and Gus even exist."

Hayden gritted his teeth in frustration. Gent had said ever since she woke up from the drug induced sleep, she had been a bitch to deal with. She refused to do anything she was told and only the threat of having Rodgers sedate her again stopped her from bursting into a fit of violence.

Even now, Hammock was on his way from Washington, D.C. to pick her up. He needed to have her ready. He couldn't present her looking like she had been wrestling cows and smelling like a horse.

The problem was she refused to cooperate, even under threat. She had laughed at him and told him to bring it on. She was going to sue his ass anyway for kidnapping, assault, and a multitude of other offenses. He cursed, giving Gent free rein on using whatever method he needed to bring her back but he had been desperate.

"Indiana, I have a signed document by the judge giving me guardianship over you," he began.

"Save it, Hayden. We'll see what the judge has to say when he finds out you falsified information to obtain that guardianship. No judge in his right mind would have agreed unless you gave him some trumped up documentation," she snorted. "By the time I get done with you, I'll have more than enough money to buy back the ranch if I want to!"

Hayden slammed his hand down on the desk in front of him scattering papers. He cursed the fact he had been detained. Gent had delivered Indiana late that afternoon, but he had not been able to get home until ten minutes ago due to a court proceeding that didn't finish until late. He opened his mouth to retaliate when the phone on his desk buzzed. He picked up the receiver, his eyes darkening even more as he listened to the voice on the other end.

"Rodgers, get your ass in here," Hayden demanded loudly glaring at his sister.

A saccharine smile creased Indy's lips. "I called the police," she said gleefully.

"I know," Hayden bit out, seething with fury.

The door to his office opened and Rodgers came in. Indy took several steps away from him, keeping him in her sight in case he tried to knock her out again. He glanced at her with cold, dark eyes before he turned to address her brother.

"You called," he drawled out dryly.

Hayden shot him a heated glare. "You were supposed to watch her! She called the fucking police! I want you to stay with her until I get rid of them," he snapped out before pointing his finger at Indy. "You and I are not finished."

"Like hell we're not," Indy muttered under her breath as she watched him slam out of the room.

She turned to look Rodgers over from head to toe. He was no longer dressed in his faded jeans and button-down shirt, but in a pair of navy dress slacks and a black long-sleeve pullover that was stretched tight over his bulging muscles. He was a good-looking man in a rough, predatory kind of way.

"Like what you see?" He asked, a slight smile tugging at the corner of his lips.

Indy's eyes narrowed as she slowly returned them to his. "Not really, I'm imagining you and Hayden as cell mates and wondering who is going to be on top," she replied sweetly.

Rodgers chuckled at the blatant insult. "Top or bottom, both positions have their advantages," he replied, enjoying the blush that rose up into her cheeks before she warily turned away from him.

"Are you in this just for the money? If so, I have a little. If you help me get out of here I'll give you every dime I have," Indy said suddenly, turning to look at him to see how he took her offer. "Hell, I'll even sign over my future income if Hayden doesn't find some way to steal it first. I won't need it where I'm going anyway."

Rodgers took a step toward her. "How much do you know about what your brother has planned for you?" He asked suddenly in a harsh voice.

Indy took a step back in alarm at the intense coldness that came into his eyes. "I…. I don't know anything," she began, but stopped as his face grew even harder. "But…. But I suspect he is going to try to use me in some way. I'm just not sure how. I mean, legally he can't force me to do anything."

"But what about illegally?" he demanded, taking a step closer to her. "What makes you think what he wants is within the law?"

Indy paled at the implication of his words. "He's an attorney. He wouldn't throw his career away by doing something illegal…. Would he?" She whispered.

"You tell me?" Rodgers said coming to a stop in front of her. "What would he do if he wanted something badly enough? Something like the U. S. Senate."

Indy stared into his eyes for what seemed like an eternity, her vision clouding as her mind worked.

What would Hayden do to get to such a powerful position? Would he do something illegal to get it? There were always rumors about things like that. About kickbacks, bribes, and even worse, but surely he wouldn't take a chance of ending up in prison by doing something so stupid. Surely he wouldn't sacrifice one of his own family members? Doubt filled her as she thought about what he had done to their grandfather.

She jerked out of her thoughts when she felt a pair of warm hands on her arms, shaking her gently. She frowned up at him, she shook her head. She knew Hayden was a greedy son-of-a-bitch, but it was hard for her to believe he would take such a chance.

"No, I don't think he would. He might be a greedy bastard, but he is also a cautious one," she replied. "He wouldn't do anything that might come back to bite him on the ass."

Rodgers released her arms and took a step back. "Are you willing to bet your life on that?" He asked.

Indy shoved her hand through her hair in aggravation. "What are you talking about? Why should my life be in danger?"

Rodgers stood frozen in indecision for a fraction of a second before he glanced briefly at the closed door. "Your brother is using you as a bargaining chip. You and your money in exchange for support from a very powerful man who likes sweet, innocent little girls," he bit out in a low voice. "You are payment, a commodity, a prize, Indiana Wild, nothing more, but a plaything for a rich man who has decided he wants you."

Indy stood frozen in horror. If what Rodgers was saying was true, her brother was selling her to the highest bidder. Everything started clicking into place as her mind sifted through different events in her life and Hayden's subtle manipulations.

That was why he wanted control over the ranch. He knew Matt and Gus were desperate for money and would do whatever they had to in order to get it. But, he knew Indy would have fought tooth and nail to keep it. By convincing a judge she wasn't capable of taking care of herself, he had effectively taken control of her money and her body. A shiver of fear ran down her spine. She looked at the door judging the distance.

"You won't make it," Rodgers stated. "He has at least four other men between you and freedom."

Indy started and she glanced at him, biting her lip in indecision. "I won't let him get away with this. Jonathan won't let him. We'll fight him," she hissed out. "If I don't kill him, I know Jonathan will if he lets some slime ball touch me."

Rodgers frowned. He had forgotten that she said she was married. That might change things, but he wouldn't count on it. He knew Hammock. The man wouldn't care. He would simply quietly order Indy's husband permanently removed so there would be no messy strings left untied. Of course, he would make sure it looked like Indy's husband met with an untimely accident.

"You need to find out exactly what your brother wants," Rodgers said making a decision to do what he could without jeopardizing his assignment. "I'll stay as close as I can to protect you."

"Why?" Indy asked, puzzled. "I just want to go home," she said huskily, suddenly very tired. She turned to stare out over the city. "All I wanted was to live on the ranch where I felt like I belonged. When Hayden and my other brothers sold it out from under me, I knew it wouldn't stop me from living the life I wanted. I might not have the Wild Ranch any longer, but I knew with my experience I could always get a job on another one somewhere. Hell, Sam would hire me in a heartbeat without me even asking." She looked back at Rodgers again. "I just want to be left alone," she finished in a small, tired voice.

Both of them turned when Hayden came back in followed by several other gentlemen. She didn't recognize any of them, but Rodgers must have as he stiffened and moved away from her. She watched warily as the men came into the room.

"Jerry, this is my sister Indiana," Hayden said heavily looking at Indy's disheveled appearance with a disapproving eye. "Unfortunately, she has not had time to get cleaned up. She was just about to do so. Indiana, I've taken the liberty of having some clothes delivered for you since you didn't have any."

Indy's mouth tightened as she watched the man called Jerry look her up and down like she was a prized mare at auction. She noticed the other two men who entered with him stood close to the door. It didn't take a brain scientist to realize they were his muscle.

The man standing before her was in his mid-fifties. He was still lean for his age. He stood several inches shorter than her brother, but there was an air about him that told her size was not an issue. The man reeked of power. His hair had just a touch of gray at the temples and his piercing brown eyes drilled into her, as if in warning.

This was a man used to giving orders and expecting them to be obeyed. Unfortunately, she wasn't the kind of girl to follow orders very well. As far as she was concerned, he could take his 'look' and shove it up his ass for all she cared.

Indy turned her attention to her older brother with a sneer to her lip. "I told you once before you could shove your liberties up your ass, Hayden. My suggestion hasn't changed. I'm leaving here. I don't know what you told the police and personally I don't really give a damn. My husband isn't going to be happy that you have kidnapped me. You'll be lucky he doesn't put a bullet in you for doing so," she said, lifting her chin in defiance.

"Husband," Hayden said falling back a step. "You can't be married!" He exclaimed, his eyes moving to her left hand automatically.

Indy raised her hand, showing off the simple, yet elegant ring. "I can assure you, I am," she said with a triumphant smile. "I told you. You should have just let me walk away."

Hayden's face turned a dark red as he stared at the ring on his sister's finger. A sharp command stopped him when he took a menacing step toward her. Instead, she found her hand captured by the man Hayden had introduced as Jerry.

A dark smile curved his lips, as he studied the ring. "You are worth more than this thin piece of gold," he said, glancing over to where Hayden stood in indecision. "You were not lying about your sister's beauty. Even under the dirt, I can see it," he said in amusement. He released her hand, capturing a strand of her hair between the long, slender digits. "I like the fire in your eyes. I wonder if you are as passionate in bed."

Indy gave him a nasty smile. "You haven't seen fire yet, asshole. Now, let go of my hair or you'll be eating your balls for dinner," she snarled.

Jerry chuckled as he withdrew his hand. Only he didn't let it drop to his side like Indy thought he would. Instead, he backhanded her sharply across her cheek.

The blow sent her stumbling sideways and falling to her hands and knees. She put her hand to her mouth, tasting blood from when the inside of her lip busted from the blow. The two men near the door took a step forward when Hayden yelled out a protest. Rodgers just stood frozen, his eyes focused on the man who had hit her.

"You sorry-ass son-of-a-bitch," Indy said, rising up to stand trembling before him as she put the back of her hand to her mouth. "If you ever hit me again,

I'll gut you the first opportunity I get!" She threatened, lowering her hand and clenching her fists tightly.

Jerry chuckled again. "Such fire," he said, nodding in approval. "Yes, it will be interesting to see it while I'm fucking you." He turned to look at Hayden who had paled considerably. "I am disappointed she is not the virgin I was promised, but I won't take that out on you, Hayden. You can expect my support in the upcoming race," he said smugly. "Pour us a drink and we can discuss the finer details while your sister gets cleaned up. I hope you bought her something in red. I do love the color," he added, moving to sit down on one of the plush chairs near the windows.

Indy stood shaking as she stared at the man in disbelief. She opened her mouth to tell him what he could do with his likes when she felt the sudden pressure on her shoulder, warning her to be quiet. She turned to look at Rodgers, who shook his head briefly at her, a dark warning in his eyes for her to remain quiet.

"I'll make sure she is ready for you," Rodgers said with a nod to his head. "Move it," he snapped out in a tone that warned her not to disagree.

Indy glanced at her brother one more time, but he refused to look her way. Whatever he had done, he was now in too deep to get out of it. She started toward the door before she turned to look at him one last time.

"Hayden," she called out softly, waiting for him to acknowledge her. When he turned his head at last, she stared coldly into his eyes. "I hope you enjoy the prison cell you are going to end up in. You are no longer my brother. Family doesn't sell out family. Ever!" She said before she turned, stiffening her shoulders before she walked quietly out the door.

Chapter 16

Jonathan let out a loud curse while Jacob bent over the bag he was holding and tried to breathe through the nausea. It would appear they did 'fly' in this time. When Allie had driven to a tall building set off a ways from the ranch earlier this morning, neither one of them could figure out what in the hell was going on.

She had parked outside a large, metal building. An older man came out with a grin on his face and spoke briefly to Allie who nodded. She had told him and Jacob to stay put while she did a 'flight check'. Since neither one knew what she was talking about they chatted for a few minutes with the man called Allen.

He explained he was a mechanic and worked on just about anything on the Whitewater ranch that needed fixing. He joked with them for a while, telling them different stories of some of the mishaps that had happened over the years. Jonathan had just nodded his head, listening with half an ear while Jacob kept glancing toward the building. Jonathan suspected his brother wanted to know what Allie was doing.

After a few minutes, Allen's cell phone rang. He talked for a couple of minutes into it before he hung up with a sigh. He told them he needed to head out, that one of the tractors had broken down and the guys couldn't figure out what was wrong with it. Jonathan watched as the old man climbed into an old blue, dull looking truck and drove away.

"I don't know how they can talk into little boxes and someone can be on the other end and hear what they are saying. I know it would be handy but I like seeing the person's face when I'm talking to them. That way I know if they are telling me the truth or not," Jacob said leaning back against the silver truck. "Sam said that Indy's brother took her to his place in California," he said with a frown on his face. "I don't know how he expects us to meet up with this man, Trey, at noon today. It would take us weeks of hard riding to get there and that's if we don't run into anything."

"It wouldn't if we go in one of these metal wagons," Jonathan said, tapping the truck with his knuckle. "You saw how fast it can go and with the black roads they have, it shouldn't be that hard of a journey." Jacob opened his mouth to respond, but Allie stuck her head out of a side door and called them.

"You guys ready to go?" Allie said, pressing a button so the door to the hanger would open. "The plane is ready and my flight plans are filed. We're wasting daylight," she called out over the rumble of the door.

Jonathan and Jacob had both been puzzled and leery as they got their first view of the metal wagon Allie called a 'plane'. It was shaped a lot differently than the other vehicles they had seen so far. She opened the door to the Cessna Turbostation and motioned for them to climb in. It was a roomy, single prop plane that could carry up to six passengers. Allie stood aside and waited as the two men approached the plane with a worried frown on their face.

"You don't have to be nervous," Allie said with a roll of her eyes. "I'm a damn good pilot."

"Yeah, well, I hope you really are better at driving this thing than you were the other one," Jacob said jerking his head toward her pickup truck. "You damn near hit another metal wagon yesterday," he added with a snort.

Jonathan decided that was probably not the best comment to make before they all piled in the metal beast. He reached for one of the little bags that Allie pointed to shortly before she jammed the black things over their ears. He couldn't help but think some of the rocking and rolling was due to Jacob's comment about her driving.

Both of them had been alright until the damn thing started to lift off the ground. The moment it did that, they were both cursing loudly before the praying began. A chilled sweat coated his forehead as he tried to breathe deeply through his nose. Jacob sat beside him, muttering the Lord's prayer and every other prayer their momma had taught them when they were little.

Allie's giggle reached both of them through the black device they had over their ears. "You both can open your eyes. If you want, I can give you a little bit of information about what we are flying over. It might take your minds off the fact you're both scared shitless of flying," she said with a twinkle in her eye. "I've made this flight hundreds of times since I was about twelve. Papa used to let me fly some. He said it was a good thing to know in case something happened to him. I got my pilot's license by the time I was sixteen and have been making trips a couple of times a month to different places, checking out the horses for the ranch or going to cattle sales. I haven't crashed – yet." She couldn't resist adding that last part.

Jonathan's throat worked up and down as he stared out the window at the ground far, far below them. He heard Jacob's swift draw of breath before his brother pushed his nose against the glass in fascination.

"Where are we?" Jacob asked in an awed voice.

"We're skirting Yellowstone before heading down to Salt Lake City, Utah. I have to drop something off and we'll refuel before heading down to Las Vegas for another refuel then Los Angeles. We'll do the same on the way back. It is almost twelve hundred miles and we'll be reaching speeds of 174 mph. We should be there around noon – one o'clock at the latest- if all goes well," Allie replied.

"Twelve hundred miles," Jacob said under his breath, looking at Jonathan with a shake of his head. "This is unbelievable."

Allie laughed and gave them both a strange look. "Haven't either one of you ever flown before?"

Both of them shook their head and looked back out the window. Allie spent the time between the stops giving them an overview of the landscape and the history of the regions as they flew. Jonathan was amazed at the huge salt deposit outside of Salt Lake

City. Neither one of them knew what to think of Las Vegas as they flew over.

Whoever would have thought that such a large city could exist in the middle of a desert? Both men climbed out to use the restroom while Allie took care of the refueling. She rolled her eyes when Jacob came back to the plane with both hands filled with quarters from the machine in the bathroom.

"I think that one is mine," Jonathan said, plucking one of the quarters that threatened to spill out onto the runway.

"It is the most amazing thing I've ever seen. Well, except for the silver wagon and this flying machine and the lights that come on without a flame and the water out of the wall," Jacob was saying excitedly. "Who would have thought a machine would give you money if you pull on its arm?"

"It doesn't always," Allie replied buckling back up. "Guess you guys live pretty rustic lives back home?" She asked as she glanced down at the checklist in her hands.

"Yes, you could say that," Jonathan replied, looking at his brother whose face suddenly closed up. "But, we wouldn't have it any other way."

Allie looked up and raised an eyebrow when she heard the defensive tone in his voice. "I know what you mean. All this could disappear tomorrow and I wouldn't miss it. I love to fly, but to live where…." Her voice faded as she shook her head.

Jonathan smiled at the intense look on Jacob's face as he studied Allie for a moment before a small smile curved his brother's lips. Jonathan watched as Jacob nodded to him before sitting back in his seat. He knew his brother would enjoy this time as much as he could, but he had no doubt where Jacob's heart lay. He could only hope that his brother wouldn't be alone for much longer.

* * *

Indy shivered as she waited in the bedroom of Hayden's townhouse. The guards had been posted at the door all night. She had tried to sneak out, but they had blocked her way before she had even taken more than a couple of steps.

She had spent most of the night pacing before she barricaded the door with a large dresser to make sure no one could come in while she took a quick shower. She had finally fallen into an uneasy sleep just before dawn. Her heart ached at what Jonathan must be thinking.

She hoped Cal and Jake let him know that she would not have gone if she could help it. She also worried about if she would be able to return. Her chest hurt so bad from the thought of never seeing him again that she had to sit for a moment to catch her breath.

No, she thought fiercely. *I will see him again. I will get back to him. I will not give up!*

She jumped up off the bed when a loud knock sounded on the door. She looked down at the glittering red dress that had been laid out for her and grinned with devious delight. There wasn't much left of it. She had shredded it last night as soon as she had seen it. After taking her frustration and anger out on the dress, she had washed out her undergarments.

Luckily, they had dried during the night. Now, she wore them under her dirty jeans and top. She would be damned if she would dress up like some Barbie doll for a dirty old man.

"Unless you are letting me walk out of here you can go to hell," she yelled out, standing near the window.

"Open the door, Indiana," Hayden growled out. "You can't stay in there forever."

"I don't need to stay in here forever," she yelled back. "Only until Jonathan or the police come. If you have the police out there with you I might consider opening it."

She heard muffled voices on the other side of the door before Jerry Hammock's deep, menacing voice sounded. "Open the door now, Indiana, and I might not get too upset with you."

"Go fuck yourself," she snarled back. "Or better yet, go fuck Hayden. He seems to want to be in bed with you."

A shiver went down her spine when she heard a low order given right before the door shook. She moved toward the bathroom as the sound of splintering wood echoed through the room. A few minutes later, a hole opened up large enough for a hand to appear. Indy decided another door between her and the force of the men breaking through into the room might be wise. She bolted for the bathroom wishing Jonathan was there to help her.

"Damn it," Hayden's voice echoed as she slammed and locked the bathroom door. "Indiana, you might as well give up."

"Never!" She called out, sliding down and bracing her legs against the wall.

It wouldn't help much, but it was better than nothing. The flimsy lock on the bathroom door wouldn't hold anyone out for long. She let out a whimper when the door shook and the lock shattered from the kick on the other side.

She slid forward a little and immediately scooted back, pressing as hard as she could against the door. Another hard kick and the added weight of the muscular shoulders of Hammock's bodyguards were more than her slender body could hold back. No matter how hard she tried to keep her weight against the door, she was still being pushed forward.

"No!" She wailed in anger, fear, and frustration as one of the men squeezed through the opening and lifted her body off the floor.

"I've had enough of this," Hammock bit out coldly. "Drug her."

"No!" Indy screamed out again, this time louder, as she began struggling fiercely to break free of the tight arms around her. "Hayden, you have to help me! You can't do this!" She cried, tears running down her face. "You can't do this."

Hayden stood near the door of the bedroom. His face was pale, but resolved. He was too far indebted to stop the events from unfurling. If he tried, he would not only lose his chance at the Senate but possibly his life. He had signed a contract with the devil in exchange for his soul and the devil had come to collect.

Her eyes moved from her brother to Rodgers, who was standing silently beside the man holding her. He refused to meet her gaze, instead his eyes were fixed on Hammock. She was suddenly overwhelmed with everything that was happening and the depth of her brother's betrayal.

"I'm sorry, Indiana," Hayden said quietly. "If you don't fight, things might go easier on you. He's a rich man. He can buy you anything you want."

Indiana stood still for just a moment as her brother's words sunk in. The bodyguard who was standing near the door came toward her with a hypodermic needle filled with a sedative in his hand. Something inside Indy exploded as the unfairness of having found love, only to brutally lose it, swept through her in a crushing wave of fury.

She burst out in violence as the wave reached its peak inside her. Slamming her head back against the bodyguard holding her, she caught him off guard when she had calmed for just that brief moment. She felt the pain exploding in the back of her head at the same time as she heard the crunch of his nose breaking from the force of the blow.

His arms loosened around her and she broke free, kicking out her leg at the other guard. Her foot caught the arm holding the needle and it went flying across the room. She rolled under his outstretched arms, even as Hammock roared out for Rodgers to grab her.

Indy continued rolling before jumping to her feet. She had only taken a few steps when Hayden stepped in front of her. She didn't think twice about raising her knee and slamming it as hard as she could into his groin. His strangled cry echoed through the room, even as his knees hit the floor. He fell forward clutching his balls in agony.

Indy thought she might actually make it out of the room. She would have if Hayden hadn't gotten in her way, delaying her escape. Those few precious seconds gave Hammock just enough time to come up behind her and grab her by her long hair. He jerked her around roughly, wrapping his fist tightly in the silky strands and pulling until her head was bent sideways, forcing her to look at him.

"You have been a very, very naughty girl," he tsked out coldly. "I am going to enjoy beating you. You will learn to obey or you will pay for your disobedience."

"You sick bastard," Indy choked out hoarsely. "You'll never get away with it. My husband will find me and when he does, he'll kill your ass."

Hammock laughed and twisted her hair even harder in his fist, making her cry out and drop to her knees. "Silly little twit, if your husband shows up, he'll end up dead just like the last bitch who got in my way. He'll meet with a tragic accident and I will be there to help his grieving widow," he whispered with a cruel grin.

"Really?" Indy asked huskily. "You forgot one thing, though," she whispered as he pulled her up by her hair until she was standing in front of him.

"And what's that?" Hammock asked with a raised eyebrow.

"This," Indy muttered, shoving the syringe into his side and depressing it. "Sleep tight, asshole. When you wake up, I'll be long gone."

Hammock's eyes widened in disbelief even as his legs trembled, then collapsed under him. Indy pushed his body away from her and scrambled over Hayden, who was still moaning on the floor. She didn't even look back as she rushed out of the townhouse.

The elevator opened at the same time as she was running for it. She slid to a stop, losing her balance and falling to the floor. A cry ripped from her throat as four figures poured out of it, rushing toward her.

Chapter 17

Trey Randall waited while the Cessna Stationair taxied to the hanger. He pushed off from the side of the dark green SUV he was leaning against, folding his arms across his chest as he waited for Allie and her passengers to disembark. When Sam had called him late last night, calling in a favor Trey owed him, he knew it must be serious.

After Sam explained what was going on, he realized it was more than serious, it was going to be explosive. Trey worked in the local FBI office and had been following a possible lead on corruption, bribery, and the murder of one of their fellow agents. He had been shocked when Sam mentioned Hayden Wild. While the prominent attorney had a squeaky clean record so far, the man he was dealing with did not.

Trey watched as three people climbed out of the small plane. He knew Allie from numerous visits out to Sam and Claire's ranch. He did not recognize the two tall men with her.

Sam had said they were Jonathan and Jacob Tucker from Montana. Trey had done a search for them, but had come up empty-handed. He studied both men carefully as they approached. Allie had an easy grin on her face, but the two men looked serious and dangerous.

"Hey Allie," Trey said, leaning down to kiss her. He jerked back in surprise when she was pulled backwards against the chest of one of the tall men before he had a chance to brush his lips across hers in greeting.

"I wouldn't," Jacob drawled out darkly, ignoring Allie's startled squeak. "Jacob Tucker," he said, studying the equally tall man standing in front of him.

"Trey Randall," Trey said with a wry grin.

"I'm Jonathan Tucker. Sam said you could help me get my wife back," Jonathan said, pushing forward. "He said you would know where she is being held."

Trey frowned and nodded. "Let's get going. I can tell you what I can on the way to Hayden Wild's townhouse. We've had him under surveillance for the past year. While he hasn't done anything against the law per se, he has brushed the line more than once. Your wife was seen being carried inside and the police responded to a call she made from his home," Trey explained as he pulled out of the gate of the small, regional airport and headed for the freeway.

Allie leaned forward from where she was sitting in the back seat with Jacob. "Why didn't the police help her?" Allie asked furiously. "Why didn't she go with them?"

"Hayden told the police that Indiana was a recovering drug addict and had called because he refused to give her money for her next fix. We called them off as we knew something was going down. We needed to see what would happen next," Trey responded, glancing at her in the mirror before letting his eyes slide back to the road in front of him.

Allie gasped in shock, sitting back. "You are using her for bait?" She asked in outrage. "What if something goes wrong and she gets hurt?"

Jonathan's fist clenched as he fought for control. It was a good thing Trey was driving, otherwise he might have beaten him to a bloody pulp. He swore under his breath before he turned in the passenger seat to look at the man who Sam said they could trust. If trusting a man who would use an innocent woman as bait was considered normal during this time, then he couldn't wait to get back home. A woman was meant to be protected at all cost.

"What the hell does she mean you are using my wife as bait?" Jonathan gritted out between his teeth.

Trey looked uneasily at the man sitting next to him. He knew a predator when he saw one and this guy reeked of it. He glanced in his side mirror before changing lanes wishing he could move away from the barely controlled fury of the man next to him. He debated how much he could reveal to his three passengers without compromising his assignment any further than he had.

"Hayden was expecting company, powerful company, from Washington, D.C. last night. I can't tell you much as it is an ongoing case, but I can tell you this man is dangerous. We suspect this man contacted Hayden Wild to help in Wild's bid for a seat in the U. S. Senate. This man has helped a number of other men get seats which he then controls through them. His corporation has received some questionable contracts both domestically and in our foreign venues. While the corporation is legitimate, some of his business practices he hides under its umbrella are not. We are hoping he will make a mistake with Wild so we can issue a search warrant," Trey explained as he took the exit marking the downtown area.

"What does my wife have to do with any of this?" Jonathan asked. "She has been gone from your time for the past four months."

Trey glanced at Jonathan, puzzled by his choice of wording. "We believe Wild offered your wife up on a silver platter for this man. The suspect likes beautiful, young women. I've seen photos of your wife," Trey said with a brief grin. "She fills all of the man's requirements plus some. She is hot!"

"She is my wife," Jonathan replied coldly. "She isn't just an image or bait or whatever in the hell you want to call her. Her name is Indy and she is mine."

Trey chuckled and nodded his head. "I'm just jerking your chain, man. I talked to one of our men that is on the inside just before you arrived. She was safe as of first thing this morning," he promised. "Our inside man won't let anything happen to her."

"Does Indy know about this man, your inside agent?" Allie asked anxiously.

Trey shook his head as he took another right at the intersection then slowed for a light. "No, it would be too dangerous for our agent. The last one we had was compromised and we found her dead. The initial ruling was a car accident, but we have evidence that she was dead before the car went off the shoulder and down into the ravine," he said, his voice hardening.

Jonathan flexed his fists as the SUV started moving again. "I can't believe you left my wife within reach of that bastard. If he has touched one hair on her head, I'm going to kill the son-of-a-bitch," he snapped out, his eyes flashing. "I suggest you don't get in the way."

Trey looked at Jonathan, his eyes widening when he saw that he had pulled a gun out from under the long coat he was wearing. Between the coat, the cowboy hat, and the way he was handling the gun, Trey felt like he was sitting next to a cowboy from the last century.

"Shit!" Trey responded, barely swerving to miss a car that was turning in front of him. "What in the hell do you think you are doing? Put that damn thing away! What do you think this is, the wild west or something?" He asked with another curse on his lips when Jonathan smiled.

"Where we come from if a man threatens what belongs to one of us, we kill the bastard," Jonathan said coldly.

Trey gave a nervous laugh as he drew to a stop in front of a large, towering building covered in steel and glass. "Yeah, right, and I guess you hang horse thieves and murderers too," he said opening his door.

"If we don't shoot them first," Jacob said with a shrug as he opened the door and slid out.

Trey turned to look at the twin from the back seat and paled even further when he saw the set of guns hanging from around his waist as well. Both brothers had unbuttoned their long coats and tucked it behind the holsters strapped around their slender hips. They looked like they were not only used to wearing them, but that they knew exactly how to use them.

"Is this where Indy is supposed to be," Jonathan asked in an emotionless voice, staring up at the massive building.

"Yes, Wild has a townhouse on the twentieth floor," Trey said looking at both men cautiously. "We also have an agent in there. I don't want you guys going in there guns blazing and shooting the wrong person."

Jacob laughed as he pulled his gun and whipping it around between his hands before sliding it back into its holster within a matter of seconds. "We don't waste bullets. We only hit what we are aiming for, isn't that right Jonathan?"

"Time's wasting," Jonathan said with a nod to his brother. "Let's go get Indy."

Jonathan motioned for Trey to step ahead of them. He bowed his head to hide the grin when he heard Allie make a comment to his brother as she walked by. It sounded suspiciously like she said 'show off' before she moved to walk behind Trey.

"You haven't seen anything yet, darlin'," Jacob responded, drawing a heated look from Allie.

* * *

Jonathan realized two things as they moved upward. One, he decided he hated heights and two, he hated this thing they called an elevator! His stomach felt like he had left it on the ground floor.

He didn't know what to think when Trey had pressed the button on the wall. He had watched a light blink out numbers, but he couldn't figure out what it meant. When the metal doors slid open and Trey and Allie walked into the small box, he and Jacob had looked with skepticism at each other. They had waited so long the doors to the damn box had started to close. He and Jacob had to hurry through the opening before it closed without them.

Trey had then pressed the number twenty and it lit up. It wasn't until the damn box started moving that he felt like he had left a part of his body back on the other side of the box. Jacob had started muttering curses again and glaring at Allie, who just shook her head in amused disbelief while Jonathan prayed he wouldn't end up at heaven's gate when the box opened again.

Jonathan stumbled out of the doors as soon as they opened, sucking in a deep breath. His eyes widened when he saw a figure running straight for him. He would have recognized Indy's slender figure anywhere. She had a look of terror on her face as she charged toward the box they were exiting. Her eyes widened for a moment before she lost her balance and slid on the glossy surface of the marble foyer, a strangled cry ripping from her throat.

Jonathan rushed forward, lifting her into his arms while Jacob pulled his gun with one hand at the same time as he pushed Allie into a nearby alcove to protect her. Jonathan vaguely recognized that Jacob stood protectively in front of all of them, making sure his body was between them and any threat that might come at them.

Jonathan's arms tightened around Indy as she buried her face into his chest, huge gasping sobs escaping her as she tried to mold her body against his. He wrapped them tightly around her trembling figure and rose with her securely caged against his tall frame.

"Don't let me go," she gasped out in a husky, frightened voice. "Don't you ever let me go!" She cried out again fiercely in a voice barely above a whisper when he made to shift her so he could free one of his hands so he could grip one of the guns at his hip.

"I won't, darling," Jonathan promised, moving back away from the area she had run from while Jacob continued holding the man who had charged after her within his sight. "I need to use my hands, Indy. I need to set you down behind me, honey. Just hold on to the back of my coat. I promise I won't let anyone take you again," he murmured, trying to get her to let him go enough so he could protect her.

"For crying out loud, don't shoot!" Trey growled out above all the confusion. He stepped in front of Jacob with his arms spread out wide. "What the fuck is going on?" He bit out to the man standing in the long hallway with his hands raised.

"We have him," Rodgers stated calmly, slowly lowering his hands. "He confessed to killing Evelyn."

"Did you get it on tape?" Trey asked harshly.

Rodgers nodded, his eyes focusing on Indy's partially hidden figure. He took a step forward only to stop when Jacob pulled the hammer of his gun back. He looked into Jacob's eyes and nodded, raising his hands in a gesture to show he wasn't going to do anything stupid while taking a step back again and standing still.

"Is she alright?" Rodgers asked in a quiet voice. "I tried to do what I could to protect her. She doesn't make it easy, you know," he said with a small smile.

Jacob's eyes narrowed and he glanced briefly at Trey, who nodded his head at the silent question in Jacob's eyes. "He's our inside man," Trey responded in a low voice. "Agent Spencer Rodgers, FBI. Where's Wild, Hammock, and Hammock's bodyguards?" Trey asked curiously, turning back to look at Rodgers, who relaxed his arms down to his side again.

Rodgers' lips curved with a ghost of a smile and he nodded toward where Jonathan was holding Indy protectively against his body. "Let's just say Wild should have listened to his sister when she told him he needed to let her just walk away. Hammock is knocked out. He won't be waking up anytime soon. His guards aren't in much better shape and Wild will be lucky if he ever walks straight again after his sister busted his balls," Rodgers stated. "You can read about the details in my report. Right now, the clean up crew are on their way and should be here shortly."

Rodgers looked over to where Indy and Jonathan were talking quietly, wanting to make sure she was alright. He paused when the tall man who had been holding the gun on him stepped in front of him with a glare. Rodgers raised his eyebrow and waited for the cowboy to make up his mind as to whether he was to be trusted or not. It took almost a minute before Jacob slid his gun into the holster at his side and stepped back with a glint of warning in his eye.

Allie, who had been pushed to the side by Jacob, stepped out of the small alcove. She walked up to Jacob and smacked him in the chest to get his attention. She waited a moment before she reached up with both of her hands to grip his cheeks. She didn't give him a chance to say anything before she pressed her lips to his in a fierce kiss that lasted only a few seconds before she pushed him away.

"If you ever - and I mean ever – do a stupid stunt like pushing me out of the way and putting yourself in danger again, I'll bust you in the gut," she growled out before walking over to see how Indy was doing.

Trey stood looking at Sam's petite, dark haired daughter with a grin on his face before turning to look at the stunned expression on Jacob's face. "You know, she'll do it too. I once saw her break a chair over a guy who thought he could beat his girlfriend at the local bar. She beat the shit out of the guy with it."

Jacob just stood watching Allie with a silly grin on his face. Hell, she could get pissed at him any time if that was how she wanted to let him know she was mad. He wasn't about to complain, not one damn bit!

Chapter 18

Jonathan stood holding Indy, rubbing her back and whispering how much he loved her. He had tried to convince her to let him set her down and get behind him, but she was trembling so badly he realized she probably wouldn't be able to stand on her own. He also realized almost immediately that the situation appeared to be under control.

Jacob had them covered, Trey was talking quietly to the man who had been coming after Indy, and no one else came out of the door she had run from. Jonathan assumed the man must have been the one Trey told them about. He really didn't give a damn. He was just relieved to have Indy back in his arms.

"I don't like your world very much," Jonathan murmured softly in her ear. "As soon as we can get back to Sam's ranch, I'm taking you home."

Indy shuddered as another wave of adrenaline caused from the fight or flight reaction swept through her. "I don't like my world very much either," she admitted with a shaky voice. "I was so scared you would think I wanted to come back. I didn't."

Jonathan tilted her chin up and brushed his lips against hers. The soft, trembling breath that caressed his lips pulled a groan from him. He pressed a hard kiss to her lips only pulling back when she winced in pain. His eyes narrowed on the bruise on her chin and the slight swelling of her lip where Hammock had struck her.

His eyes darkened dangerously. "Who hit you?" He bit out harshly, gently examining her face.

Indy shook her head and gave him a shaky smile. "I told him you would want to kill him. You don't have to worry, I gave him a dose of his own medicine," she said with a twinkle in her eye at the inside joke.

Jonathan's mouth tightened in anger. "Who hit you, Indy?" He asked again in a low, dangerous tone.

"Leave it be, Jonathan," Indy said with a tired sigh. She could feel her body on the precipice of crashing and burning from too much adrenaline and not enough rest. "Jonathan, hold me," she whispered as her eyes suddenly felt like someone had put lead weights on them and her muscles turned to jelly.

"Shit! Indy!" Jonathan cried out as her head suddenly rolled back and she folded.

* * *

"Aleaha said all Indy needs is a few days of rest," Allie murmured, brushing Indy's hair back from her forehead. "She knows what she is talking about, Jonathan. I promise. She would never do anything to hurt Indy."

"It's been almost two days!" Jonathan exclaimed, lifting Indy's delicate looking hand to his lips.

"Yes, and she has been through a lot," Claire said in a gentle voice. "Come downstairs and I'll fix you something to eat. You haven't eaten hardly anything since you got back."

Jonathan looked at the three women staring down at him as he lay on the bed at the Whitewater ranch. One of the paramedics had checked Indy out and said except for the bruise on her chin, she appeared to be fine. She was just exhausted.

Afterwards, Allie had convinced Trey into letting her borrow his SUV so they could get back to the airport and fly home. She promised him they would be available for any testimony that the FBI might need, but she wanted Aleaha to check Indiana out. Trey had gotten approval on the condition that none of them left the country. Jonathan and Jacob agreed, after all where they were going was still part of the U. S. as far as they were concerned.

It had been late the day before last when they touched down. Sam, Claire, and Aleaha had met them at the hanger. Jonathan had carried Indy, refusing to release her to anyone else. Even once they were back at the ranch house and he had laid Indy down in the bedroom he'd had before, he refused to leave.

Aleaha had checked Indy thoroughly under Jonathan's watchful eye. Once she affirmed the paramedic's diagnosis, he had sent everyone from the room. He locked the bathroom door between his room and his brother's room before he gently peeled Indy's dirty clothes from her body.

He took his time washing every speck of her soft, delicate skin, even washing her hair. She slept through the entire thing, not even moving when he washed and rinsed the silky strands. He had taken his time drying her as well, memorizing her body all over again as he made sure for himself that she had not suffered any other physical injury.

The time he spent caring for her pulled at something deep inside him making him realize he could never live without her. After he was done, he slid into the bed beside her and drew her against his long, hard length, holding her as if he would never let her go again.

His words started out soft.... hesitant. He told her about the first time he saw her, before he knew she was a girl, and how confused he was about his attraction to her. He admitted he sent her to the old cabin by the river as a way to punish her for the confusing feelings he had felt.

He told her of how beautiful she was standing so defiantly up on the roof in barely any clothing and how confused he was that she didn't realize that she was almost naked. He even confessed about seeing Maikoda coming out of the cabin later that night.

He explained how he had been determined to protect her in case any of the other cowpunchers had seen her. Instead, he found he was jealous that she was with the Indian and was shocked at how comfortable she was around him. He drew in a deep breath and pressed a kiss to her temple before he told her how he had watched her in the small wash tub, her skin glistening like gold.

His voice broke as he admitted to watching her bathe, wishing he could touch her skin, and his reaction to the most beautiful sight he had ever seen. He knew without a doubt that she was his. He planned to marry her as soon as he realized she was a woman.

He told her of how she made him lose control with just a simple smile and how much he missed it, that he desperately needed her to wake up so he could see it again. He told her he never expected to find a woman as warm, passionate, or beautiful as she was and he swore he would always love and protect her. He shared the devastation at finding her gone and his fear of never seeing her again. By the time he finished, tears fell unashamedly down his cheeks, soaking her hair where he held her tucked protectively under his chin.

"I love you so much, Indiana Tucker," Jonathan admitted. "You are my life, my heart, my soul. Don't leave me," he whispered. "Please don't ever leave me," he begged, running his trembling fingers down along her shoulder and arm. "God, I love you!" He choked out in a thick voice.

Throughout it all, Indy lay peacefully in his arms. Her soft breath and warm body the only things reassuring him that she was, indeed, alive and well. It took a long time before the emotions he had been holding back finally faded away leaving him drained. Sleep slowly overtook him as his body finally gave in to the need for rest. Even in slumber, his arms remained tight around her slender form, holding her close to his heart.

He had repeated his words to her again that next night and he would repeat them every single night until she woke and could hear them. He wanted her to know how much he loved her and needed her. He wanted to make sure there would never be a single doubt in her mind or heart about his true feelings for her. He ignored everything but her. She was his world. She was his everything. She was his Indiana.

Now, he looked up into the soft, concerned eyes waiting for his response and shook his head. "Thanks Claire but I'm not hungry," Jonathan said, tiredly rubbing his hand over his face.

"I am," Indy said in a groggy voice. "In fact, I'm starving. What are you fixing?"

Jonathan drew in a sharp breath as Indy finally opened her beautiful, dark green eyes. She blinked several times before she focused on his face with a trembling smile. She started to raise her hand so she could touch it and was surprised by how hard it seem to be. She looked at him in confusion.

Jonathan grabbed her hand when it started to fall back to the covers. "You can have anything you want," he promised her, raising her slender fingers up so he could press his lips to them.

"Anything?" She teased.

His eyes filled with tears as he gazed down at her twinkling ones. "Anything," he promised.

She frowned for a moment before she turned her gaze to look at Claire who was also looking tearfully down at her. Her eyes shifted to where Aleaha was standing near the window, smiling before moving to Allie, who was impatiently brushing at her cheeks with the sleeve of her shirt.

"What happened?" Indy said, struggling to sit up. "Did someone die?"

Jonathan chuckled as he quickly pulled the covers up with her. She was still naked under them. He liked the feel of her bare skin against his and hadn't bothered to put any clothes on her. She looked down as if realizing she felt the soft cotton of the sheets against her skin instead of clothing. She blushed as she looked up and caught Jacob staring at her from the doorway with a huge grin on his face.

"Ah shucks, Jonathan," Jacob teased. "You didn't have to be so quick. I'm curious to see how far her 'tan' goes down."

Allie jerked away from the wall where she had been standing with a low growl and pushed past Jacob, muttering under her breath as she walked by him. Whatever she said wiped the smirk off his brother's face. Jonathan chuckled as Jacob turned to follow Allie, calling her name as he pounded down the staircase after her.

"He's in deep shit now," Indy said, looking at those remaining in the room. "What happened?" She demanded even as she weakly leaned back against the pillows Jonathan hurriedly tucked behind her.

* * *

Indy sighed deeply later that night as she listened to everyone sitting around the table talking. Jonathan, in tune to everything she did, immediately slid his arm around her and rubbed her shoulder. She squeezed his leg to let him know that she was okay. Jonathan had explained everything that happened after she passed out outside of Hayden's townhouse. He teased her about getting there only to find out she had already kicked some major ass. His smile died, though, when he thought about what could have happened to her if she hadn't been so fierce and his guilt at not keeping her safe nearly choked him.

"Stop," she leaned closer to him and whispered. "You have nothing to feel guilty about. Shit happens. The main thing to remember is that you were there when I needed you most."

Jonathan smiled down tenderly at her and brushed a kiss against her temple. "Have I told you how much I love you, Indiana Tucker?"

"Only about a million times.... today!" She giggled softly, a light blush turning her cheeks a rosy color.

"And I'll tell you a million times a day for the rest of our lives," Jonathan promised huskily.

"I'll keep you to that, cowboy," she responded looking up at him through her lashes. "I'll remind you if you miss one."

Both of them turned to listen as Sam filled in some of the missing pieces that Jonathan had missed while he cared for Indy. Sam smiled at Claire when she poured him a cup of coffee. Loud groans could be heard from all their kids when he swatted her lightly on her ass, drawing a blush and a giggle.

"Ah, Papa," Taylor groaned out. "Get a room, will you? You are doing some serious damage to your kids' minds."

Sam pointed his fork at his youngest son and shook it. "Mind your manners, Taylor. One day you will discover a woman who makes you feel happy and you will know what it feels like to have her near you," he said before taking a bite of the peach cobbler Claire had made earlier. "As I was saying, Trey called me earlier. Indy, you don't have to worry about Hayden bothering you ever again," he said with a twinkle in his eye. "He is not the only one who knows a few powerful judges. I hired a private investigator shortly after Hugh died. I knew something was off. Your grandfather had an appointment to make sure the Wild Ranch went to you. He had set up trust accounts for Gus and Matthew and a lump sum for Hayden."

"But....," Indy said, shaking her head. "I don't understand. Hayden had the will drawn up when Grandpa had his stroke."

"He may have drawn it up, but your granddad didn't sign it," Sam said. "Three days before your granddad passed away, he called Allen Halbrook in town. Allen's been away for the past six months dealing with the death of his daughter's husband and helping her with the kids. He came back a couple of weeks ago, but has only just now gotten caught up on all his paperwork. That paperwork included your Grandfather's Last Will and Testament. Hayden knew about your grandfather's desire to give you the ranch."

Indy sat stunned, looking down at the table while her mind raced through everything she was being told. "But," she said again. She pushed her hair behind her ear when it fell forward in irritation. "How did Hayden get the power of attorney? How could he have a signed copy of the Will?"

"He forged it," Sam replied quietly. "It is probably the only thing he ever truly did that was illegal. He made a bad choice of buying into what Hammock was promising him. He saw the prestige, but not the hidden strings attached. Your brother has always been ambitious and self-centered. Hammock doesn't do anything without careful research. He used your brother's weakness against him. From what the investigator could piece together from the evidence the FBI collected, Hammock met you when you were about sixteen. It was when you visited Washington D.C. with your grandfather to attend a dinner sponsored by the Cattlemen's Association. Hammock must have known you would grow into a beauty and he set about capturing that beauty for himself."

Indy rolled her eyes. "How could you know that? I certainly don't remember ever meeting the creep before. Why would you think he had any big desire for me?" She snorted in disbelief.

Sam's eyes softened as he took in Indy's disbelieving look. "When Hammock's home was searched they found a room with pictures of you at different stages of your life posted all over one wall. He had been very careful in making sure you were kept isolated. I remember Allie telling me once that you were upset that the few guys you dated during college never asked you out more than once. I suspect Hammock had something to do with that."

Indy was silent as she absorbed the fact that she had been stalked for years and never knew anything about it. Her hand trembled as she reached for the hot tea Claire had set down in front of her. She looked up into Sam's compassionate eyes, the question trembled on her lips before she forced it out.

"You.... You said I would never have to worry about Hayden bothering me again," she said. "What did you mean by that?"

Sam sighed and pushed his empty dessert plate away from him as he searched for the right words. "You could contest the sale of the ranch in court but it would be a lengthy and expensive fight." He looked at Jonathan who nodded once to let him know he should continue. "Jonathan... and I talked to Allen who agreed that it would be difficult to get the ranch back. Personally, neither one of us thought you would want it anyway for several reasons. Hayden has agreed to terminate his request for guardianship and release all monies, including his share of the sale of the ranch, over to you. In addition, he has promised he would never voluntarily seek you out unless you requested to meet with him. In exchange, you will agree not to prosecute him for fraudulently signing a Will in your grandfather's name or press kidnapping charges against him."

Indy sat stunned. "But, that's millions of dollars!" She said hoarsely, looking at Jonathan.

Jonathan held her hand tightly in his, his heart pounding in his chest in fear as he waited to see what she would do. Would she choose to stay here, in her time or would she choose to return with him to his? His gut clenched as the seconds turned to long minutes as they stared at each other.

A smile curved her lips as her eyes softened. "I don't want the ranch," she responded in a strong clear voice. "I already have one. It's called the Twin Rivers. Where I'm going Hayden won't be able to find me anyway." She turned her head to look at all her friends sitting around the huge table. "I want to go home."

Sam smiled and reached for Claire's hand which clasped his tightly in return. "I'll take you to Spirit Pass tomorrow. We can leave at first light," he said.

Indy grinned, turning to gaze at Jonathan, who let out the breath he was holding. "Not tomorrow. I plan on taking a few things with me this time," she said mischievously. "We're going to need a few pack horses, Sam. Do you think you can help out?"

"I can take care of the pack horses," Allie said with a frown. "But, why in the hell do you need to go to Spirit Pass?" She asked looking around the table. "Papa said that place was haunted and we were to never go near it."

Jonathan, Jacob, Indy, Sam and Claire all laughed before Indy erupted into a mountain of things she wanted to purchase and take with her. Jonathan looked at his brother who was staring intently at Allie as she joined in making a list with Indy. Jacob turned to look at his brother and nodded with determination, a wicked smile on his face.

The next few hours flew by before Indy started yawning like crazy. Jonathan finally pulled her up, wrapping his arm around her. They were almost to the door of the dining room when Indy stopped suddenly as another thought occurred to her. She turned back to look at Sam.

"Sam," she called out softly. "I almost forgot. You said there were several reasons why you thought I wouldn't want to fight for the Wild Ranch. What was the other one?"

Sam raised his eyebrow at Jonathan who gave him a brief nod. "Because I don't think Colt and Dalton Tucker would give it up without a fight," he replied with a grin. "The brothers are the direct descendants of the family that started the Twin Rivers ranching outfit."

Chapter 19

Indy tightened the strap holding her saddlebag on Midnight. Chester and Tweed were jumping around, trying to get her attention. It had taken almost two weeks to get everything finalized. She had converted the almost two and a half million dollars from the sale of the ranch into some form of wealth that she could use in the past.

Most of it was in the form of high bred horses, precious stones, and some gold and silver. The rest went into other necessities that Jonathan, Jacob, and she thought would help make life a little easier, including several crates of medical supplies. She had also added fabric and Jonathan had added a trunk full of lingerie that Taylor had shown him how to order on the Internet.

Jonathan had grudgingly admitted he would miss two things about the future – the bathroom and the Internet. He and Jacob had already decided they were going to see about building a bathroom or two in the ranch house. They had researched instructions on how to do plumbing and building a septic tank on the Internet and printed them out.

Both men had spent an informative evening locked in Sam's office with Taylor. They both decided they had learned way more about Sam's younger son than either one of them needed to know. At twenty, Taylor had more knowledge of the opposite sex than Jonathan and Jacob combined thanks to the damn box.

"What are you thinking so hard about?" Indy asked, coming up to wrap her arms around his waist.

Jonathan started and gave her a wry grin. "Taylor and the Internet," he admitted.

Indy laughed out loud. "Say no more! Just putting Taylor and the word Internet together tells me way more than I want or need to know," she snickered.

Jonathan looked suspiciously at Taylor, who was joking around with Jacob. "What is that supposed to mean?" He asked, looking at the younger man through narrowed eyes.

"I'll tell you about it later tonight," Indy said, mischievously letting her hand slide down his chest to the front of his pants. "I'm impatient to get home," she murmured as she stood on her toes to press her lips against his.

"Hey you two, get a room!" Taylor called out.

"Don't worry," Allie said as she walked by leading her horse. "I'll kill him before he reaches twenty-one."

Indy frowned at her best friend. "What do you think you are doing?" She demanded.

Allie raised her eyebrow at Indy. "Get real, do you really think the three of you can handle this on your own? You have over forty horses and mules here, Indy. Add that in with the sixteen puppies you bought yesterday and you have your hands full. I told Papa I would come and help you guys get home. God knows why we can't just trailer everything instead of doing it the old fashioned way, but if this is what toots your horn, who am I to complain? It isn't like this will be my first trail ride. I told Papa and Mama I'd be back in a couple of weeks. I wanted to make sure everything is cool with you and I thought it would be neat to check out your new place," Allie said before she suddenly stopped, a look of doubt creeping across her face. "You don't mind, do you Indy? I mean, if you do, I can just help you part of the way and come back," she added hurriedly, turning away so Indy couldn't see the hurt in her eyes.

"Oh Allie, you know I would love to have you come with me," Indy said cautiously. "I'm just not sure it is going to be what you expect. I mean...." Indy paused to look at Jonathan for guidance.

"We are traveling a long way from your time, Allie," Jonathan said. "Where we live, where we are going to, is a different world from what you are used to."

Allie looked at both of them before she glanced at Jacob who was watching them intently from where he was standing next to Taylor and Aleaha. She chewed on her bottom lip for a moment before she shrugged her shoulders, breaking his gaze. She looked back at Indy and Jonathan and smiled.

"It can't be much worse than this one," Allie replied lightly. "Besides, it's not like I'm going to be staying or anything. I'm just visiting for a couple of weeks."

Jonathan nodded, putting his hand on Indy's arm when she opened her mouth to protest. "We appreciate your help, Allie. Let's load up. We have a long way to go," he said lightly, squeezing Indy's arm and nodding slightly toward Jacob, who was still gazing at Allie, a hungry, possessive look in his eyes.

Indy smiled and turned back to Midnight, mounting him in one graceful move. With a sharp whistle, Chester and Tweed bounded over to her. Aleaha and Taylor would take up the rear with Jacob while Sam and Allie lead the way. Indy and Jonathan would take the middle. Sam, Taylor, and Aleaha would not continue on once they reached Spirit Pass. After that, it would be up to Jacob, Jonathan and Indy to lead the way back to the Twin River ranch and - home.

They were all so focused on leading the long train of horses and pack mules that none of them noticed the dark figure sitting on a rock ledge off to their left watching them. The dark eyes moved over the long line of horses tied together before stopping on one of the figures towards the back.

Maikoda's blood heated as his eyes ran over the slender figure of the woman who was talking to the twin who had saved his life several years before. He almost gave his position away when the tall white man smiled up at her as she mounted her horse.

He listened carefully to the words that were being spoken. He had come through Spirit Pass searching for this woman. He knew she was destined to be his, what he had not expected was to find her quite so easily. His eyes followed the line as it moved past him. From the conversation he had overheard, the one called Aleaha would be coming back this way.

Maikoda smiled. He would be ready for when she did.

* * *

It took almost two full days of riding to get home. Allie had ridden up to Indy shortly after they made it through the narrow Pass to talk. She had confided to Indy that she had been a little spooked going through it and was glad when she could see the opening on the other side.

Taylor had wanted to come, but Sam had put his foot down with his youngest son, telling him he had much to learn before he could even think of traveling to the 'other side'. Allie had joked that her dad had sounded like Rod Sterling from the Twilight Zone for a minute when he talked about Spirit Pass.

They reached the western pasture and were greeted by several of the cowpunchers that Indy recognized from her first few weeks out on the range. Trace and Butler had the grace to blush a little when they saw Indy again but their eyes opened and grins lit up their faces when they saw Allie.

"Howdy ma'am," Trace said, pulling his hat off his head and nodding.

Allie grinned back at the two men. They looked like some of the rodeo clowns that hung out with Taylor after an event. Both were trying to smooth their hair down before wiping their grubby hands on their pants.

"Hi guys," Allie said with a chuckle. "How's it going?"

"It's going just fine," Jacob snapped, stepping closer to Allie. "Don't you two have work that needs to be done?" He demanded, giving both men a look that told them in no uncertain terms that Allie was off limits.

Allie rolled her eyes at Jacob before she turned back to check the straps on several pack mules. "You need to get a life," she muttered under her breath to Jacob before moving away.

"I'm going to...." Jacob started to say before he bit his tongue.

"She's like that with all the guys," Indy assured him. "They are drawn to her like a bug to a bug light and then she zaps the hell out of them," she added before walking over to help Allie.

"What the hell is a bug light?" Jacob asked absently to Jonathan, who had come to stand next to him.

"Damned if I know," Jonathan said, appreciating the way his wife's pants hugged her sweet little bottom. "I have a feeling it is one of the million things we missed on our trip and not one I would regret failing to learn about."

They only rested long enough for Jonathan and Jacob to catch up a little on what had happened at the ranch while they were gone and to give the horses and dogs a rest before they finished their last leg of the journey. Indy stopped next to Allie on the small rise above the ranch house. She heard Allie's gasp at her first sight of the beautiful homestead.

"Gosh, Indy," Allie muttered. "This looks just like the Tucker place over near Meeteetse. You didn't tell me that Jonathan and Jacob were related to them. They own one of the biggest ranches in the Montana/Wyoming area. It makes Papa's ranch look like a kiddie farm."

Indy had never paid much attention to the other ranches in the area. The Wild ranch wasn't as profitable so Indy and her granddad had their hands full running it with fewer hands. Sam's ranch was almost twice as large and he had turned to adding crops as well as breeding horses and cattle.

"I never thought of it," Indy replied honestly. "Allie, there is something I need to tell you," she said hesitantly.

Allie turned, looking at the serious expression on Indy's face. "What?" She asked curiously. "If you are afraid I'll act all weird because your hubby is related to one of the richest families in the country, you don't have to worry. I mean, I don't really give a damn if a guy has a lot of money or not," she said awkwardly.

"It's not that," Indy replied, gazing down at the ranch house. "Do you remember telling me about how weird you felt when we went through Spirit Pass?"

Allie frown in concentration. "Yeah, it was all misty and cold and stuff. The hair on the back of my neck was like standing on end. Even the animals were all freaky. What was up with that?"

Indy drew in a deep breath and released it before giving her closest friend a smile. "You are no longer in 2013, Allie. Welcome to my new home. The year, by the way, is 1867."

Allie's mouth dropped open before she snapped it shut. "You're shitting me, right?"

Indy shook her head. "Nope. I felt the same way too. You should have seen the preacher and his wife's face when Jonathan was tying me up so he could marry me. I don't think she liked the comment I made about her dress," she said with a grin. "It shocked the shit out of me when I signed the marriage certificate."

Allie's shocked expression turned to anger. "What do you mean, when he tied you up? Why the hell did he do that?" She demanded.

"Because a woman's reputation is ruined if she is with a man and has no chaperone," Jacob said riding up behind them. "Jonathan had to marry Indy to protect her."

Allie turned sharply in her saddle to glare at him. "That's bullshit. Shit like that doesn't really happen," she snorted. "It would be a cold day in hell before I let some guy tie me up and force me into marriage just because I spent some time alone with him! Hell, I'd have been married dozens of times by now if that were the case."

Jacob's face darkened and a look of grim determination glittered in his eyes. He moved his horse closer until his leg brushed against Allie. He smiled as he looked down at her defiant face.

"There is one thing you forgot about, Allie," Jacob said in a low, deep voice.

Allie tossed her head, refusing to give into the urge to move her horse away from him. "Yeah, what's that?" She asked sarcastically. "That all guys are assholes?"

"No," Jacob replied, reaching around her suddenly and pulling her off her horse and into his arms. "That you are no longer in your time, but mine," he whispered in her ear as he wrapped the cord he had hidden in his hands around her wrists.

Allie's frustrated scream and loud curses filled the air as Jacob kicked his horse. Indy started in surprise at Jacob's sudden behavior. She would have chased them, but Jonathan had come up on the other side of her and grabbed Midnight's reins, holding the huge horse in place.

"Jonathan," Indy said worriedly, looking at him, then back at the fading figures on horseback. "Jacob…. Allie…." She half way wondered if she should be more concerned for Jacob's safety since she knew what a handful Allie could be when she was riled. She also knew Jacob would never hurt her friend. She was just worried about whether Allie felt the same way about Jacob as he obviously did about her from the heated looks he had been sending her friend.

"Let him handle it," Jonathan said quietly. "I want to take my wife home."

Indy didn't resist when he lifted her off of Midnight's back and onto his lap. She slid her leg over his horse's neck and leaned back with a groan as his hand moved up to cup her breast. He let the reins rest on the arched curve of the gelding's neck and used his knees to guide it down the slope towards the house while his other hand moved to rub her intimately.

Her soft gasp and arching into his hand, spurred him to increase the speed home. He had known his brother had something up his sleeve when he saw the determined look on his face as he rode over to Allie. He also knew his wife would jump to the defense of her friend. Now, he didn't give a damn about anything but getting them down to the ranch house. Tweed and Chester moved up and down the long line of horses. Several of the men, including Jake, Ed and Carl had ridden out when they first spotted them coming in. Jonathan moved his hands when Jake came riding up to them.

"Howdy boss, Indy," Jake said, spitting tobacco out onto the ground. "Glad to see you made it back safely. We was getting worried something might have happened," he said, before glancing at the long line of horses and pack mules. "Hell, if you come back loaded down like this every time Indy gets kidnapped, we might have to build more corrals," he added with a grin.

"Hi Jake," Indy said with a grin at the old cowpuncher who reminded her so much of her grandpa. "How is the training going?"

Jake smiled beneath the covering of silver whiskers covering his face. "Good, there are only about a dozen left. The men have been working real hard to get them ponies ready. The commander of the fort and a couple of his men came out a few days back. They seemed real pleased with them," he added.

"That's good," Jonathan said. "Anything else I should know about before I take Indy down to the ranch house?"

Jake leaned over and spit again before he glanced worriedly at Indy. "There's been talk that some of the Indians are getting stirred up by all the military coming in. They have attacked a few of the smaller homesteads, running off with some of the cattle. Ed decided to move some of the cattle in a little closer just in case."

Indy's mouth tightened in disapproval. "What do you expect when their lands are being taken from them and their food sources wiped out?" She started in angrily, only stopping when Jonathan gently rubbed her stomach in warning.

"Let me know if there is a problem," Jonathan ordered Jake. "Spread the word that under no circumstance are the men to fire on any Indians if they come onto Tucker land. That includes if they see them taking cattle. I want to be informed immediately and I'll deal with it."

Jake's eyes widened in surprise, but he nodded. "I'll spread the word, boss."

They watched as Jake pulled his horse back and headed back to Ed and Carl. "Now, if anyone else tries to stop us before I get you to our bedroom, I think I'll shoot them," Jonathan murmured in her ear as his hand slid up to cover her breast again.

* * *

The only one who stopped them was Wally, who was beaming from ear to ear and talking non-stop. Jonathan was able to get a request for hot water in between the Chinaman taking a breath.

He even helped out by carrying the huge copper tub upstairs and then hauling buckets up as fast as Wally had them heating. Indy fixed them a light meal of cheese, biscuits, and sliced beef that Wally had cooking and carried them upstairs. She couldn't help but roll her eyes when she saw the large box that Jonathan had marked 'For Jonathan's eyes only' marked on it. That was the one full of lingerie that he had ordered. She turned to look at him with a raised eyebrow as he and Wally brought in the last buckets of steaming water.

Jonathan grinned and wiggled his eyebrows back at her, forcing her to turn around to hide her laughter from Wally. "Thank you, Wally," Jonathan said in a deep, husky voice. "That will be all for now."

"What of Mr. Jacob?" Wally asked puzzled. "Jake tell Wally Mr. Jacob was with you, but he not now. Should Wally heat more water?"

Jonathan shook his head and placed his arm around Wally's shoulders, gently steering him towards the bedroom door. "No, Jacob had something he needed to take care of. He might not be back for a few days."

"Oh," Wally said, glancing over his shoulder and smiling again at Indy who waved to him. "Wally go see if men need help."

"That is an excellent idea," Jonathan breathed out in relief. "I'm sure they need a lot of help. We brought a lot of things back with us. Just put the boxes downstairs in the living room and we'll take care of them later."

"Wally take care of all that for you, Mr. Jonathan," Wally said with a quick nod before he disappeared down the stairs.

Jonathan let out his breath as he finally closed and locked the door to their bedroom. "Final....ly," he said before his voice faded and his eyes lowered as he drew in a sharp breath.

"You weren't the only one who did a little shopping before we left," Indy admitted as she let her shirt slide down her arms to fall to the floor. "I never got to show you what a bathing suit looked like while we were at Sam's," she whispered as her fingers went to the button of her jeans. "Do you want to see what I wear when I go swimming?"

"Holy shit, Indy," Jonathan croaked out as her jeans slid seductively down her legs. "I saw women in the flat box wearing things like that but...." He swallowed as she stepped out of her jeans and raised her arms to release her hair from the ponytail she was wearing it in. "I hope you never wore that in front of other men," he muttered hoarsely. "I think I just might have to kill them."

Indy's laughter filled the room as she walked toward him. "I'm afraid you would have to kill a couple of thousand then," she admitted in amusement. "This might be a little more daring than the ones I normally wear, but not by much."

"Ah hell," he swore under his breath before he pulled her roughly against his hard, very aroused body. "How do you take it off?" He muttered against her lips.

"Pull the string."

That was the last words she was able to say rationally before he kissed her with a wild passion that scorched her from head to toe. In the back of her mind, she could actually feel her toes curling as he tugged at the strings of her two piece. In a matter of seconds, she was standing in front of him dressed the way she was the day she was born. Her loud moans blended with his as his calloused hands ran over her sensitive skin.

"You have too many clothes on," she muttered as her hands worked desperately to fix the issue.

Jonathan cupped her breasts in his hands, pulling back just enough so he could suck on the engorged nipples. Her hands fisted in his opened shirt and a low mewling sound broke from her lips at his tugging. She threw her head back, closing her eyes as hot liquid formed between her legs. She cried out when his fingers slid between the silky folds, testing her.

"Damn, you are so ready for me," he whispered, standing up and pulling back away from her. "Get in the water, honey. I need to wash some of this trail dust off me before I take you the way I want to," he demanded. "And Indy," he paused, waiting for her to open her eyes again and look at him. "I mean to take you every way I can."

Indy's eyes darkened at the promise. She smiled and ran her finger along his chest, flicking one of his nipples that hardened immediately in response. She turned and walked over to the huge copper tub. Bending over, she stuck her ass up in the air in invitation as she tested the water. It was perfect. She glanced over her shoulder just in time to see the last of Jonathan's clothes hitting the floor and a fully aroused male coming at her with the promise of retaliation in his eyes.

His fingers bit into the soft skin of her hips as he lined his throbbing cock up with her moist lips. He was so hard he didn't even have to guide his cock to her slick channel. It was as if his cock knew the way and couldn't wait to bury itself inside her heated channel.

Both of them groaned as he pushed forward along her vaginal sheath, not stopping until he was fully buried deep inside her. Jonathan swore he could feel her gripping him, as if daring him to try to pull out. He was panting loudly as he did.

The pleasure and pain of being so aroused stroked every nerve ending. Hot waves of ecstasy ran through him as he began moving faster. In the back of his mind, he knew he was holding her roughly, pounding into her too hard but the primal need to mate, to claim, to possess overwhelmed all rational thought until all he could do was feel the heat, smell their combined arousal, and hear her soft pleas for more. When her body exploded around him, he couldn't contain the cry that ripped from his throat as his own body surged forward in answer to her. The orgasm was so intense he actually had to lean over her and wrap his arms around her to keep from collapsing to his knees as his legs gave out underneath him.

"Oh baby," he groaned over and over as his cock jerked in response to the continued spasms along her vaginal walls. "Oh baby!" He groaned loudly, trying to draw in a breath.

He let his head drop down, resting his forehead on her shoulder as his body shuddered over and over until he felt as weak as a newborn babe. He kept his arms wrapped tightly around her bent form, his eyes pressed closed as he felt the last wave of his seed pulsing deep into her womb. The thought of them creating a child at that moment caused his cock to jerk one last time, pulling another moan from both of them.

"Damn, baby," he muttered hoarsely. "I've never felt anything like that before."

Indy's arms trembled as she tried to hold her body up above the copper tub. The steam from the water, combined with the sweat she had worked up during their lovemaking had turned her skin slick. The feel of his chest sliding against her skin made her want to rub against him and start purring. Damned if she didn't feel like a cat who had just been given the richest cream ever served.

"I love you, Jonathan," Indy murmured, rubbing the side of her head against his chin. "I love you so much."

Jonathan slowly straightened, cursing as he slipped from her body. Holding her tightly against him, he lifted her up and set her in the water before climbing in behind her. Once they were settled, he pulled her back against him so she was sitting snugly between his legs with her head lying up under his chin. He reached over and picked up a bar of her scented soap that she had used before her kidnapping. A shiver went through him as he remembered how close he came to losing her forever.

He slowly lathered a small cloth and began gently running it over her skin. "I love you, Indiana Tucker. I love your spirit. I love your strength. I love your passion. It is going to take me the rest of our lives to show you just how much," he said quietly. His hand moved down over her flat belly. "One day, our child will round your body. I'll still think you are the most beautiful woman in the world when it does."

Indy tilted her head back, pressing her lips against his cheek until he turned his head crushing her lips with his in a fierce, passion-filled kiss that had her twisting around to face him. He cursed at the limitations of being confined in the copper bathtub. He was going to have to talk with Jacob as soon as his brother got back about building one of those indoor bathhouses like Sam had. He had loved making love to Indy in the 'shower'.

"My turn," Indy whispered huskily against his lips. "I think if you want to see me rounding with a child, we need to practice a bit more."

Jonathan's chuckle echoed around the room as he cupped her face to pull her closer. "Have I told you I love you today?"

"Yes, but you still have about another couple of hundred thousand times to go," she answered, sliding her knees over his thighs so she could slowly sink down on him.

"How about I just show you?" Jonathan replied huskily as he lifted his hips up, sealing them together forever.

To be continued…. Spirit Warrior: Spirit Pass Book 2. (Read excerpt below)

If loved this story by me (S. E. Smith) please leave a review (just keep swiping, LOL). You can also take a look at additional books and sign up for my newsletter at **http://sesmithfl.com** to hear about my latest releases or keep in touch using the following links:

Website: http://sesmithfl.com
Newsletter: http://sesmithfl.com/?s=newsletter
Facebook: https://www.facebook.com/se.smith.5
Twitter: https://twitter.com/sesmithfl
Pinterest: http://www.pinterest.com/sesmithfl/
Blog: http://sesmithfl.com/blog/
Forum: http://www.sesmithromance.com/forum/

Additional Books by S. E. Smith
Paranormal and Science Fiction short stories and novellas

For the Love of Tia (Dragon Lords of Valdier Book 4.1)

A Dragonlings' Easter (Dragonlings of Valdier Book 1)

A Warrior's Heart (Marastin Dow Warriors Book 1.1)

Rescuing Mattie (Lords of Kassis: Book 3.1)

Science Fiction/Paranormal Novels

Cosmos' Gateway Series

Tink's Neverland (Cosmo's Gateway: Book 1)

Hannah's Warrior (Cosmos' Gateway: Book 2)

Tansy's Titan (Cosmos' Gateway: Book 3)

Cosmos' Promise (Cosmos' Gateway: Book 4)

Curizan Warrior

Ha'ven's Song (Curizan Warrior: Book 1)

Dragon Lords of Valdier

Abducting Abby (Dragon Lords of Valdier: Book 1)

Capturing Cara (Dragon Lords of Valdier: Book 2)

Tracking Trisha (Dragon Lords of Valdier: Book 3)

Ambushing Ariel (Dragon Lords of Valdier: Book 4)

Cornering Carmen (Dragon Lords of Valdier: Book 5)

Paul's Pursuit (Dragon Lords of Valdier: Book 6)

Twin Dragons (Dragon Lords of Valdier: Book 7)

Lords of Kassis Series

River's Run (Lords of Kassis: Book 1)

Star's Storm (Lords of Kassis: Book 2)

Jo's Journey (Lords of Kassis: Book 3)

<u>Magic, New Mexico Series</u>
Touch of Frost (Magic, New Mexico Book 1)
<u>Sarafin Warriors</u>
Choosing Riley (Sarafin Warriors: Book 1)
<u>The Alliance Series</u>
Hunter's Claim (The Alliance: Book 1)
Razor's Traitorous Heart (The Alliance: Book 2)
<u>Zion Warriors Series</u>
Gracie's Touch (Zion Warriors: Book 1)
Krac's Firebrand (Zion Warriors: Book 2)
Paranormal and Time Travel Novels
<u>Spirit Pass Series</u>
Indiana Wild (Spirit Pass: Book 1)
<u>Heaven Sent Series</u>
Lily's Cowboys (Heaven Sent: Book 1)
Touching Rune (Heaven Sent: Book 2)
Excerpts of S. E. Smith Books
If you would like to read more S. E. Smith stories, she recommends <u>Abducting Abby</u>, the first in her Dragon Lords of Valdier Series
Or if you prefer a Paranormal or Time Travel with a twist, you can check out <u>Lily's Cowboys</u> or <u>Indiana Wild</u>...

About S. E. Smith

S. E. Smith is a *New York Times*, *USA TODAY* and *#1 International Amazon* Bestselling author who has always been a romantic and a dreamer. An avid writer, she has spent years writing, although it has usually been technical papers for college. Now, she spends her evenings and weekends writing and her nights dreaming up new stories. An affirmed "geek," she spends her days working on computers and other peripherals. She enjoys camping and traveling when she is not out on a date with her favorite romantic guy.

Made in the USA
Middletown, DE
15 July 2015